Venus & Her Thugs: Fifteen Weird Tales

by

J. A. Nicholl

Counter-Currents Publishing Ltd.
San Francisco
2017

Cover image: Ramon Casas i Carbó
Nu femení d'escorç, 1894

Cover design by: Kevin Slaughter

Published in the United States by
COUNTER-CURRENTS PUBLISHING LTD.
P.O. Box 22638
San Francisco, CA 94122 USA
http://www.counter-currents.com/

Hardcover: 978-1-940933-82-5
Paperback: 978-1-940933-83-2
Electronic: 978-1-940933-84-9

Library of Congress Cataloging-in-Publication Data

Names: Nicholl, J. A., 1984- author.
Title: Venus and her thugs : fifteen weird tales / by J. A. Nicholl.
Description: San Francisco : Counter-Currents Publishing Ltd., 2017.
Identifiers: LCCN 2017028525 (print) | LCCN 2017028880 (ebook) | ISBN
9781940933849 (electronic) | ISBN 9781940933825 (hardcover : alk. paper) |
ISBN 9781940933832 (pbk. : alk. paper)
Classification: LCC PR9619.4.N53 (ebook) | LCC PR9619.4.N53 A6 2017 (print) |
DDC 823/.92--dc23
LC record available at https://lccn.loc.gov/2017028525

CONTENTS

AUTHOR'S NOTE

Earlier versions of some of these stories have been published elsewhere: "The Baby Shower," "Dry Leafless Trees," "Empathy," "The Horrible Thing," "Lions," "Miss Polly," and "The Second Marriage" appeared online at Counter-Currents/*North American New Right*; "Eternal Sleep" appeared in *Unsung Stories*.

The epigraph for "Analogue" is from *Schopenhauer's Parerga and Paralipomena,* trans. T. Bailey Saunders.

The text reproduced in "Eternal Sleep" is from Kropotkin's *The Great French Revolution,* trans. N. F. Dryhurst.

Special thanks are due Greg Johnson and John Morgan of Counter-Currents.

This book is dedicated to my wife.

J. A. Nicholl

BIOPOIESIS

Perhaps the authorities might have been summoned, but for the mouse plague that caused the whole building to stink like an overheated charnel house that summer. Nor was it particularly noteworthy to anyone that the woman had not been seen in the hall or elevators for over a fortnight; she had always been a recluse, making her shopping trips when most of her neighbours were at Mosque.

The discovery of her body fell to a pair of these neighbours, boys in their teens who had surmised that the apartment was likely vacant, and wanted to check on the off-chance that there might be something worth stealing.

". . . Or if it's empty you can use if to pimp out your slut cousin," Da'uud said to Bilal.

"Shut the fuck up," the other responded, punching the shoulder of his friend, who was engaged in picking the lock. "I'll take my *kafirah* here and fuck her. If you're lucky you can have sloppy seconds."

"Whatever. Fucking stinks worse here than on my floor," remarked the one standing guard.

When the lock-picker pushed the door open the foetor was released from within, and the discoverers found themselves sickened by what, vastly intensified, struck them viscerally as an odour of despair so intense that they could form no words to express their shock. The boy on his knees remained there a moment; the other swayed a little on his feet, both of them slack-jawed. They stared ahead, without exchanging glances, into the filthy, miasmic apartment.

The elevator rattled in the corridor behind them. Their response, instead of running away, was to enter the apartment of death, closing the door behind them. Stranger still, neither made any effort to shield his nostrils from the violently assaultive stench whose source they progressed towards.

Whatever volatile compounds had triggered so unaccustomed an emotion in the erstwhile jovial boys was now, moments later, producing a quite different affect. The fruity sweetness, which they could taste in their open, drooling mouths like the steam from a *shisha* pipe, was intensifying as they walked through the dishevelled lounge room (the dead woman having suffered from a congeries of physical and psychological illnesses that had long made house chores difficult), glancing neither at the piles of dirty dishes and clothes that lay about, nor the football regalia on the walls, nor minding the flies that harassed their faces and filled the air with ominous buzzing.

Like their salivary glands, their genitals responded enthusiastically to the horrible aroma. If the normal activity of their frontal lobes had not been suppressed, no doubt shame, bafflement, and disgust had been theirs.

The woman's quarters were small. On the far side of the living room was located the door that would reveal the source of what had drawn the intruders hither. Da'uud turned the knob and entered first.

On a double bed, as expected, lay a human corpse in a state of black decay, glistening and swarming with maggots in the semidark. Beside it lay a heap of something also resembling carrion, which, over and above the congealed effluvium that had puddled in the rumpled bedclothes about the corpse, suggested evisceration.

In that dark corner, something moved while the boys remained, staring fixedly. The creature lifted its head, which rotated at an unnatural angle to face the visitors, and howled.

The foetor intensified with the howl, as though reserves of it were now released by the puncture of some distended organ. To the receptive minds of the two boys, the animal seemed at once to express both emotional pain of the most abject degree, and the most exquisite triumph. As before, they registered these emotions with passive empathy. Somehow it was apparent from the noise they made that those sub-bestial vocal chords had never before sounded a note; that the creature had not been conscious of its own existence until the moment it had been disturbed.

Its toothless mouth hung open, pus-coloured gums and lolling tongue on display. The features were vaguely canine, but almost hairless, except in irregular patches.

Now this canid thing stirred its legs, seeming thereby to resolve itself more completely out of inchoateness. As much as a dog, it was like some weird sea creature flopping around on the deck of a ship, the darkness, the rumpled bedclothes, and the woman's remains making it difficult to discern the shape of its body and the number of its limbs. It howled again, more loudly.

Then it flopped down onto the carpet and ran, in a manner of speaking, towards the onlookers, its tail dislodging maggots with each wag. Certainly no guard dog, it meant to welcome the intruders with all the means at its disposal, chiefly its bruise-coloured tongue that glistened with a vile lethean fluid. It had no eyes, but the boys had the distinct impression of being seen by it.

In the normal course of events, Da'uud and Bilal would certainly have disabused any dog of such affectionate presumption. This time, they were powerless.

When others came along several days later, in search of the boys who had gone missing, they smelled only the natural, albeit atrocious stink of death. They found the corpse on the bed in an early state of butyric fermentation. The bodies of the two boys, fly-blown and swollen where the skin remained intact, had been partially eaten and strewn about the room. The unclean animal that met them had now solidified its form, though its flesh remained decidedly putrescent. It lifted its head, turning a pair of superficially blind-seeming, yellow eyeballs on the new intruder, Bilal's father, who stood in the doorway, and bared its similarly pus-coloured teeth to emit a sort of wheezing snarl. Two newborn pups were wriggling at its teats.

Dry Leafless Trees

I see them crowd on crowd they walk the Earth
Dry leafless trees no Autumn wind laid bare;
And in their nakedness find cause for mirth,
And all unclad would winter's rudeness dare;
No sap doth through their clattering branches flow,
Whence springing leaves and blossoms bright appear;
Their hearts the living God have ceased to know,
Who gives the springtime to the expectant year;
They mimic life, as if from him to steal
His glow of health to paint the livid cheek;
They borrow words for thoughts they cannot feel,
That with a seeming heart their tongue may speak;
And in their show of life more dead they live
Than those that to the Earth with many tears they give.

—Jones Very, "The Dead"

"Al" was short for Aloysius, a name indicating clearly enough his family's religious background, though liable to mislead as to its intensity. In fact, it was only his middle name, but that was the one he had preferred since a dream in which the Virgin had appeared and blessed him led to his becoming an altar boy at the church his parents attended on holy days.

That enthusiasm lasted for about a year before disillusionment set in. The priest had been unable to answer his questions about the Real Presence and other theological matters to the boy's satisfaction, and worse, had spoken as though such questions hardly mattered.

A short time afterwards Al was studying world religions in RE class. It was not the first time he had heard the basic tenets of Islam, but on this occasion, in the context of his acute disappointment with Catholicism, they impressed him as profoundly satisfying in their simplicity. As he conducted further research, they grew on him more and more, until soon he began secretly learning Arabic and actually thinking of himself as a confirmed Muslim, even going so far as to reject pork products (ostensibly on animal welfare grounds: a genuine concern of his that gave rise to some cognitive dissonance over the issue of *halal* slaughter).

This nascent devotion grew to the point where in his mind "Al" had become the Arabic definite article, in preparation for the day when it would find itself sandwiched between a traditional Islamic first name and the geographical adjective "*Australi.*" Then he would have to remind himself, in the words of the *Sahih Muslim,* that "He who has in his heart so much as a mustard seed of pride shall not enter paradise."

Al told no one about his spiritual revolution. His parents would not be enthusiastic, and as for the handful of acquaintances who passed for his friends at school, he had never shared much with them besides a passion for *Dungeons and Dragons, World of Warcraft,* and so on. There were few Muslims at the Catholic school he attended, and they were obviously not devout. That left only online forums, and these tended to confirm and galvanise his increasingly radical understanding of Islamic doctrine.

The public declaration of his new faith occurred without premeditation in the same venue where his conversion had begun just over a month previously. The class was discussing the recent phenomenon of large numbers of outwardly assimilated migrants re-migrating to fight in order establish an Islamic Caliphate in the Middle East.

"Can't we just send 'em all back and bomb the fuckin' place!" exclaimed Cody Newsom, a notorious troublemaker.

"Cody! Can you please not be so . . . intolerant?" came Miss Cowper's flustered response.

But Al, blood pounding in his eardrums, stood up and turned to face the same boy who had once pushed his head into the narrow space between the shelves of lockers outside the classroom and slapped his buttocks with a ruler. "There is no God but Allah, and Muhammad is his Prophet!" he shouted, holding up a single index finger. Throughout the room there was silence. He continued, surfeited with adrenaline and the presence of Allah,

"You should be beheaded for saying that!"

"What did that little prick just say?" Cody chuckled uneasily to one of his confederates at the rear of the class. "Come on and behead me then! What are you waiting for?" he taunted as best he could; but then he was the first to look away.

The initial outcome was a visit to the principal, followed by referral to the counsellor, a young woman named Evie Quinn. Perhaps he escaped reprisal from Cody and his "crew" because the issue had been too high-profile for that to go unnoticed. Al preferred to think it was the look of conviction, of *jihad* in his eyes.

"This is nothing but Islamophobia!" he complained in the first session. But Evie was a skilled and sympathetic counsellor—and pretty as well, with strawberry-blonde locks in a tumble-down bun, and those endearing spectacles that magnified her bright green eyes. She was twenty-five, but looked about the same age as some of the senior students. Al began joyfully to anticipate their meetings, and to dream of certain scenarios, such as one in which he confessed his feelings, and she responded by taking his hand and placing it on that generous bosom that struggled against the buttons of her blouse.

He had tried to explain the reasoning behind his conversion, and to impress Evie with the admission that he had "thought about joining the *mujahedin*."

"Wow, okay . . ." She bit her soft, pink lip. "Have you talked about this with anyone else?"

"No." He only half-lied.

"Not even online, with these . . . contacts you've talked about?"

"No, but I've been thinking about it—*a lot*," he added with lame emphasis.

She looked at him softly but intensely, and it made him uncomfortable. Far from impressed by Al's warlike resolution, she was worried for him. "You haven't ever thought about . . . hurting yourself, or anyone else, have you Al? I mean, like the boy who was in the news the other day?"

It struck him forcefully that for her there was nothing, however grudgingly, to be seen as heroic in the case of one "Jihadi

Josh": to her he was just another maladjusted teenager whom she wished she had been there to help. For the first time he saw himself clearly through those lovely, caring eyes, and felt ashamed.

He tried to wish that Evie were covered in a *hijab* and hidden safely away so as not to tempt him, but apostasy had already risen like a tide in Al's breast, and soon he was left wondering how he could ever have been so foolish as to mistake the religion of a seventh-century desert bandit for the transcendence he was seeking. For the first time he questioned whether the latter was even within his reach as a human being, or if it was, whether he personally had been granted the constitutional ability to grasp it.

So he went back to the internet and developed an interest in Far Eastern religion. They were the more esoteric and exotic forms that attracted him most in this new phase of sensibility. Whereas Islam had seemed like an obvious, simple answer to the riddle of existence, these doctrines promised something harder to grasp, yet more profound and, paradoxically, more immediate. He began to search for gurus to whom he might be able to offer himself as a disciple, but found that at best he might be able to join a community of fellow aspirants, and occasionally participate in meditation retreats if he saved his pocket money or got a part-time job. Later, perhaps, he might make his way to the US or India or somewhere, and begin his spiritual career in earnest.

Al began attending a local *gompa* after school and taking a beginners' *vipassana* course before trying out the more advanced concentration and visualisation exercises. Before long he was able to evoke on demand a limitless compassion for the entire world of sentient beings, and almost to silence his doubts regarding the mathematical possibility of achieving liberation after a "beginningless" eternity already spent in *samsara,* among various other conceptual incongruities. He stopped eating meat in principle, although, equally in accordance with Buddhist teaching, made an exception for meals prepared by others.

All the while he came and went without making much of an impression among his fellow seekers. They were friendly (though somewhat patronising on account of his age), and he supposed that he was part of their *sangha*, but in a way Al felt no more connected to these strangers whose meditation practice he shared than to the billions of sentient beings to whose liberation they were working towards. He would imagine himself surrounded to the limitless horizon with holy *bhikshus* and *bhikshunis*; but then the conversations he had with their real-life counterparts confirmed, at least to his *klesha*-afflicted mind, that these people were all rather self-absorbed and their knowledge of *dharma* generally superficial.

Then one day Al met someone whom instantly he could see was different. He had not noticed her in the meditation room; if he had, he might not have been able to concentrate. She appeared only slightly older than him, which was somewhat unusual here, where the average age was probably between forty and fifty. It was she who first spoke to him, at the communal meal. He was trying to concentrate on the precise sensation of the slightly stodgy rice and the flavourless, rubbery tofu in his mouth, in order to experience its *tathata*, while at the same time generating a sense of gratitude and compassion to all the numberless sentient beings who had contributed their suffering to his nutrition. But his eyes kept finding out the intriguing girl on the other side of the table.

With her wide face, high cheekbones, and long, straight, black hair she might have been an Asiatic, but her grey, wide-set, eyes were round as any Occidental's. In fact, they were the largest and most striking eyes he had ever seen. She did not exactly smile, but, against his will, held Al's gaze for longer than he had thought it possible for him to lock eyes with a girl without blushing and looking, if not running, away. He wondered if it was the equanimity he had attained through meditation; but if he were calm, why was his heart thrashing around in his chest like trapped animal?

"Hi," she said, without smiling. It was like a single and surprisingly deep note blown on a woodwind instrument.

"Sorry," said Al, embarrassed, and his cheeks flushed.

"What for?"

He apologised again, and laughed uneasily. "Nothing I guess. I don't know . . ." He introduced himself, wondering confusedly if he ought to extend a hand across the table, which he only just decided against. There was a pause in which the girl did not look away but continued staring disconcertingly into his eyes.

"You can call me Akasha." She spoke without a discernible accent, but very deliberately, as though attempting to conceal one.

"Akasha . . . That's an interesting name. Where does it come from?" It sounded familiar but he could not place it.

She shrugged. "Nowhere in particular."

While the same sluggish movements and murmurs went on around him, Al was immobilised. The ambiance of the place, with its low lighting and mixed aroma of kitchen smells and earthy Tibetan incense, seemed suddenly quite depressing. His senses were definitely heightened following the meditation session; he could see the warm, mellow light bouncing off Akasha's unblinking eyeballs, and hear acutely all the dinner table noises to the extent that they suddenly began to irritate him. She blinked, and he came back to himself.

"How long have you been coming here?" he managed.

She seemed to think this was an odd question, but answered anyway. "A long time, but I come and go. This place is alright, but I know better."

Was that "a better place" or just "better"? In any case, such a judgemental tone was unknown here, and certainly no way to speak about anything connected with *dharma*. No doubt the *sangha* members were all imperfect beings outside these walls, but there was a certain etiquette observed within them that entailed evincing the *brahma-viharas* in one's speech and manner. Sometimes it looked a bit like pusillanimity; for example, when a visiting *geshe* had remarked in a talk that it was pointless trying to explain the *Heart Sutra* to Westerners, but that even by hearing his teaching, the seeds of a more advantageous rebirth were being planted in the listeners' mind-streams. No one had been overtly offended by this, or dared to question it. Nor did anyone seem offended by Akasha's words just now, though they had been loud and clear enough.

Akasha went back to her food, chewing it in a way that failed to disguise her displeasure, before confirming, "This is awful." Al felt very uncomfortable. Then she stood up, gently shaking her silken, coal-black hair, and tucking a strand of it behind her ear. He noticed that she was dressed, beatnik style, in a black skivvy and jeans as well. She was very thin and her figure rather androgynous, but although he would not have called her his "type," was far from unattractive. "Do you want to come with me?" she asked in a tone whose indifference was belied by the deep gaze of those eyes that might have belonged to a spirited horse appraising a new rider.

Al's heart beat with an untoward passion. Was she trying to seduce him? Like any other young man, especially one of his shy temperament, Al had often dreamt of a girl who would walk into his life unexpectedly and offer herself in some overt, implausible way.

She moved slowly behind the row of diners, towards the door. Again, no one seemed to notice her rudeness. She did not repeat her offer. Anxiously, yet apparently covered by her invisibility spell, he followed Akasha's example, inconsiderately leaving his unfinished meal and uttering the fragment of a lie to no one in particular: "I'll be right . . ."

"So, do you, like, go to school, or . . . ?" he asked as she waited by the front door for him to tie his shoes. It was a mild *non-sequitur*, but Al felt he must say something.

"It's a house," she replied, seeming to have misunderstood the question, "like this one, only older. It's where I live. That's where we're going, if you're coming."

She walked ahead of him at a brisk pace on her long, almost bony legs, while Al wracked his brain for more potential conversation starters. In a minute or two they reached the end of the tree-lined street, turning onto a busy main road just as a bus pulled over to the sign a few metres ahead, in front of the hotel with its flashing "pokies" sign. "This is our bus," she said, and walked towards it with no trace of hurry. The sky was still light, but would not remain so for long. It was cold and looking like rain.

Akasha got on the bus without a ticket. No one seemed to mind, but Al fumbled in his pocket for his day pass, almost falling over when the engine started. They travelled via a different route than he had ever taken before. He had no sense of direction or geography anyway; all he knew was the area in which he lived and went to school, and the bus route from there to the central business district, on which the *gompa* was located about halfway. The peculiarity of the circumstances coupled with the slight novelty of the scenery created a complex ferment inside him, the autumnal atmosphere also contributing its part. Al could not stop looking at his companion, who now seemed to him to be the most darkly beautiful creature he had ever seen. Akasha seemed not to mind being stared at, so he did it more and more boldly. She wore no perfume of the conventional sort, but a pleasant smoky scent clung to her that was distinct from the incense back at the *gompa*.

He knew little about girls and less about how to interact with them, but Al gathered that his job was somehow to keep talking so that she would not grow bored with his company. He was also, naturally, curious and a bit nervous about where, and possibly to whom, this strange dream incarnate was taking him.

"So, do you have a teacher, I mean, like, a guru?"

"No," she said, turning to face him with a smirk. "There is no guru."

"Is that, umm . . . You mean in your sect, like in Pure Land Buddhism, or the Nichiren School . . . ?"

"I'll show you what I mean, don't worry."

His every conversational overture was rebuffed. It was just the sort of test one would expect from a genuine teacher, and the fact that this one looked just like a beautiful young girl might be a further test. Were his feelings toward her sacrilegious, in that case? On the other hand, whilst he knew that *tantra* was not always sexual, Al knew also that it certainly could be . . .

He remembered the stories of the great *yogis* who had searched high and low for a teacher and were often rebuffed or, once taken in after days of sitting out in the cold, begging for acceptance, put to work for years on some menial task. Al felt compelled to show off his erudition by speaking once more into the silence, "It's funny, I was just thinking how Milarepa had to build and demolish three towers before Marpa would take him on as a disciple. But here, you've come along, right when I wasn't expecting, and offered me . . ." What had she offered him, exactly? How to finish the sentence? "I don't know—but, like, this . . . invitation. Know what I mean?" He knew that he ought to shut up, but rambled on: "All I'm saying, I guess, is it's just really weird—I mean, like, 'weird' in a good way, don't get me wrong!" He chuckled pathetically.

"It sounds like you've read a lot of books," she observed with a faintly contemptuous smile, leaving him to wonder if she was being sarcastic, given his collapse into inarticulacy.

In silence Al began to wonder more intently whether perhaps some third party was to be involved in whatever revelation was in store for him at Akasha's house, and whether the transaction his unlikely guru had in mind would be to his advantage at all.

"So, like, where are we actually going? I mean—"

"I told you. My house."

"Sorry, I know, but . . . it's just I don't know this part of town, and . . . I mean, you didn't exactly tell me why we were going; I just assumed, and maybe I'm wrong, so . . ."

"I'm going because I live there. What about you?"

"Uh . . . you asked me."

"So, would you do anything I asked? Good to know." She smiled, appearing so much more human for this little piece of mockery that Al felt immensely reassured.

In any case, he got no further. Who was she? Was she the bait in a sordid trap, or an emanation, a *nirmanakaya* of some *dakini* come to lead him on the *bodhisattva*'s path? Or might she be something even better?

Al reflected silently that a few months ago he had been confessing the *shahada* with, as he then thought, all his heart and soul; he sensed now that the next phase of his spiritual life was about to begin, similarly discontinuous with the preceding one.

The other passengers, of whom there had been many to start, gradually exited until there was no one left but the pair of them. After the bus had left the high road, it had taken them through an upmarket commercial district of cafés, antique shops, Pilates studios, dog groomers, and so forth. Then they went over a bridge, and their environs changed. Soon came the ethnic neighbourhood, full of dingy-looking restaurants of various nationalities, spice-and-video shops, pawnbrokers, and hairdressers advertising extensions and straightening. Among these there began to appear a steadily increasing proportion of shopfronts that were probably or definitely unoccupied. These Al found very affecting, with their crumpled tin awnings, peeling paint, and remnants of old advertising. Yes, the feeling swelled in him, it was necessary to escape from this world corrupted by becoming; and in an odd way, it seemed that this had been achieved in the almost ghostly locale through which they now travelled, transcending time by succumbing to it.

"Do you like the view?" she asked, taking him by surprise.

"Huh? Oh, yeah, in a way. I guess it makes me feel . . . nostalgic, if that's the right word."

"You'll love my place, then."

The bus was now winding through residential streets. There were cars and furniture in various states of decrepitude stationed on lawns overgrown with weeds, the houses in matching condition. Akasha pulled the cord and stood up as the bus began slowing down. She continued looking straight ahead and said nothing, so that as for most of the journey Al felt invisible. He had lost all sense of time, so engrossed had he been in his companion and their surroundings.

If not for the streetlights it would have been dark by now. It was autumn, towards the end of daylight-saving, the air chilly. The rain that had seemed likely had not eventuated. What was reassuring, though certainly odd, about this suburban district was the presence of so many people out on the street under the pathetically mutilated plane trees, telephone cables, and the streetlights with their dirty, yellowish beams. They were strolling around, walking dogs, and sitting on verandas and fences. He noticed in particular a pair of children holding hands and leaning in opposite directions, playing a balancing game, and an old man sitting on his gate post, smoking, whose head rotated slowly to follow Akasha and Al as they walked past. Those who were close enough that it seemed they should be conversing made no sound that he could hear, not a fragment of a word, only the rustle of leaves overhead—which was odd, since there were so few of the latter.

"Kind of like a creepy street party," he remarked.

"They're always around," his guide replied in what might have been a contemptuous tone. "Here we are," she added a moment later as they reached the gate of a very large and heavily built bungalow with a double-arched portico facing off to one side, away from the street and towards what was probably once a garage. The side of the house facing them was shrouded in the dense, twiggy remains of some climbing plant that had completely overrun it. The house was very imposing, the grand entrance looming into view as they ascended the terrace that had buckled the brick fence, almost ready to collapse onto the footpath. There were overgrown garden beds and one dead tree. Slim chance she lived in this squatter's mansion alone.

She took his hand.

The house was incredibly similar to the one where their journey had begun, only tremendously dilapidated. "It looks just like . . ." he began to remark, but just then she took him by the hand, and he lost his train of thought. It was a hand of flesh and blood, sure enough; a little cold, but real, human.

Akasha pushed open the unlocked door which creaked in predictable agony. It was dark inside. She picked up a kerosene lamp that lay on a table in the long entry hall, and lit it with a match. Al's attention was on the physical contact this living miracle had initiated on the garden path. It was the first time a girl had ever held his hand since he had been old enough for it to mean anything. The lamplight disclosed an open door to their right that in the house's twin would have led to the meditation room, but he saw as they passed that there was nothing inside that room but a huge hole in the floor and some cracks and dirty smears on the walls. The cracks were large and ubiquitous. The floorboards creaked loudly. He felt a sudden fear that the edifice might collapse and bury them. "Do you live here alone?" he managed finally to ask, in a high-pitched voice.

"In a way. There are others who come and go, but I'm always here, except when I'm not. Don't worry, Al, we'll have the place to ourselves tonight." His heart beat faster.

She took him into one of the rooms off the hallway that, in the *gompa* were marked "private." It was a bedroom, yes, but what a comfortless one! Apart from a fireplace and ornate mantelpiece there was nothing there but the bed itself and, apparently, one of those old wooden cupboards whose doors would never stay shut, since they were swung open now to a disconcerting wingspan. The bed was metal-framed and bare, as though today had been laundry day (which must also explain the empty cupboard). Al wondered if they would be lighting a fire; he could smell ashes, and there were burn marks on the threadbare carpet. On the wall behind the bed someone had smeared charcoal from the fireplace into a quite perfect, fuzzy-edged oval shape about a metre high. Perhaps it was just the low lighting, but it seemed extraordinarily black in the centre of that monolithic smudge.

"What's in here?" he asked in a voice that hardly resembled his own.

She did not answer but, as he almost had the right to expect by now, after setting the lamp down on the mantel, pressed her body to his and kissed him, open-mouthed. Although it was incredibly exciting, the tanniny taste of her mouth brought back the feeling he had had on the bus when going past the seedy old buildings.

They gravitated towards the bed, her hands methodically caressing and undressing him, while he hardly knew what he did. The excitement was almost more than Al could bear. She said nothing else until, having pulled him on top of her, the incredible moment arrived in which they were joined. There, beneath him was her massive heartbeat so powerful it seemed to negate his own, an oddly slow and powerful bass drum despite both the act in which they were engaged and her delicate figure.

But as soon as Al experienced the immediate certainty of their union, it evaporated. Her heartbeat now seemed to recede far away amid a whining, equally distant chorus of bedsprings; nor could he quite manage to feel the girl's body as actually present to his touch. The idea of Akasha as an emanation body, or *nirmanakaya,* returned as his hands wandered, in a compulsive effort to summon her back. She responded as enthusiastically as he could have wished, and yet he felt almost nothing; it was like those dreams in which the blessed moment of sexual fulfilment would arrive, and the next Al would realise that he was dreaming. He tried to concentrate on the essential zone where their bodies were joined, but it was no use.

They had tumbled about for some time, and she was now on top, facing him. Above his head the black smudge loomed on the wall, he remembered. In fact, the wall behind him seemed to tilt forwards, or the bed to tilt backwards, as now he stared up at it in the flickering lamplight, until the blackness began to merge with the silhouette of the *dakini* straddling him, as if both she and the wall were folding down over his prostrate form. Now Akasha was submerged from behind as in a body of black water. He called her name, but heard nothing. The dark oblong occupied his field of vision completely as the light from the kerosene lamp slowly dimmed and went out. The shape was blacker than the blackness in which Al floated. Around the periphery glowed a trace of very cold, silvery-blue light, like daylight peeping through between a door and its frame.

Now the shape—the portal—descended over him, and after a spasm of terror, followed by a moment of the most suffocatingly luxuriant darkness and vacancy, as of an ocean of velvet night, Al found himself again outside the house, standing in the street he recognised from what could only have been minutes before, though it felt far longer.

The sky seemed to agree. It was bright yet overcast: a chilly autumn morning. He remembered something his friend Euan, who laid claim to some sexual experience, had told him: "Your first time, it's so different from what you imagined, mate. Believe me."

And the people were still there. If anything, there were more of them, but this time none were strolling or sitting down at leisure. All were standing, all facing him with an intense interest he could feel even before his eyes had adjusted to the light sufficiently to meet theirs. In fact, it seemed that they wanted desperately to run at him and do God-knew-what, but apparently some invisible force was holding them back.

Al blinked at the silver Sun fiercely struggling through a thick blanket of clouds. The crowd's eyes were lidless, with an expression of something that might have been panic or avidity, or a combination of both. It was impossible to read it in any other way, since the flesh of their faces and bodies was shrivelled like the flesh of ancient mummies: lipless, noseless, and sallow. Only their eyes were alive. They stood leaning forward precariously and, as it seemed, pulled upward by invisible puppet strings that kept them on their toes, wasted limbs jerking and twitching like the branches of trees in the wind—though the actual trees around them did not move at all in the total silence.

He spun in a circle, seeking Akasha, who was nowhere to be seen. The house in which he had just been was a pile of rubble, utterly demolished. Staring at it as panic grew within him, he knew that she was now far away, having abandoned him here in this hellish realm. He wanted to go home to his mother, his father, his bookish and virtual, introverted life!

Al started moving, briskly but warily, not wanting to look at the hideous spectators, but knowing that he must keep as wide a berth around them as possible. They reminded him of the cowskin rocking horse his mother sentimentally had refurbished years ago, and that he could remember appearing to rock by itself, terrifying him as a child. They had hair and clothes like normal, living people, but their mad eyes were glossy as marbles, and big as Akasha's had been. They might have been botched taxidermy mounts but for those horrible, hesitating signs of life. This one might have been an old woman to start with; the one beside her—no, to judge from her clothes and hair it must be—have been—her granddaughter! And with them was the most terrifying dog Al had ever seen . . . !

Their bulging eyes followed his movements as far as they could. Ahead was the intersection where the bus had stopped. Could it be that on the other side of the blasted, overgrown-hedge, he might find the road that led back to his familiar life?

No, there were only more of the horrid mannequins.

He was running now, almost colliding with one as he swerved to avoid another. Behind the painful beating of his heart was another pulse, a heavier, slower rhythm that was not inside his body, he knew, or his mind only, but everywhere and nowhere. It was the heartbeat of this world, Akasha's world, into which he had fallen.

A wind began blowing behind him where none had been before. It was her breath, and the loss of her made him feel an unexpected poetic sadness: perhaps he would find her again somewhere ahead on this mysterious journey, which now began to seem like a tantalising adventure. She would not be found among the scarecrow-mummies, occupying as she did a higher plane of existence.

The wind also made running easier, almost lifting Al's feet up from the ground as in those dreams he had always had at intervals in which he would discover miraculously the ability to tread on air like water, to glide like a leaf on the breeze: almost actually to fly. Those dreams were always set in gloomy, autumnal landscapes like this one – minus the watchers.

But the wind was there to serve purposes not his own; it soon grew unpredictable, multiplying its forces from every direction until soon he was caught between powerful cross-currents that lashed him so that he began to stagger, doing his best to recoil before contact with any of the vile figures, one of whom, he was sure, managed briefly to grab the fabric of his jumper before another gust blew him in the opposite direction.

Al felt and heard himself crying out; then, just seconds later – drying out.

He could not have stood up by himself under such buffeting, but now that an equilibrium had been reached, he swayed in one place, feet oddly rooted to the ground but without the least sense of a firm purchase. His skin stretched tight against his skull, as with difficulty he fought to raise an enervated hand to his face to feel its papery surface, lips and eyelids receding as his nose crumpled in on itself.

MOTT'S PLAIN

Yeah, I'm a country boy; grew up in a place called Mott's Plain, up in the Mallee. I fitted in okay when I lived there, after a bit of a rough start, even played footy after starting school at thirteen. I don't ever plan on going back again, though. I'm not alone in that: from what I gather the population's shrunk by about half just in the last decade.

They had their educational theories, my folks, and they were pretty well-positioned to put them into action, with Mum, ironically enough, being a primary teacher. Dad was retired philosophy lecturer ("retired" as in couldn't get a regular academic job; he wasn't that old). He was definitely a polymath and a bit of an eccentric; designed and to a large extent built our house by hand, for one thing. The socialisation aspect was difficult for them to arrange, though, in the absence of any other home-school families in the area. I suppose they'd had to compromise and live where they could afford, with only Mum bringing in a wage.

There were some hippies in the mix, but mainly the other families I can remember us meeting were religious; didn't want their kids learning about evolution or sex or non-Christian religions, essentially. We were different. I remember Dad describing Christianity as, what was it? "a degenerate, plebeian manifestation of the solar cult."

So while Mum went out to work at the local school, he stayed at home with me, and we looked after the garden, the chickens, the dogs, the cow, and the odd goat or sheep that we had. The aim was self-sufficiency in food, though I don't think we ever reached it. I learnt a fair bit working with Dad; for example, he taught me Pythagoras' Theorem by using it to plot where to build a new chook house. I had formal lessons too, of course, studied Latin and German as well as the usual subjects. Dad and I used to philosophise about everything, like, I remember him telling me about the Great Chain of Being and us discussing the ethics of keeping animals and eating meat one time when the slaughterman came for one of our calves. A fair bit deeper than what I learned in first year uni, in fact.

And we all loved music: classical music, that is. That was Mum's main contribution to my education. She taught me piano, which I'm not a bad hand at to this day.

So one day when I was eleven, she took me to visit a boy called Josh Ryan. We were going to see her family in Bendigo after, I think, while Dad stayed home to look after things. Josh's family lived quite a drive away, on a real farm that was so far off the public road I couldn't even believe it.

Maybe the distance was why we'd never visited the Ryans before. I'd begun to embrace my outsider status among the widely dispersed home-school community by this time, and being obnoxious about their religion was an aspect of it, I guess, to pre-empt rejection. I used to tell other kids that I didn't believe in Jesus or God, and in the same breath, that not only did I hate footy, I loved classical music and art and theatre and all that.

Josh was an only child, like me, but at thirteen he was a couple of years older. He seemed starved for company. As I recall he was big and strong-looking, with dark fuzz on his upper lip, and the type of undercut hairdo that was the style at the time. I remember his mouth hung open a lot of the time. It was the 90s, so he was wearing a Hypercolour T-shirt that changed colour throughout the day, showing the sweat under his arms.

"Who do you follow?" was the first thing he said after I was deposited in his room. There were footy posters and pictures of cars on the walls; no crucifix or anything.

"I don't."

"Huh. I got some footy cards I was gonna show you."

He seemed so disappointed that I immediately decided not to be a prig, after all.

"Just kidding, footy's alright. I follow the Cats, kind of."

He made some comments about players and how apparently we, that is, Geelong, weren't going to do so well this year without some Dazza or Bazza or Smokie or Pokie, or whoever, who'd defected to some other animal species for whatever reason. I agreed and asked him who he followed, which took the onus off me a bit while he went on about his favourite players. Josh had lots of cards that he kept in a brimming shoebox under his bed. I didn't know any of the players but pretended I did, while he mainly just read their stats off the back, and drew comparisons between them that I nodded and agreed with. I did get caught out to some extent, though, when I compared a back pocket's goal scoring stats to a full-forward's. I remember thinking Josh seemed young for his age, at first. It was hard to believe that he was actually two years older than me.

So then it was time for lunch, and we met around the table for roast lamb. It was delicious; one of their own. They said Grace but didn't make a big deal about it. Normally I was incorrigible: one time I remember saying at someone's dinner table, "But if God is a spirit then he doesn't have ears, so how can he hear you?" My parents cut me a bit too much slack, I'd say, when it came to things like that. Oh, I was their little genius!

Our mothers seemed to be getting on well, talking about us, mostly, and about our fathers, until Josh's came in late from working somewhere on his vast property, apologised, and tucked in. His wife did most of the talking, along with my mum, and it was mostly about Josh and me, our interests and achievements. Josh and his dad were fixing up a motorbike; they'd made a sheep feeder; he was on the local football team, as I'd already gathered, and got along well with the other kids who all went to school together . . . Mum under-emphasised the academic focus of my education, which I felt made me come off second-best.

After lunch Josh said, "Hey Harry, wanna play Sega?" I did actually like videogames; it was a guilty pleasure I enjoyed so rarely because my parents were against it. So I lost badly at *Super Mario Kart* (Josh said regretfully "I'm not allowed to have violent games 'n' that"). His comments on my skills were encouraging after I told him I had no console at home. Then his mother came into the room and said, "Why don't you boys go and get some vitamin D?"

Josh explained, "Mum always says vitamin D when she means outside."

It was a nice day, and, as it turned out, there were practically no flies around, which is practically a miracle up that way. I think I said something autistic like, "Did you know on high UV days you're at risk of sunburn, even if it's cloudy?" A nice thing about home-school kids is that they're pretty tolerant of others' weirdness. Josh seemed okay.

No, there was no pool. We went to the dam, which was a big puddle of water with a lonely eucalyptus casting a snaky bit of shade. It was only waist-deep and lined with orange plastic. But to get there or anywhere else on the Ryans' enormous property, you had to ride a motorbike. This was before the big drought, by the way; people don't have dams like that anymore. So Josh lent me a pair of bathers that were a bit too big, and I rode pillion over the bumpy ground, gripping him around the middle and feeling very awkward about it.

Then we were paddling around on an old tyre and a boogie board. (Josh was polite enough to give me the board.) I asked him where the water came from, because my dad had told me the water under the ground hereabouts was saline. It seemed a grown-up thing to talk shop like that about living on the land. Josh said the water was from the town catchment, delivered by pipeline. "It's for the sheep. We get some in after harvest to clean up the stalks, then we send 'em away to get killed. Probably won't be able to have a dam anymore soon, though. Me uncle Shane—he's not me real uncle, just this bloke Mum and Dad knows—he topped himself last year, 'cause of the drought 'n' that." Then, after a short pause he exclaimed, "Just wish I had a stubby of VB right now! Be-yewtiful!"

Well, we were supposed to be back at the house by three so Mum and I could get to Bendigo at a reasonable time. On the way, Josh asked me if I wanted to stay over. He suggested I could stay while Mum did her thing and came back the next day. I really didn't want to, and I wished I hadn't told him we were only going for one night. The very idea of staying over in someone else's home without my parents made me uncomfortable; I'd never done it before.

My mother was only too happy to let me stay. I had to restrain a real sense of panic, waving goodbye to her from the veranda. I remember looking out to the horizon with wheat stalks and bits of miserable Mallee scrub stretching out in every direction, and trying not to panic. Then inside there were all other-people's-house odours of different food, different cleaning products, different bodies. I was squeamish about things like that. And even if my hosts were hospitable, the landscape wasn't, even compared to our place. I felt as if I were staying over on the Moon.

After that we had a piece of cake and a Milo for afternoon tea and went back out to play. It calmed me a bit. Josh's mum was really nice, I decided. She asked me lots of questions and spot-cleaned my face with a hanky (not with spit, though!). It didn't seem out of place, given her natural, affectionate manner.

We still had a good few hours of daylight, so Josh wanted to go and do some shooting.

"I thought you weren't allowed to play violent games?" I said.

He seemed not to understand.

It was new and a little daunting to me, though I didn't feel like admitting it. I was afraid I'd be asked to shoot something living, which I was fine with on a philosophical level, but in real life . . . I'd seen Dad kill a chicken or two, but refused to watch when the slaughterman came to kill something bigger. Josh and I took turns shooting a pellet gun at some tins and bottles dangling from bits of string from a tree. "Last time I went shootin' with this piece I hit a rabbit right in the head, here." He pointed to his temple. "Me and Dad, we go shootin' sometimes with proper guns. Sometimes we kill 'roos, but mostly it's just rabbits. You ever been ferretin'?"

I said no, and he explained.

I couldn't seem to hit anything, which was embarrassing because Josh was a crack shot. I felt the dynamics shifting. He was showing off to a younger kid who, he was starting to suspect, was a bit useless.

Josh exclaimed, "Jeez, ain't you ever shot a gun before?"

"It's getting dark," I said, grinding my teeth.

And it was, to an extent. The sky was greying except for the blaze building up on the horizon as if there'd been a grass fire. After another awkward ride hanging on to Josh's middle, smelling his sweat, we arrived back at the shed near the house where the pellet guns belonged.

"Me dad's got heaps of tools," Josh said. "He's real handy. Is your dad handy?"

"He's building our house," I said with pride.

"Oh, is he a builder? I wanna be a builder if I can get a 'prenticeship. There's a bloke in our church might gimme one when I turn sixteen."

Then he reached under the workbench beneath the hooks where the gun was hung. "Hey, show you something else, Harry. This is the knife we use when we kill kangas, to field dress 'em 'n' that." I didn't know what "field dress" meant, but I could guess. "Check it out! Touch that, and I bet you'll cut yourself. This knife can cut paper, no joke, like one a them Samyurai swords."

I drew my fingertip across the edge and felt the prickling sensation. It was sharp alright.

Then this abstracted look came over his face. He was looking past me so intently I almost spun around to see what must have been right behind me. When there wasn't, I wondered fleetingly if I was about to get stabbed. "That reminds me of something else we could do," he said in a really wistful tone of voice, not looking at me. I remember I felt dread at those words, and excitement, though I had no idea what he was talking about. A moment before I'd been longing to call it a night and go inside.

"There's another shed about a K. away. Reckon we could get there and back before it gets proper dark. You won't believe what's there, Haz!" No one had ever called me that before, and I didn't like it. He was smiling; wouldn't tell me anything except, "wait and see."

So Josh topped up the fuel tank, and we rode over the bristling fields and into one of those patches of scrub that were scattered around the property. But this one was denser; you couldn't see right through to the other side, despite how sparse and cobwebby the foliage was. It was getting darker. Those trees, branching out from the ground this way and that, were like half-dead things, snaky and black and burnt-looking. It's like that in the Mallee, as you know.

Soon we reached a little clearing with a small, squarish

wooden shed that looked very old and rustic, the planks that made up the walls having the texture of an elderly person's skin, as I recall.

"I wouldn't show this to anyone, but you and me's friends, Haz. She's in there." I noticed his use of the feminine pronoun; Josh had called his shiny Yamaha a 'she' earlier, too. But then he added, "She's me girlfriend. Mum and Dad don't know."

There was a window in the side of the little building that we, despite not being fully grown, almost had to bend down to see into. You might have expected there to be cobwebs inside that window, and for the glass to be milky with dust, but that wasn't the case. When I looked inside, my heart thundering with anticipation, well, it almost stopped. Inside there was indeed a girl. She was sitting on a wooden chair, facing away from us, looking out of the other window opposite, so still I wondered with alarm if she was even breathing.

As far as I could see the walls were bare inside, but clean, like a house when you first move in, with a wooden floor and walls that had been clad, you know, like the walls of a house. It was basically a very small granny flat. I had a very strange impression that the room inside was bigger than the outside. There was a subdued, cool light inside that contrasted with the warm, blood-streaked gold of the sunset; didn't see where it was coming from.

The girl was just so beautiful. Now, she was seated with her back to me, so you might well ask how I got so excited right away, but there you go. I could tell right away to an extent that's impossible to explain or communicate that she was simply perfect. That fiery, sunset-coloured hair swept over one shoulder . . . marble-white shoulders and back, and a glimpse of her nape on the other side, glowing underneath it, "And all her body like a pallace fayre / Ascending uppe with many a stately stayre," okay? She was wearing a real ball gown of a dress, strapless, with masses of layered skirts cascading all over the floor. Just sitting there exceptionally still. I had this intense feeling that she was a tragic figure, and I wanted to do something to help her.

The feeling I had was the one you get in adolescence towards the opposite sex, or anyway the ones you have a crush on. Maybe you can relate, maybe you can't. It was an awe that was beyond desire, though I'm pretty sure I did desire her more than anything or anyone, ever. This was the first time I'd felt any interest in a girl, that I can recall. And remember, I hadn't even seen her face yet!

Josh gloated: "Ever seen one like her before? Here, out the way. Gizza look." For the second time that day I felt a surge of resentment, much stronger this time, but I did as he asked. I saw the dying sunlight glinting on his avid eyeballs and teeth as he licked his lips (or maybe it was the strange light coming from inside). In a minute he turned back to me, and there was this look of swaggering mastery on his face. It was like earlier with the rifle, only tenfold.

"Wanna see her face, Haz?" he teased me.

"Okay." I wanted more than anything to see the face that went with that adorable figure of a young girl probably just a little older than me, about Josh's age.

From the opposite side I saw the exact same view as I'd just seen: same girl, same angle; the only difference being that she was now facing away from the embers of the sunset. The pair of them were playing a joke on me. The big boyfriend and girlfriend against the little tag-along kid!

Josh was laughing. "Still can't see her face, eh, Hazza? Can't open that door either, eh? See that padlock? Been there bloody years. No key for it." There was indeed a large, rusty padlock on the door, which I hadn't noticed. He and I both stood for a while, heads touching, at the window. I could hear Josh's heavy breathing. He might have been forming words underneath, but I don't know. My attention was elsewhere.

Eventually he said, in a surprisingly deep, husky voice, "Get out me way. I'll show yer." I obeyed. He added, "It's worth it."

Then Josh repeated those three words to himself twice more, under his breath, the same abstracted look over his face as I'd seen in the shed near the house when he had had the brainwave to bring me there. He stood back just a bit, in a wide stance, and took the knife in its leather sheath out of his waistband. He threw the sheath down and wiped the blade, both sides, on his shorts. Then he drew it across his hand to prove its sharpness. The blood pooled in his palm. He sniggered and kept staring ahead.

Then Josh put the knife tip to his wrist and plunged it in, and ripped the blade through longways, up to the elbow joint. Blood gushed, went pitter-patter like rain on that thirsty ground.

I don't know if I managed to scream; Josh didn't, nor make any other noise. He wobbled a bit on his feet, passing the knife to his other hand and doing the same to his other arm, maybe not quite as successfully. I had to admire his willpower. He had rivers of blood streaming down his arms and all over his hands as he staggered, righted himself and raised his forearms to the window pane and smeared blood all over the glass. Straight away there was a noise inside the shed like something falling over, and more banging noises as though a wild animal were trapped inside.

And, let's just say, that wasn't the furthest from the truth. Josh was leaning against the window, trying not to let his knees buckle, trying not to go down just yet. Then another face appeared to meet his on the inside. The girl pressed her open mouth to the glass, which she appeared to be kissing passionately: lips, tongue, teeth, starving eyes. No, she wasn't trying to kiss Josh—or actually, maybe she was in a way. And she wasn't frantic over what he had done to himself, exactly. She wanted to taste his blood.

I felt the blood go out of me as well, and I absolutely wished that it was my body that was slumping against the side of that furiously rattling shed, knees hitting the dirt before I fell sideways, head smacking unconscious against the ground, then rolling onto my back, still smiling, still bleeding.

Josh was dead. I tried to think about what that meant. I stood there for ages, but really the girl still held my attention. She was still trying to drink the blood that was on the other side of the glass. I was invisible to her. I looked over at the knife that was lying on the ground, and thought about picking it up. But then I was shocked to see her banging that furiously screaming face, still so terribly beautiful, against what was obviously soundproof and reinforced glass, and looking down at Josh's body below, out of her reach. I was afraid she might hurt herself. God, those incredible blue eyes . . . the turn of her little nose . . . just everything about her!

When she dropped out of sight (less in defeat, I suspect, than to get nearer the source of the blood smell), I looked back at Josh, and it hit me again. I ran to the edge of the bit of scrub where his bike was lying, and I rode back in the direction of the house, adrenaline probably enabling me to rise to the occasion and speed up without falling off. I'd never ridden a motorbike before, but somehow I managed it. At first I was unsure of the way back, but then I could see the lighted windows and roof of the farmhouse. I ran up to the front door and banged on it. I was terrified of what Josh's parents might do or say when they'd heard what happened. What if they thought I'd done it? I was a stranger to them.

"Harry!" Josh's dad exclaimed when she saw me quivering on the doorstep.

I blubbered incoherently, apologising again and again without making any sense. He held me close and I smelled his strange smell that was like my own father's but subtly different. Josh's mother was there now, behind him. I felt so sorry for them both. It couldn't have been harder to tell them if I *had* been Josh's murderer.

Then his dad took me by the shoulders and said, "Harry, what's happened? Who's Josh?"

That was how I came to live on Mott's Plain. My new parents must have thought I was acting pretty strangely for a while, going on about this imaginary friend of mine. A lot of that early period's a blur to me now, as I gather traumatic memories generally are. Anyway, it turned out I was the only son they'd ever had, and I had no other parents; none who came back for me that I know of, in any case. For a while I thought I'd been kidnapped by crazy people, but then they were so nice to me, and the story of my life as Harry Ryan, son of Darren and Leonie, was corroborated by strange grandparents, and alleged friends who came around to play. The child psychologist made it clear where I stood, too. So after a lot of crying and runaway attempts, and efforts to phone my parents (number disconnected), I decided I must indeed have been the crazy one, that I'd just imagined a life with those other people I can still remember so clearly, even now.

I looked for the girl in the shed, too—next day, actually, and many, many times after that. I was afraid of what she'd make me do, but I wanted above all else to be with her, as I guessed Josh was now. But wouldn't you just know it? The shed had disappeared, along with the body, the blood, and the knife, and my new parents had no idea what I was talking about there either.

So a few years on, I got a scholarship to go to uni, which was handy after the Ryans disappeared inexplicably in their turn, during my second year, so they couldn't help me out any longer. I missed them as well. But that's right, their number was disconnected, so I went back there and . . . I probably don't need to tell you that story.

Anyway, here's a little proof of what I've just told you. Well, it's proof as far as I'm concerned, though it wouldn't prove anything to you if you had any doubts. See, I had no piano growing up with the Ryans, and I never played again until like a decade later, honest. But listen to this. Let me play you, let's see . . . Beethoven's Pathétique Sonata seems appropriate.

And after that, you can finally show me what I missed out on all those years ago.

THE BABY SHOWER

It happened on a housing estate in the inner city, somewhere between the uni and the zoo, appropriately enough; a piece of parkland that had been handed over to developers to build these boxy little two-storey homes for yuppies who'd come along too late to be part of the last gentrification wave. I never would've known a place like that existed, even though it was just a short bike ride away from where I live.

To start with, I was standing around with loads of others in the kitchen-dining room, just watching, listening, and trying not to look like too much of an outsider. It was pretty weird, though, attending the baby shower of the woman I was replacing in the Law Research Office while she took maternity leave. First baby shower I'd ever been to, in fact. I gathered she was "a bit of a character," as they say, mostly disliked but well-respected, and that her power derived—where else?—from sucking up to academics like the one who was throwing this party for her. That was Associate Professor Johanna Lurie, the new Dean of Research. I gathered she and Mag had studied together years ago, and Johanna had gone on to a Rhodes Scholarship while Mag, well, hadn't. But they were still close friends, and on the grapevine, I'd heard that Johanna had spoken of Mag as a "miracle worker" when it came to tracking down and honing applications for research funding, and especially how she'd helped her get that Open Society Fellowship.

Everyone loved Johanna (besides which, almost everyone was employed on a temporary contract); hence, I guess, why basically everyone from the law school who had a vagina had turned up at this very awkward do, along with a gay boy or two and a tranny. It wasn't just arse-kissing; a lot of people actually looked up to Johanna, wanted to be her, maybe, or had some kind of a crush on her. For example, recently she'd been on TV, one of these ooh-ahh-controversial panel shows, where she was arguing against this conservative journalist over hate-speech laws and whether we need them in Australia. The guy basically implied that she was a Nazi for advocating political censorship, accusing her of wanting to burn books and put political opponents in concentration camps. Well, it was a bad move on his part because those sultry, dark eyes of hers filled with tears, and Johanna started talking about her grandparents' miraculous, last minute escape from the gas chambers. The guy was totally embarrassed and had to apologise, right then and there. Discussion over. Everyone was talking about it at work afterwards, sharing in Johanna's triumph. I heard she got a standing ovation from her students when she walked into the lecture theatre next day.

Anyway, I won't bore you with a detailed description of the place she shared with the Dean of the School, who of course she just happened to be shacked up with; enough to say they had plenty of nice furniture and appliances; but it was reassuring to me as a mere plebe that the place looked hardly lived-in, like they must've had no time to enjoy it.

Another wine, and I was in danger of getting truly drunk and doing or saying something stupid. Conversations were awkward because there was a sense that you were supposed to know everyone, which was sort-of the situation, but only sort-of. You might know a voice but not the face, or a face but not the name, and so on. And they were all university people, which meant that no amount of pretentiousness or ideological flaunting was off-limits. At one point, for example, I struck up a conversation with a girl who happened to be standing beside me on her own. I had a hunch she worked as someone's Personal Assistant, or possibly in some research centre or other; but I didn't want to assume in case she happened to be some young hotshot academic.

"I love your dress!" I said.

"Thanks," then after a pause that was a bit too long, "yours too."

"So retro. What is it, '60s? '70s?" The dress looked like it was made from recycled lounge chair upholstery, with a big white doily stuck on around the neck.

She smiled. "Actually, I made it myself."

"Wow! That must have taken you ages. It looks so . . . authentic," I said, unintentionally using what must have been a red flag word.

"Actually, that's a notion I'm really into interrogating," she began, "you know, cultural 'authenticity'?" she made quote marks with her fingers, making me want to throw my drink in her face right away. "I think it's really a discourse which thrives on the social inequality between centre and periphery, and the fetishisation of the underdeveloped-as-commodity. In my thesis I'm exploring the notion of the nostalgic consumption of time as a feature of late capitalism . . ."

She was using these big words and offsetting them with a rising intonation that I guessed was supposed to stop her from sounding pompous. She went on and on, namedropping the usual suspects and trying to convince me that she was doing something important with her life. So I was right about her being admin, then.

". . . Anyway," she eventually wound up, "sorry to be such a theory nerd! What do you do?"

I told her as colourlessly as possible, then let the conversation drop, having barely managed to repress my desire to smack her in the mouth while draining my glass and saying "uh-huh, right, I see" in the required places.

Then it was a sudden feeling of someone or something standing right behind me, too close for comfort, and uttering a kind of buzzing snarl, or snarling buzz, right in my ear. It was a feeling I'd had several times over the past few days and that was starting to make me wonder if I was about to experience a psychotic episode (which by the time I've finished this story you're going to think I did). That feeling related back to a dream of about a week ago that had hung over me ever since. Even fully awake, I kept getting the urge to run away, and it wasn't getting any better with the passage of time. If I was inside, I wanted to be outside, and vice-versa. Wherever I went, it felt like an ambush, as if whatever I'd done was just what it, what that . . . predator wanted me to do.

It went like this. I was getting ready for work, anxious about being late, and so on. To begin with, it was your typical stress dream, you know, just repeating and rehearsing the days behind and ahead of me with a sense of time slowing down, days passing while you butter the toast, get distracted chasing a white rabbit, etc. But then it intensified gradually and eventually changed into something worse. Something, some threat, was materialising right behind me. I'd turn around, and it would have instantly rotated 180 degrees. Finally I got out of the house, caught the tram, which was empty except for me and this awful presence I couldn't see, that followed me when I changed seats and kept on after me when I got off at my normal stop. The streets around uni were totally empty, and there was a sense that people had taken cover, as though there was a plague or a bomb threat or something. I began to panic and ran from one locked doorway of a shop or someone's house to the next, afraid of being out in the open. Then I began to see it out the corner of my eye, like it was meeting me halfway. It was a dark figure about the size of a man, and I understood that it was basically some kind of rapist.

Of course, when I turned around it wasn't there, but then it would reappear as a blur in the corner of my eye when I began running again. The distance in front of me lengthened as I ran. There was a terrible feeling of agoraphobia, and vertigo like I was going to fall over and not be able to get back up. And even though I say it was a rapist, at the same time I couldn't have said for sure that it was male. So when it caught me I was paralysed rigid, and there was a stinging pain down there where it . . . penetrated me, and I was paralysed, certain I was going to die.

So next thing, back at the party, I thought I heard this baleful sort of crying, moaning noise, but before I could be sure or figure out where it was coming from, one of the little kids in the next room where the TV was on started throwing a tantrum. He was screaming, "You're dead! You're dead! You're dead . . . !"

Then I accidentally made eye contact with my boss, the Research Manager. We'd said hi earlier on, and I'd disappeared as soon as someone else butted in. She was looking at me without smiling, and I thought not for the first time that she might actually be a psychopath—or just really not like me for some reason. Of course, she was talking with the Publications Coordinator, probably about how incompetent I am. They talk like that about everybody. And so I remembered how just the other day I'd felt in real life something a lot like the paralytic state from my dream, like being a fly caught in a spider's web.

It was during the monthly office meeting, and they put me on the spot in front of everyone. It was the Publications Coordinator. (That's right, I'm not using their names; they're such shallow people it seems appropriate.) She'd asked me a couple of weeks earlier to undertake some kind of research project on the research projects being undertaken at essentially all the research institutions in the world. The job was initially given to her, but then she'd re-negotiated her workload with the Research Manager (on one of their buddy-buddy trips to the coffee shop, I suppose), and considering my extremely vague job description and newness, I could hardly refuse to take this half-arsed project on. "Just something for the back burner . . ." she'd said, when I asked for details.

Now I was being asked to give a report on it in front of everyone!

"Well . . . it looks like there's been a lot of research activity in environmental law," I began, unpromisingly, "and international law . . ."

"I see. And what kind of intersections are you observing between research areas?" says the Manager.

I looked at the papers in front of me, then back at her face, and saw that she'd been looking at my papers, too, probably noticing that I hadn't brought any relevant notes. The project wasn't on the agenda, which it'd been my job to compile; should I have added it on my own initiative?

"Well, I'm not really at the stage yet of . . . you know, analysing the data in detail. I'll have a closer look at those intersections and, of course, at the extent and types of interdisciplinary crossover as well, once I've finished the . . . initial survey." I waffled on until the creased foreheads began to nod along in the hope that I would just shut up. In fact, all I'd done was to enter search terms into a citation database that I guessed was authoritative, and recorded the number of results for each in an Excel sheet. I'd barely got started, what with all the symposia and the mail-outs and blah, blah, blah.

I could have sworn, though it seemed incredibly rude, that the Manager had rolled her eyes while I was speaking—I mean, quite blatantly, as if to say to everyone present, "Do you hear this?" Focusing on making relative sense and talking for what I guessed was a sufficient length of time, it didn't register when it happened; it was only afterwards that I became increasingly sure, and increasingly angry remembering it.

Anyway, back at the party, fighting the urge to just leave, I experienced an even more urgent need to go the toilet. Problem was, this was a house full of boozing women, and there was a queue. I could hardly believe it: it was like in a bar. I could see academics and admin staff having bored and awkward conversations everywhere, and resorting pretty heavily to alcohol. So I decided to just go upstairs, even though my impression was that it was out of bounds.

There was a door on one side of the corridor upstairs, which I opened just a crack. It was dark inside, and carpeted: a bedroom, obviously. There was another bedroom up ahead that was lit by a raised blind, so I felt less intrusive about going in. Well, perhaps one of these bedrooms had an *en-suite*; I was already snooping around where I didn't belong.

Success! I wasn't too worried about being disturbed as I'd just seen Johanna deep in conversation with another academic, some obvious dyke from the Faculty. As soon as I sat down and began to collect my thoughts, I heard voices approaching—and in another moment they were in the room next to me! In case either of them needed to go, the smart thing would of course have been to emerge straight away and plead emergency. I was just in the process of freaking out when I realised that the *en-suite* was what you'd call a "Jack and Jill," you know, in between, connecting the two bedrooms. So, thank God, I could always escape quickly into the next room to hopefully avoid being seen.

". . . I just don't know what to do, Sam! Maybe you could have a look at her and—oh God!—please tell me I'm crazy!" It was Johanna speaking, sounding like a bad actor, just like she had on the TV.

Whoever it was sighed. "What can you do about it either way? If she doesn't want a doctor you can't force her."

"No, you don't understand; if you'd only seen what she looks like! I knew she was unwell this morning—I mean *really* sick. She wouldn't even get dressed; I had to make her take something out of the wardrobe to change into later. I even had to pick it out for her. She was standing there, completely listless, just staring into her cupboard like a dementia patient!"

I stood up and arranged myself as quietly as I could, ready to flee, and kept listening.

"Jo, I know this may sound unkind, but don't you don't think it might be partly theatrics? I know Mag's a very competent person in her sphere, but she does have . . . let's say, a bit of a thespian streak. You said she was reciting Yeats in the car—"

"Oh, sure, that's just something she does, haven't you noticed? 'Things fall apart, the centre cannot hold' It's like a catchphrase with her."

"Yes . . . I remember when I didn't get the Ford Foundation grant last year, she told me, 'All that is solid melts into air.'" The woman chuckled. "She's a character."

I remembered finding a little "quote of the day" calendar on Mag's desk when I started. Interesting to think of her being motivated by insecurity. But who isn't? There was also that email forwarded to me where she offered some academic "an intelligent layperson's point of view" on whatever-it-was.

Johanna kept emoting: "But the thing is, Sam, it was apropos of nothing. Mag was just, I don't know, *incanting*. And she looked just, so, so terrible, like a meth addict or something. She was lying in bed doing this asthmatic breathing thing when I got there to pick her up. I was almost afraid. Then I saw her face, like Mia Farrow in *Rosemary's Baby*—no, worse, God, so much worse than that!" (I'd seen a picture of Mag on the Faculty website, so it wasn't too hard to believe that she'd look quite a bit worse than a twenty-five-year-old Mia Farrow under any conditions whatsoever.) "So I said I'd call a doctor, but she said no, she'd already seen one—well, I gathered that was what she meant—but she wasn't actually looking at me when she said it. I got the impression she didn't know what she was saying at all. One minute I had my phone out, looking up the nearest doctor, the next she was up, grinning like crazy and spitting out these kind of half-formulated phrases, and we were on our way. I just didn't want today to be a failure, with everyone coming together like this, it was supposed to be, I just wanted . . . ! There was muffled sobbing for a while before the story continued.

"But then she started coughing and doubling up when we arrived. I thought maybe she was embarrassed about it, me throwing the shower for her. I know Mag doesn't have a lot of friends, not really . . . but, God, her face! I mean, when she started showing, before she went on leave, she was throwing up all the time. You remember, we practically had to stage an intervention to get her to take some time off. But that was different, it was her first trimester. Now she actually looks . . . oh, God, it's uncanny! I can't even describe . . ."

"Okay, it's okay. Let's go in and have a look at her."

There was sobbing and mumbled acquiescence.

Of course, I now realised that Mag was in the next room, and that the shortest route there was via the *en-suite*. I leapt on tiptoes across the tiles (thankfully my soles were relatively soft) and crossed to the door without glancing at the bed in that shadowy room. If she saw me, Mag could hardly recognize me, could she? Even in those short moments, though, given what I'd just heard, the temptation to look back and possibly turn into a pillar of salt was almost overwhelming. I might have seen something, actually: something like a human figure sitting up rigid at 90 degrees. I'd certainly heard its breathing, like a puttering lawnmower engine. I flew past, ran straight down the hallway and the stairs. At the bottom I almost collided with a circle of chatting women who gave me a funny look in unison.

Before I could settle back into things, there was a cry from upstairs: an unmistakable cry of pain. In the context it struck me as like a woman giving birth. But at the same time, I recognised it as the noise I'd heard myself make when the creature from my nightmare stuck me from behind with its stinger. But it wasn't all in my head; the noise certainly got everyone else's attention, too. In a moment something or someone fell over loudly upstairs, and there was a more human and high-pitched scream.

Some feet were already rushing upstairs when a figure that must have been the woman of the hour herself appeared at the top; at least, from where I was standing, you could see her feet and the hem of her nightgown. Strangely, those rushing towards her went no further; they were putting the obvious questions to each other in hushed voices, and retreating slowly. Mag was staggering like a drunk, but her complexion suggested so much worse. Johanna wasn't kidding. She looked like a corpse with jaundice. Her eyes were inanimate, and her skin looked horribly dried out. You could see the cracks around her lips which were raw as eczema. I repositioned myself for a full-face view as she came slowly downstairs with a kind of stiff, regal gait. Her grey-yellow tongue was poking slowly in and out like she was some kind of mechanical lizard.

Everyone made way for her in awe, as she headed straight for the dinner table where the presents were heaped. (The finger-food was crowded up onto the kitchen benches as everyone had gone over-the-top in gift-giving; I'd hoped no one would find out I'd only brought a pack of plain bibs from Target.) Besides her appearance, Mag's breath must also have helped clear her path to judge from the way people nearby were shielding their noses. She began ripping the paper off and going through the boxes with extreme intensity, like she was looking for something. No one said anything; it was just too shocking. Finally, a woman from HR came up and put a hand on her shoulder. Mag whirled around and got right in her face, baring her greyish teeth and with claws ready to gouge. What came out of that evil clown mouth of hers, was totally disconnected: "You!" she spat, followed by a string of grammatically disconnected expletives: "Shit! . . . Fuck! . . . Piss! . . ." I guess her literary quote bank was beyond reach. The poor woman recoiled and burst into tears. I suppose she only escaped those yellow talons because Mag was more interested in the presents.

Johanna was being comforted a bit further back where she stood crying and bleeding where her face had been—what? Bitten? Raked with diseased fingernails? A few people were now on the phone, speaking quietly as though they were afraid to attract Mag's attention. But she was in her own world.

Out of curiosity I'd approached a little closer. Behind me some guests were edging toward the side and front doors of the kitchen and dining rooms, respectively, or running into the adjacent lounge for their kids. Some of the kids had come out and were standing around crying, or just in shock like everyone else.

Mag unwrapped and cast aside one gift after another. I saw that she was actually bleeding a little from the mouth. It can't have been Johanna's blood because it didn't look right: too pale and viscous, half-blood, half-pus, I'd guess. She spat something out. Some people had already left by this time, I think. It seemed like a kind of twilight descended that took the place of regular time, if that makes any sense. Probably all that had happened was that a cloud passed in front of the sun. Mag tossed aside nappies and teething rings and teddy bears . . . then she found the odd-man-out. There was a box of champagne flutes, and she held one up, making faces at her reflection until it broke in her grip. Then she continued staring into her palm, reading her own unpromising future, I guess.

Now someone else came up and placed a hand on her shoulder. Mag was quicker this time. The next thing, she had that hand in hers. There was a struggle, and the woman shrieked in pain. It made sense: Mag, who'd evidently discovered a love of shiny things, had decided to take the woman's ring, with or without the finger. She was shouting disjointed obscenities again, interspersed with more monosyllables, while her victim was screaming and begging for help, which no one was brave enough to give.

I'm not sure that woman escaped with all her fingers. Well, there were no heroines, but there was plenty of agitation, and in a few moments just about everyone had left the vicinity, including Johanna. I guess they were waiting outside for reinforcements.

Finished with the presents, Mag waded through the discarded wrapping paper and into the lounge room, possibly drawn by the sound and lights coming from the TV (Mr Maker was making glasses out of pipe-cleaners, I remember). She staggered forward and when she got there, actually sat down in front of the screen, on the vacant couch. It was like a scene from a nursing home. I'd followed at what seemed a safe distance—not that I was too worried about safety, oddly—and now I was standing to one side, watching Mag in profile by the TV's glow in that relatively dark room.

Something was happening inside her. Mag looked dangerously poised, sitting forward, hands clenched into fists after having scrabbled for a grip on the smooth leather chair arms. Those long nails would be hurting her, assuming she could feel pain—unless there was another, worse pain she was experiencing. Her face was like a tragic mask. Not knowing what I was thinking, I found myself walking around to stand between her and the TV.

Something was moving under that nightgown. Behind the white fabric there were several points of movement, and a spreading stain whose colour I couldn't quite make out, though it seemed oddly pale, like the stain meat leaves on butcher's paper. A gurgling, creaking sound was coming from deep inside her lungs.

Then something clicked, and she noticed me. It was as if with some small movement I'd set off an alarm. Mag stood up with a tubercular coughing noise, or growl, baring her teeth and exhaling violently through them. The bloody lumps were growing as I watched them, backing as far away as I could without falling backwards into the TV. It was difficult to see exactly what was going on under that nightgown until I saw what was flopping down onto the floor underneath.

Their blind faces were as pale—no, translucent—as their mother's—their host's. There was a putrid smell of off meat and incontinence that was getting worse as the flopping continued. It occurred to me I'd once seen something similar in a photo of an unfortunate caterpillar. It took little extrapolation to gather that Mag's midriff under that nightie would look like a crop of writhing bananas, one at a time falling ripe to the carpet and lying there wriggling helplessly enough, but when I saw one crawling energetically in my direction, my self-preservation instinct returned enough to make me stalk back off to one side.

Mag followed me with her eyes, turning that death's head after me as far as it would go; her feet stood rooted, wide apart. So, she wouldn't run the risk of leaving her brood undefended. The sounds she was making, beyond that stertorious breathing, were probably supposed to be more obscenities, but short, sharp vowels were all I could hear.

It was very primal, a thrilling sense of self-importance and responsibility that came over me. I had to destroy them, those abominations: it was my job and no-one else's. In the kitchen drawers I found a can of fly spray (funny, I thought Johanna was vegan) and a stove lighter.

I did what I felt had to be done, and the consequences, which I witnessed for as long as I could from the backyard before climbing over the fence, were pretty spectacular. The police and ambulance arrived shortly but, of course, no one had anticipated a need for the fire brigade, so by the time they arrived it was too late to save anything. There were no human casualties, despite reports. In the confusion, evidently no one had noticed that I was the last one inside the house with Mag, because in the days since then my house call from the police hasn't come, and things at work have gone on basically as normal, just with a lot more interesting gossip.

But the question I keep asking myself ever since is, what was I really doing, standing there, face to face with that walking-dead woman? What did I really feel? Wasn't it actually a kind of rivalry, instead of the simple, outright abhorrence a normal person would have felt? And then I wonder, was it really me who killed Mag and burnt down that place—or was it something inside me that was planted in a dream?

The Second Marriage

Roger sat in the gaming room of The Loaded Dog with a dwindling reserve of chips in his cup. It was one of those pubs that smells like ash, even though supposedly no one smokes in them anymore. The feeling of sinking deeper into the irremediable with every coin inserted gave him an odd thrill, even though he knew it was stupid. That was the point; he was done pretending to have any answers to the mystery of his life. An old fantasy flared up in the back of his mind: if he kept losing past the point of no return, he could always go home to his flat, pack a bag or two, jump in the car, and just drive: say goodbye to everything and maybe get a job picking fruit somewhere, cash in hand; forget the credit card companies and live off the grid somewhere. But no such escape was possible. Even one tank of petrol was beyond his means, and furthermore, he was unlikely to make it to pay day in any condition to run.

At least now Roger had only himself to worry about; he was grateful for that, even as fear pummelled him in the gut. At least his child maintenance payments had been infrequent and incomplete for a while now, and he was sure that their value to his ex-wife had always been more symbolic than material.

He had been approached at the casino at about this time last month by a man, a strange looking foreigner, who had abruptly offered him a loan at 25 percent. Now the loan was overdue, and he could not even afford the interest. He spent as little time as he could at home, now, dreading the sound the buzzer or an ambush. There were no friends or family to offer him a haven. The stocky, not especially tall, but certainly imposing man had introduced himself as "Bob," in answer to Roger's polite enquiry. He was unsure if he had heard the name correctly, so shortly and sharply was it spoken in an accent that made every of syllable like a gunshot.

Suddenly there was a scream. At first it sounded like something from a horror movie, then came a noise of cascading coins, followed by more screams that now dissolved into laughter and cries of "Oh my Gawd!" There was general agitation as people got up to go and see which machine had paid off. Oh, it was "Sugar and Spice." The most it had ever paid out for Roger was twenty dollars.

It was in the midst of this bewilderment that Roger felt a hand on his shoulder. As if to confirm that yes, his life was indeed dissolving rapidly into a nightmare, his bulging eyes confirmed that it was Bob, the man from the Casino, standing over him. But how had he known to find Roger here? There was no time to wonder just then how he had been tracked down, but since Bob had taken his address, and the Loaded Dog was the nearest gambling venue to it, it was perhaps not such an astonishing coincidence.

"Time you pay." The words hit harder than a three-punch combination, winding Roger, who spluttered incoherently before being actually physically lifted up by the shoulder and roughly escorted in the direction of the adjoining sports bar. There was that feeling of incomprehension at being the object of physical force that he had not felt while sober since high school days. His cheeks prickled with shame. No one, none of the oldies and Asians, saw fit to intervene, or likely even noticed what was happening. If they did, Bob looked very much like a bouncer with his physique, and his plain black and white suit.

But if he was being taken outside for a beating, then the emergency exit in the rear of the gaming room would have been a more logical choice than the direction in which he was being dragged.

To his relief, they went no further than the sports bar where, straight-backed on a stool in the corner, past the bar and in front of a TV showing a horse race, sat a little old man. He was staring at them and poised there in an improbable posture, as if he owned the place. His skin was finely lined, like the upper of a well-worn shoe, and like Bob's, it was yellow like a page from an old book. Also like Bob's, the old man's head was hairless–eyebrows included. Both their faces were broad and bony, with eyes like half-open mollusc shells.

"Mr Bunting talk with you."

As with Bob's own name, his boss's was hard for Roger to transliterate. Certainly, "Bunting" was an odd name for a foreigner to have, but the way Bob said it, emphasizing both syllables equally in his aggressive staccato, made it sound foreign indeed.

Bob politely pulled out the opposite stool at the little round bar table for the awkward guest. "You sit."

Roger did as he was told. Bob remained standing in an unnerving position just on Roger's visual periphery. The little man stared straight at Roger, who glanced away, then back again, then, feeling stupidly that he should speak, stuttered out an attempted introduction, "Hi, I'm—Ah, well, of course you know who I—"

"You listen. This hotel belong to me," Mr Bunting almost exclaimed in a way that made Roger feel that he was trespassing. I have many business concern, in you country, and in my country. It good you here tonight, Mr Dunn, so we meet like this." As Mr Bunting spoke, his lips and Adam's apple visibly oscillated, but there were none of the other little bodily movements and gestures that make speech seem organic and human in even the most coldly composed individuals; instead there was a kind of unnatural spasming of the lips that seemed quite incidental to pronunciation (it was actually as if the latter, including the pseudo-plosive consonants, occurred exclusively somewhere back in the man's throat, as if he had some kind of surgical implant that was doing the talking for him). The upper lip, in particular, curled up to reveal teeth as yellow as his skin, set in nasty, violet gums.

There intervened a pause, as Mr Bunting continued to stare, unblinking, as though assessing Roger or waiting to for him to look away, which he momentarily did. "Are you marry, Mr Dunn?"

"Not anymore." Lucky. He could play that up, if it turned out Mr Bunting were looking for leverage. He really had not seen his daughter Maddison or his ex-wife for months. If he were dead they would neither know nor care.

"You owe me some money." Mr Bunting seemed to gloat. "How you pay?"

"Well, uh, I can pay . . . some on Thursday."

"You make good money? Have good job?"

"It's okay." This was as close to a lie as Roger felt capable of. It paid what he deserved.

"Then why you no pay me now?" Mr Bunting was definitely grinning. "I think you a bad gambler, Mr Dunn, lose money all the time."

No answer seemed necessary. Mr Bunting rubbed it in: "Yes, always lose and lose, never win, borrow money, play again, lose again. I think you no pay even I give you one week, one month, one year." He raised his hands above the table rim and counted very deliberately on his fingers: one, one, one. "No, I think different thing. Instead of I hurt you, I give you more money."

Roger found himself flinching at the mention of hurting, and Mr Bunting seemed to smile, if his face were capable of it.

"No, I no hurt you, Mr Dunn. I give you something good. Give you beautiful new wife."

Roger began incredulously repeating back, in Standard English, what he had just heard, before Mr Bunting cut him off.

"This girl from my country, she come for work. Very pretty girl. Good wife for any man; I think you like her. Need husband for look after. I pay you $200,000 for marry this beautiful girl." Mr Bunting moved lifted an index finger to emphasise the offer by pointing first at himself, then at Roger. The bony, yellow finger, with its claw-like fingernail, almost touched the latter between his soft pectorals across the small table, not shaking in the slightest. Roger felt that it contained enough force to push him off his seat.

This was a pleasant surprise. He mentally went over the dangers of what he was being asked to do, and came up with only a vague but potent sense of trepidation. Still, he mumbled some words of agreement and searched for approval in Mr Bunting's countenance. There was only that same hint of a smile that was anything but trustworthy. All that was required, apparently, were his bank details, which he was able to provide by rote, having learned them well in the course of his ongoing money troubles.

The masterful old man did not offer his hand, but merely nodded and said, "Good," thin lips lowering themselves crookedly like cheap blinds. That approval was apparently addressed to Bob, whose hand Roger immediately felt on his shoulder. He stood up quickly to avoid being further manhandled. What had just happened felt a bit like making a pact with the devil, but then Roger had more than once imagined that, given the opportunity, he would probably accept the offer.

"Keep you phone switch on, Mr Dunn. We call you any time." Mr Bunting called, as Roger left, not daring to look back.

* * *

Having gradually come down in the world from his low-flying corporate days, Roger now worked for an "outsource provider" in a call centre that ran various "campaigns" on behalf of a number of private and public-sector clients. In terms of call centre jobs, this one was quite a peach, however. Immediately before getting it he had lasted a fortnight in an outbound place after making less than 50 percent of his sales quota; here, on the other hand, there were quite a few "lifers," fat, middle-aged, and either sour or sorry-faced. He probably counted as one by now.

The customer Roger was currently listening to had spent minutes detailing the number of times he had previously called about the phone data for which he alleged he had been overcharged, the names of people he had spoken to, and recapitulating the minutiae of those conversations. Roger had stopped listening minutes ago. He kept on thinking about the deal he had made with Mr Bunting two nights ago. "Well, I can imagine how frustrating that must be," he said as sympathetically as possible. "I'd better escalate this one to our complaints resolution department so we can get a positive outcome for you ASAP."

The nature of this "campaign" was that his employer, Service Flow, took enquiries from customers of a mobile phone service run by a company called Arbitel. That company was practically unreachable by phone at any time, while Service Flow employees were not empowered to do anything in the way of complaint resolution. Transferring a call to Arbitel was tantamount to hanging up on the customer, which was of course not allowed; but in the event a customer insisted, one was supposed to wait on the line with them indefinitely. This was a good way of passing the time without having to talk to anyone, but if one's break was coming up, as Roger's was, that could result in an indefinite delay, especially with a customer as dogged as this one seemed to be. Hence a better course of action, though not allowed, would be to simply cold-transfer the call.

He did so, then clicked the "end call" button on his computer screen. He took another couple of short calls before it was time for his lunch break. Then, just as he was about to take it, Tim, the so-called "subject-matter expert," appeared at Roger's side in an attitude of agitation. Tim was inoffensive enough, as long as one did not mind his effeminacy or the fact that, despite his job title, he knew very little about anything he was supposed to. Roger had the impression that he was an inoffensive brown-noser who had got a promotion by talking celebrity gossip with the women who ran the place.

"What's up, Tim?"

"Oh, umm, Tina wants to have a word with you about cold-transferring calls to Arbitel. You know we're not supposed to do that, right?"

Damn, how had that customer got through in, what, under fifteen minutes? "Oh, of course! But, uh, Tim, I'm actually fifteen minutes late for my lunch break, so maybe I should take it first so I don't mess up the roster?"

"Umm, yeah I guess . . ." Tim said with great uncertainty. "Just go and see her first thing afterwards. It's super important, okay?"

"Okay, sure thing. Thanks Tim."

Besides wandering around looking lost, Tim was also in charge of the breaks roster, so it was a good tactic to use with him. Delaying probably was not a good idea, but there was no way Roger could face Tina before smoking a cigarette. Damn, he had been slack with the call notes too! That was a hanging offence in and of itself. And, of course, that damn customer kept a record of everyone he spoke to.

Tina was a miserable bitch whose tolerance for anyone who made trouble for her with management or clients was zero. It gave Roger that burning, ice-cold feeling that had never got any easier to deal with since he had been a little boy waiting outside the Principal's office. Then as now it had always been unskilful efforts at evasion that got him into trouble.

Since then he had been a married man with a family, at least for a while. And now here he was working alongside a crew of backpackers, students, and semi-employable freaks (for some reason the Indians were mostly segregated on a separate floor), afraid of some stupid girl who had been a teenager back when he had had a place in the world. Roger looked around at the stuffed toys and action figures that were posed along the work-station dividers, the montage of pictures from various staff parties with Tina dressed as Wonder Woman . . . She did have a nice body, he had to admit.

He went downstairs and out into the real world, where he rolled and lit a cigarette, then dragged on it gratefully. It would be his last one until the day after tomorrow, unless he wanted to go around picking up butts off the pavement. Yes, it would probably come to that.

Checking his phone, he saw a missed call from a silent number. That took him instantly to the brink of panic; but just as it did so, the phone rang in his hand.

"I call you two time." The voice was calmly hostile.

"Sorry, I'm at work. You can always leave a message."

"Mr Bunting tell you answer you phone."

"I know, sorry. I'm sorry."

Bob, if that was who it was, got straight to the point immediately at hand. "You wife come in airport 6:15 p.m. Her name Annie. I text you picture. You money come tomorrow."

He assented and Bob hung up abruptly, imparting no further information, such as whether anyone else was to be at the airport, or if any arrangements had been made for Annie's accommodation. There was no number for him to call back either, had he dared. Obviously, these people did things in a very foreign way.

But where his heart a moment before had been pumping with anxiety and the nicotine rush from an overdue smoke, now it was bounding with elation. Roger went back up in the elevator, swiped his card, and made for his desk. He collected his coat and looked about for anything else that he owned of value. There was nothing. Then he looked across the room at Tina, who was sitting up on her little corner podium-like work-station. She stood up, hands on hips, and stared at him with the contemptuous hostility that was her trademark expression; he stared back, thought "why not?," and gave her the finger, before turning his back and walking out. He had seen her expression change so beautifully to baffled dismay that Roger could hardly forbear to spoil the effect by looking over his shoulder to see if there was another cause.

The promised picture did not immediately arrive, and when finally it did, it was extremely overexposed; so much so that really all you could tell was that the girl or woman awaiting him had a heart-shaped face, big eyes, and dark hair. She was either very young, or keen to be so perceived. From the days before he had given up all hope, Roger remembered the tricks women used on dating sites to obscure their age and their less attractive features. There was even something a little disturbing about those really huge, dark eyeballs without a visible centre, set in that pallid face framed between curtains of pitch-black locks. The only real worry was whether he would be able to recognize her in a crowd.

Another lay in the question as to how he was going to arrive at the airport in time.

Bob would have assumed that Roger had a vehicle based on the fact that he had seen his driver's license. Technically he did, but it was far from certain that the old Focus would be up to the task. He had hardly driven it since failing to renew the registration a few months back; it was overdue for a service, and the tyres were bald, but Roger was almost sure that there was enough petrol in the tank, provided it would start.

The first setback, predictably, was a train delay. He paced up and down the platform, unable to quell his rising fears; but when it appeared, Roger was able to comfort himself that, by his calculations, he was not yet actually running late. That changed when the connecting bus also kept him waiting. By the time he got home it was approaching four-thirty already, and he had still to get across to the other side of town in what would soon be peak hour. The journey could realistically be expected to take ninety minutes, leaving a very slender margin for further delay, assuming the plane was to land on time.

Roger guessed he would be bringing his bride-to-be back to his apartment to stay, otherwise why was it his job to go and meet her? Or was he entertaining that notion just because, in a fond, pathetic way, he dared to hope that the "marriage" would come to approximate a real one? He was lonely, to be sure, and bad at coping with it despite all the practice he had had. He stacked the dirty crockery that lay around the living room where there was room on the kitchen sink, sprayed some of the pine-scented aerosol he had bought that time the toilet overflowed, and took the rubbish downstairs with him, racing against time.

Traffic was worse even than he had expected. The freeway was clogged, so Roger took a gamble with a suburban detour before getting onto the ring-road and the freeway that led directly to the airport. Here traffic was better, but the petrol gauge began seriously to menace him. There were literally no funds he could draw upon until pay day, having withdrawn his last twenty dollars at the ATM in the gaming room the other night. In the meantime, he had been evading ticket inspectors, turning a deaf ear to the remonstrations of bus drivers, and living practically on air. There was nothing left that could be pawned; the bloke who had taken over the pawnshop (of the same race, incidentally, as his new associates) had rejected the TV last time, which was also the last time he had driven the car.

A few kilometres down the freeway, a smell of burning began to fill the vehicle. This had happened before a couple of times, Roger remembered. He shut off the aircon that was keeping him warm, and kept driving into the grey horizon.

Then he felt the car struggling. No, not struggling, but giving up. The needle on the speedometer was quite calmly dropping to zero as the car smoothly decelerated, and Roger realized that he had only a few seconds to pull over. A horn sounded behind him. He put on the hazards and sat there, numbed by the predictable malice of fate. It was a long time since he had paid his roadside assistance membership. In a moment, Roger was standing in the rain and looking uncomprehendingly at the engine, waves of heat hitting him in the face while the cold and wet ate into him from behind. The oil was fine, and he could see the water bubbling away in its plastic reservoir. One vehicle after another swooped past him like beasts of prey hunting something of greater account than him. It was spitting rain again, so he got back inside the car to attempt to spin some strategy out of thin air.

It was already past six. Whom could he call upon? Who might be able to come and pick him up and take him to the airport, not to mention chauffeur both him and Annie back home again? The only possible answer was obvious, but he choked on it.

The only person he could conceivably call was his ex-wife, Brenda. They were supposed to be enemies, he supposed, but Roger was long past blaming her; it was only her contempt he feared exposing himself to. She might possibly be home from work by now, having collected their daughter from after-school care. Or perhaps her partner, a half-Mauritian landscaper called Gus, was looking after the little girl.

As far as he knew, the family still lived in the house he and Brenda had bought as newlyweds. On their estate you could hear the rush of the freeway like waves at the beach, he remembered. He used to find that noise almost relaxing when he had lived there, too, though the same noise now, at closer range, was enervating.

Concentrating hard on the money that would soon be coming his way if he could complete the manoeuvre, Roger punched the first letter of Brenda's name into his phonebook. (Incredibly, it was the same mobile phone he had owned as Brenda's husband: an ancient Nokia with a green and black screen. He had a couple of dollars of prepaid credit remaining.) He would simply not think about what he was doing; it would be no different to talking on the phone at work; placidly and humbly he would do his best to transact the business at hand.

The call went straight to message bank. He sighed and looked out across the four adjacent lines of traffic, all going in one direction. Maybe he could report himself to the police as some weirdo he had seen staggering around on the margin of the freeway. That should get him a lift, though not the one he needed.

Then his phone rang.

Brenda's response to his introduction was only a slight chuckle of surprise. He remembered how, during the breakup, he would sometimes read an affectionate tone into her speech and manner that turned out to be really a kind of half-amused contempt.

"I hate to ask, but I need a small favour. Nothing to do with money, don't worry . . ." Roger explained with more concision and coherence than he had thought possible, while she listened without butting in or hanging up. There was silence for a moment. He held his breath.

She sighed. "Okay, Roger. Where are you?" Helpfully, he was just past the pedestrian overpass that spanned from the cluster of factory-direct shops on one side to the train station on the other.

It took her about half an hour to get there, during which time his hopes faded almost to nothing that he would be able to perform his duty in the expected timeframe. If Annie was waiting, though, word had not yet reached him. The worst thing would be if by the time he got there it was too late. And if it was not, could he ask Brenda to take them back to his place, all the way across town? Surely not. One way or another, Roger was in for an evening of extreme embarrassment.

Brenda managed to spot him and pull over onto the freeway shoulder without any mishap. She sat there unsmiling, staring ahead while waiting for him to let himself in the passenger side. He was reminded vaguely of numerous occasions in the course of their marriage, especially in the early months, when had had just one car between them, her old one, and there would be a smile and a kiss when he got into the passenger seat. The car she had now was much nicer.

Roger kept thanking her and apologising, making vague excuses while trying still to think up a plausible story about what he was doing. He was almost going to say that it was his mother he was going to meet, but then he remembered that the old woman still kept in touch with Brenda; fair enough, given that she had sole custody of her sole grandchild. His mind refused to work. They were still stranded; it would take Brenda literally several minutes to find a gap. Tension rose.

"So, how is Mad—?"

"Can you wait a minute, Roger? I'm trying to execute a bit of a challenging manoeuvre here!"

At length they were moving, and it was she who next broke the silence. "So, what's the story?"

"Sorry?"

"We're going to the airport, you said. You don't have any bags, unless you left them back there in the boot. Who are we picking up?"

Roger hesitated. "It's a bit complicated. I'm doing someone a favour–"

"Is it the kind of favour that could put me in jail as an accessory? Because Maddie needs at least one parent to look after her."

That struck him as unfair, since she had no reason to think him involved in any criminality—unless she was thinking of what he had done with the family finances. He stuttered and mumbled, trying to decide what line to take. "Yeah, it's probably better if you . . . I mean, look, it's nothing that could get you into trouble, don't worry, it's just—"

"Save it, Roger. I don't care. I don't know why I'm here, to tell the truth. You can find your own way back, by the way. I'm not chauffeuring you."

"No problem, that's cool. But could you maybe drop us off at Warramarina station?"

She said nothing to that, and Roger chose not to push a non-existent advantage. At length, he dared to ask after Maddie.

"She's sick, actually."

"Oh, is it anything serious?"

"What would you do about it if it were?"

A good question. "Sorry, I was just asking if she's okay. So Gus is looking after her, then?"

"No, Roger, I left my sick child home alone so I could take her deadbeat father to the airport for some bloody dubious purpose."

He did not try again. When they reached the airport, Roger had to apologize and promise to pay Brenda back the exorbitant price of parking. "Whatever!" was her reply.

Miraculously, the plane had been late. It was almost half-past seven by the time Roger arrived in the terminal lounge, and the woman at the desk informed him that the flight had arrived just half an hour ago, which meant that Annie had had time to go through customs and quarantine. Roger had forgot about that part. Thank God. The immediate difficulty now lay in recognizing his future wife in the crowd.

Brenda was there behind him, talking on her phone. He was a little surprised that she had wanted to enter instead of waiting in the car, or just driving off. Perhaps she was motivated by curiosity. What she would think of Annie he dreaded to contemplate.

Roger had scrutinized a few faces that might conceivably have been his future wife's, when suddenly the ghoulishly pretty one from the photo—no mistaking it—jumped out of the crowd towards him. She was unearthly, like a generic vision of an extraterrestrial, though taller, more attractive, and far from bald. That hair of hers was as striking as anything else. Her eyes were large, with their dark irises and pupils seeming to merge to form a pair of big, dark blots. (She must have been wearing contact lenses.) Her figure was otter-like, a little short-legged, but otherwise very shapely. She was wearing a fitted dress with black and creamy-white diagonal stripes, and he noticed that her skin was even paler than those stripes.

Who was that with her? Was it Bob, or another of the same tribe? He appeared to speak a word or two into Annie's ear before moving off into the crowd, quelling Roger's fear somewhat. Perhaps they had not been together after all. Anyway, she had recognised him. He supposed that she had been shown his license photo; though that was little enough go on. Probably they had looked him up on Facebook.

Roger introduced himself and was about to extend a hand before leaning in for a kiss on the cheek, despite his nerves. Her skin was surprisingly cold. "And this is Brenda, a friend of mine. I had some car trouble, so she helped me out." Mercifully, she was still on the phone, and he could not hear what she was saying over the ambient noise.

His future wife evinced the submissive manners of a courtesan, smiling and dipping the darkly arresting headlights of her eyes to nod in acknowledgement. She was wearing a strikingly sweet, musky perfume with a surprising hint of artificial cherries.

Seeing that she said nothing, he asked gently, "Do you speak English?"

"No," she said, softly, shyly.

"I thought that to get a mail order bride you had to at least have a job. Is that what this is?"

Roger paused, uncertain how to answer.

"Hi, I'm the ex-wife. I'm here because his car broke down, and he had no money for a taxi."

He had almost forgotten that Brenda could be so horrible; and given that it was she who had created an online dating profile while they were still nominally together, he found her "mail order bride" comment rather hypocritical. But clearly it was not his place to argue with her now.

And there was no need to engage with her hostility anyway. Annie's gaze was solely directed at him; she seemed not to have heard, let alone understood, Brenda's comment. That was so gratifying he almost burst into laughter. Brenda scowled and muttered something under her breath.

He remarked upon the one, small suitcase Annie had with her and offered to take it, but she seemed not to understand his meaning.

"I'll drop you off at the station, then," Brenda confirmed sharply once they were in the car. "Let this poor girl get a taste of what kind of a life she's in for with you."

It was a long, strange journey home via two train trips, with lengthy wait times either side. Roger apologized, but tried to make light of it as best he could. As time went on he became less concerned about the impression he was making since Annie's attitude appeared somewhat less judgemental than that of a stray dog. Further, her answers to his questions and conversational assays conveyed mere incomprehension. Her unblinking eyes were trained on Roger the whole time, as if she were in love with him; and yet her face was quite expressionless.

She said little, but what she did say was in an accent recognizably akin to that of Mr Bunting and Bob in its unaccented monotony, but fortunately much softer. She spoke quietly, her tone breathy rather than sharp, as though she had difficulty getting enough air into her lungs to turn into syllables. With her compatriots she also shared the ability to sit as still as a lizard.

It started raining heavily; fortunately, there was shelter at the station, and the short, violent shower had finished by the time they disembarked to walk home to Roger's. There was a strange moment when he stepped into a deep puddle, then turned around to warn Annie a moment too late, and found her wading straight through it without seeming to notice. It was a little unnerving.

They walked down the alleyway behind his block of flats, through the carpark, and approached the rear entrance. There was a human figure standing silhouetted by the security light. Even at this distance Roger could see that is was not Bob, which could not but be reassuring. The posture was too submissive, and the figure shifted its weight from one foot to the other nervously. It might still represent danger in the form of a junky or some kind of hoodlum, though, and there might be more of them around the other side of the building.

As he and Annie drew closer, Roger puffed out his chest and clenched his fists, feeling marginally strengthened by Annie's presence and a tenuous sense of association with a real-life crime syndicate.

"You right there?" he asked the figure as it stepped back from him.

It was a smallish, middle aged man who stood with the attitude of a child caught shoplifting. His eyes did not meet Roger's, and at first he said nothing. Roger had a feeling that if the man had been wearing a hat of any kind, he would have taken it off and wrung it between his hands.

"Excuse me . . . I sorry . . ." he began in breathy tones similar to Annie's. "I wait here, you know Mr Bunting . . . My English—so sorry—my English no good."

Roger was naturally nonplussed by the situation. He looked behind at his feminine shadow, who offered no hint of recognition or reassurance. There seemed nothing to do but take the money and show the gentleman upstairs.

"I wasn't expecting anyone, so . . ."

"Oh, sorry, so sorry" the little man whispered from behind Annie and Roger as they ascended the staircase.

When they entered the apartment, Roger looked behind him and saw Annie and her client holding hands. She had transferred her gaze to him, and he returned it, grinning.

"It's in there," Roger pointed towards the bedroom. "Straight ahead," he added, grunting in annoyance as nicotine deprivation, fatigue, stress, and wet feet caught up with him in a rush. Mr Bunting had spoken.

"Thank you, thank you," came the response as the little man pulled Annie after him.

Alone, Roger went to find a drink of the appalling wine that remained in the kitchen. He switched on the oil heater, and his anger surged, reflecting that he had not been allowed even the opportunity to change his wet socks.

There was a faint knocking and squeaking noise as the two strangers coupled on Roger's old double mattress-and-base. He had bought it from the Salvation Army two years ago, and, he reflected, this was the first time it had seen any action. It reminded him of an incident when he was a teenager hosting a party and a couple had used his bed in that way. It had only occurred to him next day what an insult that had been.

It was over in a couple of minutes. When the little man came out, Roger stood up from the couch and went to open the door to facilitate his exit. Catching sight of him, Roger did a double-take. The shoulders were pulled back, the eyes were cold and their stare direct. It was a changed man who had exited that bedroom, Roger could tell at a glance, more like Bob that the diffident John of minutes before, even with narrower shoulders and hair on his head. Roger was happy to play the doorman and see him out, but apparently he did not move fast enough. The two of them collided in front of the door, and Roger received the worst of it, actually tumbling backwards as he lost balance completely. There was no apology.

* * *

His phone woke him. It was work, calling to see where he was. Roger hung up. He had fallen asleep on the couch after enough time had passed to reassure him than there would be no more callers that night. There had, in fact, been a second one, practically identical to the first in his appearance and schizoid demeanour. Roger now wanted nothing to do with his new "wife," and only to get away from a home which apparently was no longer his. Having no internet connection, he had no way of checking whether the promised money was in his account yet. Probably not, but given how abruptly the other side of the deal had moved ahead . . .

Anyway, he had to escape the claustrophobic scene of last night's humiliation. If there was no money he would go to the park and try to find some butts he could harvest and roll into a cigarette. Fortunately, he had left the previous day bar-one's clothes on the bathroom floor, so there was something to get changed into without disturbing Annie.

First, he went to the ATM at the supermarket a block away and found $1,587.21 in his account. Only that? What was the idea? Had he misheard the offer? Or was he to be paid in instalments to circumvent the bank's compliance reporting? Still, it was not much. And why the random figure? He tried to think of some automatic debit that might have come out. There was supposedly no monthly fee on the account.

He went inside for tobacco, also buying a packet of doughnuts for breakfast. As he sat on the bench outside the entrance, smoking and vacantly watching the people pass in and out, his relief began to grow into dread. Something told him he ought to be at home.

Minutes later he was at the door to what used to be his bedroom. The smell of Annie's perfume crept under the closed door. He listened for a moment, made up his mind, and knocked. When she failed to answer, Roger poked his head in and would have called to her, but found her sitting up, hair covering her face and cascading down between her widely spread legs.

She looked up, face half-curtained. "I go work?" she said in that breathy voice.

What a relief! She would be *going* elsewhere to work. So last night had been an anomaly. "Sure, I'll . . . I'll see what I can do," he said, remembering his car beside the freeway. What to do about that? Roger guessed that he would be receiving a notice in the near future. For now he could walk Annie to the station, accompany her where she needed to go.

"Do you want breakfast? There's doughnuts," he asked affably.

Annie looked at him, uncomprehending, from behind the processed cocoon of her hair, which she did nothing to rearrange. Roger made eating and drinking gestures to show his meaning. "Oh, no, no," she said, shaking those black silk strands groggily.

"I'll just make you a coffee, then."

"No, no. Work . . . I need work . . ." she gasped plaintively. A slight shake of the head and her incredible, midnight hair was back in order as though freshly brushed. Roger felt a flash of sympathy for this strange girl. He hated to think how her words reflected on the probable relationship between Annie and her employers. Her body was not even her own for the purpose of taking meals.

"Help me, Roger" she said. "Watch me." She mispronounced his name the same way Bob and Mr Bunting had. Somehow he had been unable to appreciate the cuteness of that until now.

"You want me to . . . ?"

"Watch me, please."

His groin responded, and he obliged, standing there, baffled and silent, as she got up, went to her suitcase, unzipped and spread it open. That perfume of hers enveloped them in a heady cloud. It was growing on him.

Annie's luggage was actually a portmanteau, like the ones that must have been used by travelling performers in the olden days. Dresses hung on their hangers on a collapsed rail like the stand of an ironing board, which she now extended. She then pressed a clip and out popped a little compartment for shoes. She went about her business deftly, seeming to repose her whole attention on him. She was without modesty where nudity was concerned, also, which was perhaps not so surprising. Roger, who had not seen a naked woman in the flesh in years, found her beauty quite affecting.

"Don't you want a shower?" he asked as Annie began pulling on her clean dress: low cut, electric blue.

"Oh, no, no, thank you."

Especially given the type of work she did, the refusal of a shower seemed very odd. And how could she not be dehydrated? Perhaps she had showered while he was asleep, without waking him up. Actually, her perfect, rather too heavy makeup, along with her well-groomed hair, would argue that she had. Roger stared. Were those big eyelashes fake? He thought of Bob's and Mr Bunting's hairlessness. Now she was dressed.

"When do you have to be there?" he asked, mentally crossing his fingers.

"Ah?" She tilted her head slightly to one side.

And immediately, the buzzer sounded. It was a hideous sound, like receiving an electric shock to the temples. They must have come to collect her.

Roger went into the kitchen and answered it, Annie remaining behind. The voice on the other end made diffident noises. He went down the stairs, suddenly resigned (the key-button being broken), and opened the door.

"Hi, Annie's ready. Would you . . . ?"

"Oh, thankyou, thankyou" came the aspirate reply.

Roger came home late that night, considerably poorer and with a hangover starting to set in. In the living room everything was as he had left it, the TV on the same channel, chattering away at low volume. It was at once cold and stuffy (that was inevitable, because if you opened a window the heat would go out, and there was precious little of that). He had propped open the outside door with a brick, a lame half-measure considering that several other people came and went to and from the apartment block throughout a typical day.

It was with trepidation that he stood before what used to be his bedroom door.

"Excuse me," he piped.

No response.

"Excuse me, is there anyone in there?"

He reached in and turned on the light before entering.

Annie pulled herself upright on the edge of the rumpled bed, just as she had done that morning. The movements of her slender body reminded him of a spider, especially of one that appears to be dead, having been swatted or sprayed, but then comes back to life unexpectedly. She soaked up his gaze as presumably her dark eyes focused in the twilight.

"Annie, sorry, I . . ."

"Roger," she said, staring into her lap, "please . . . help me."

She was still wearing the dress she had put on that morning. She must be tired after a long day's work, he thought, pitying her.

She raised her arms like a child who wants to be picked up and carried away, or like a ballerina in some scene of mythic pathos. He approached and went to pull the dress over her head. The sensation of touching her skin was very strange, but certainly not unpleasant. She seemed to be hot and cold at once, or one after the other in quick succession, as when frostbitten extremities are warmed by a fire. Roger was somewhat alarmed as the best explanation for what he was experiencing was probably some circulatory, or cardio-vascular disorder. His father had died of a stroke at about his current age, and he had felt a little dizzy and short of breath coming up the steps.

When he picked her up, she was almost totally limp. Further, she did not seem to be breathing—and, he was no doctor, but where was her heartbeat?

"Annie! Are you okay?"

A pause while she drew breath with difficulty, then "Yes, I okay."

Leaving her on the couch, where she reclined bonelessly, he left her side momentarily in order to fill the bath.

"What have you been doing all day?"

"No work." That worried him.

Have you eaten?"

"Uh?"

He repeated the question.

"No, no." she shook her head.

"Can I get you anything?"

"No, no, I okay."

So it went. Annie was not much of a conversation partner. When the bath was ready, Roger carried her in and laid her down in the tub, propping her head considerately on a folded towel.

Then the buzzer sounded with its inimitable harshness.

His stomach folded itself into a paper crane. "Hello?" Nothing on the other end at first; then a harsh voice that practically shouted, "Annie!" and nothing more. Funny, he thought, looking for some regularity amid the chaos, the ones last night and this morning had both been shy—at first, anyway. It took him a moment, but he found himself saying: "I'm sorry, look, she's in the bath." The caller replied "Annie! Now!"

When Roger opened the outer door, he saw three men by the security light. On the left one was as bald as Bob or Mr Bunting, while on the right was one whose hair was in the process of falling out, which gave him a highly unattractive appearance in conjunction with the mummified quality that those two gangsters' skin possessed. They were wearing the plain suit that was apparently the uniform of their kind. Between them was an anomalous figure with carrot-red hair whose facial features put him in mind of a Neanderthal, or a donkey.

The baldest man stepped forward immediately, and Roger turned perforce to lead the way. The men followed him closely up the stairs, then, once inside, the hairless man pushed past him, causing Roger to stumble more drunkenly than he felt, and made a bee-line for the bedroom door. The other two stayed between him and the door, hemming him in most uncomfortably. He called out, "I'm sorry guys, Annie's not in there. Like I said, she's in the bath right now." Their faces were inscrutable as carven monoliths as he looked from one to the other. "Sorry, I didn't—we didn't—know you were coming. It's late," he pled, rubbing his hands together.

The hairless leader pointed towards the bathroom door and said something foreign with an incredulous intonation. Roger nodded. This one entered the bathroom, while the balding one and the asinine one hung back. The latter displayed an unmistakable look of fear and submission in his dully enquiring eyes as he shifted from foot to foot. His minder's eyes were locked sternly on Roger. The bald man now exited the bathroom, strode straight up to his host, who struggled with himself not to flinch. He then threw some sharp syllables in his face before grabbing Roger's shirt front and pulling him across the room. Too shocked to protest, in a moment he stood by the side of the bath where Annie lay, eyes open, face submerged while her hair floated like seaweed. Roger was thrown to his knees, which probably would have broken had there not been a mat over the tiles. He cried out in pain and fear.

"They're going to kill me!" he thought in that moment, imagining a gun held to the back of his head while he knelt there, looking down at Annie, who stared back up at him from under the bath water with a gaze that might have been either dead or alive.

The man behind him barked some harsh foreign syllables. Good, they would hardly waste words if they were going to kill him, would they? Then he lifted Roger up by the armpits and bundled him back into the living area, throwing him face-forwards into the coffee table, which tilted forward as it caught him in his gut, so that he tumbled over face-first in an undignified half-somersault. Winded and in shock, Roger managed to turn himself around and sit up, propped against the underside of the table.

On managing to get up and turn around, he saw the bald man holding Annie in his arms, still dripping wet, carrying her into the bedroom. The others followed.

In moments the knocking and squeaking started. Roger listened, incredulous.

Then, minutes later, the bedroom door opened, and the balding man stood before him once more. He thrust his phone at Roger, and grunted.

"Hello?"

"I say you no answer my call, I tell Mr Bunting."

"I . . ." Roger had nothing to say to that. His phone had had a flat battery when he left that morning.

"You job stay with you wife all day. No go away!"

That much he remembered verbatim when replaying the

conversation in his mind later, after the intruders had gone. Then he would sort through the fragments of broken English, and find that Bob's instruction had been without qualification.

When the other two clients emerged, Roger was standing up as best he could with a pair of badly bruised kneecaps, unsure, since he was unable to make himself invisible, of how to proceed. The man with the unfortunate face walked in between the others on the way to the door. It appeared he had been struck blind and was shaking violently all over. He was also dribbling copiously, his jaw hanging slack and eyes rolling back in his head as he lumbered forward like an animal walking on its hind legs. Roger could hear his laboured breathing, too—a sort of hee-hawing, indeed. The man in the rear had to guide him at one point when he lurched violently to one side and collided with the book case, knocking off a framed picture of Maddie, the only one Roger had on display. Perhaps the man was an epileptic or had some other neurological condition, and the excitement of the encounter with Annie had proven too much for him?

Roger peeked through the door to check on her after the men had left. As she did not move, he approached the bed. She was lying on her belly, seemingly dry despite where she had just been. Perfume seemed to diffuse from her pores, subtly comforting Roger's nerves, while he noticed that her makeup remained unsmeared. When Annie began to stir, Roger swiftly and quietly exited, closing the door.

He pondered all that had happened as he lay on the couch that night, unable to sleep, listening for the buzzer.

He watched them as they came and went, singly and in groups. The pattern was that established on the first night: first-timers were comically nervous before being transformed into dangerous, cyborg-like automata who would walk through him should he fail to get out of their way. It was apparently no part of Roger's job to receive money from these clients; at first they required nothing more of him than to answer the door.

Very occasionally, though, there was one who apparently had some sort of painful reaction to Annie's embraces. When this happened to a solo visitor, it fell to Roger to assist him. He would not sit down, nor would he respond to any verbal solicitation, but just kept on drooling, rattling, and bumping into things until Roger helped him out of the apartment and downstairs. By the time they would reach the bottom, the visitor would have stopped dribbling and seemingly regained his vision and muscle-control as he was able to shuffle off by himself, but with how different a gait to the others! They were easy to spot in advance, these unfortunates who seemed a lower caste, a breed apart. Roger would have issued a word of warning once he noticed the pattern, but knew that it was not his place to do so.

There was no knowing when the last client of the day or night might come. Once or twice he had been able to go to bed on the couch after midnight and sleep through till mid-morning without interruption, but more often there would be a caller or two, and he must be ready for them. Of necessity he slipped out occasionally for supplies. When inevitably this resulted in callers being kept waiting, he would receive a physical admonition such as a cuff across the face and a pro-forma expostulation from Bob, over the phone.

The laundry was not a problem. A woman as far unlike Annie as was imaginable while being of the same race took care of that, treating him almost as roughly as Mr Bunting's goons should he cause her any inconvenience. Like the others, she might come at any time, and also like many of them, spoke not one word of English.

What his neighbours must have thought about the comings and goings Roger could only imagine. The inhabitants of Roger's building kept to themselves, and he had long ceased to greet or look them in the eye. In any case, Mr Bunting and his minions would no doubt be capable of handling any situation that might arise in that regard.

He had grown psychologically enthralled to an extent perhaps out of proportion to the violence so far suffered. It was more the way these increasingly glamorous, exotic beings saw through him for the worthless coward and fool he knew himself essentially to be, than it was any physical aggression or threat. On the other hand, perhaps he was supposed to rise to this inner challenge, to brave the possibility of that terrible buzzer raking over his being at the crucial moment while he claimed his conjugal right. Roger's one, far-fetched hope now was that it was some kind of initiation test.

But the hypothesis gaining the most ground was that they intended to torture him to death.

As the weeks progressed, the attitude of Mr Bunting's men towards him began to change. Now, their only weakness besides sex—assuming that was what they did—with Annie seemed to be enjoyment derived from tormenting him. For example, he was now being more severely beaten for being away from his post. Once a big group surrounded and took their time with him in the foyer of his building. (If anyone came by they did nothing to stop it.)

What had happened was that the previous client demanded a martini—if Roger had heard him aright—which was the first time any of them had expressed an interest in refreshment, though that particular visitor, in contrast, had seemed offended at not being offered anything. Roger had run to the bottle shop, and by the time he returned that client had left and several more had arrived. Their erstwhile blank faces now began to smile at him in a way reminiscent of Mr Bunting's, so long ago.

And when they beat him, Roger knew that it was with much of their power held in reserve. They could have punched through him like steel through paper with those burning, hot-cold hands of theirs, even though not all of them were as well-built as Bob. (Out of curiosity, Roger once shook hands with a solitary visitor, pre-initiation. His grip was clammy and weak, but otherwise normal.)

The final development came when Roger's presence began to be requested in the bedroom, where he was instructed to take his turn with his "wife." Too nervous to oblige, he became the object of a chorus of laughter similar to the noise emitted by the apartment buzzer.

Now, the amount Mr Bunting had agreed to pay him was finite, and Roger was growing convinced that the term of these payments was intended to set a term to his life. For evidence, he could point to the fact that these payments, though regular each fortnight and ever-increasing, were of mathematically unpredictable amounts that seemed to correspond to the extent of the insults and pain inflicted on him in the preceding period. Time was running out. It seemed a logical progression from here to physical castration, to death, Roger told himself. Not for the first time in his life, but with more conviction than ever before, "Nothing to lose" became his silent mantra.

So late one night after what he hoped would be the last visitor, Roger entered the bedroom, where Annie instantly woke and looked up at him, raising herself from the pathetic position in which she had been discarded by the last gentleman caller.

"Annie . . . Get into bed, under the sheets . . . please," he fumbled. There was no time to change the bedding, if that had occurred to him.

She did as she was asked. Roger turned off the light.

Cheeks burning, he was relieved that she seemed not to discriminate against him. There was none of the "What are you doing?" or rather "What you do?" that he had feared. Her movements under the sheets were like those of a snake waking up in the springtime. He had been afraid of a repeat of his previous impotence, but touching Annie's skin was thrillingly erotic, like ice applied to an erogenous zone at the right moment. He felt a tingling numbness spread over him, but knew that he was hard and ready. Her sweet perfume was powerful, filling his sinuses and brain with wistful, subliminally recalled memories.

Roger had never been the type to be turned on by a woman who went limp in bed, and despite impressions, that was not Annie's style at all. She gazed, now expressively, into his eyes. Without nostalgia, Roger remembered how it had been at first with Brenda, all those years ago. Now, just as he was about to take her, she surprised him further by wrestling him underneath her with surprising strength, straddling him. She was smiling now, as if enjoying his surprise. Then she held him with her dark eyes in the semi-dark, the city lights outside the first-floor window lighting the room enough for him to see and marvel at her beauty. This was their wedding night.

He was inside her—and then a split second later, with the first movement of her hips, it was as though a hypodermic needle penetrated him in turn. Then, before he could respond in any way, it was compressed and emptied, the contents entering his bloodstream in a burning, freezing-cold rush. Joy became terror; bliss, agony. The stuff he had been injected with was alive with a horrible, alien life-force, and it was in the process of seizing its rightful throne within his body and mind, having overrun them both in an instant. His treacherous heart played the part of its artillery.

And in the same moment the metallic noise of the buzzer cut through his soul like a serrated weapon, resounding, echoing louder and louder without end.

Roger gasped, and his lungs seemed to fill with the unbreathable air of the outer universe, into whose blackness he was suddenly banished. But it was far from peaceful there. Even if the noises were all in his head, his head was eternally in the process of exploding, like an unfortunate astronaut's in a science fiction movie he once saw. An unending crescendo of discord built up and plateaued on a level far beyond anything he had ever known or imagined, blotting out all thought and external awareness. Before his mind ceased entirely to be his own, the last thing he could comprehend happening to him was a complete involution of consciousness from head to a heart that seemed to be pumping mercury.

How this second marriage would compare to his first, Roger would never find himself in a position to reflect.

Miss Polly

They were sleeping apart after Yusuf had yet again failed to stand up to his parents, who still refused to acknowledge their son's *de facto* relationship with her. Maureen had just overheard heard him yet again tactfully and without remonstration decline to be set up with someone more to their liking, who would make him a "good wife." They would sleep apart that night.

Her bed was a raft out in a pitch-black sea reminiscent of an illustration in a book of nursery rhymes she remembered from childhood. There was no sight of land anywhere, but a mysterious columnar object on the horizon which might have been the vortex of a tornado, but which turned out, provisionally, to be a lighthouse. When she saw it, having almost given herself up for dead, she wept tears of relief. Besides its disturbing blackness the ocean was full of sharks, their fins breaking the surface, and it was only a matter of time before they got her; also, the wind was starting to blow, summoning huge, opaque swells that threatened to graduate into breakers.

The lighthouse was drawing her to it, getting bigger and bigger—faster, in fact, than it grew closer. She began to experience vertigo from looking up at its light, while continuing to pray (as she never did in waking life). It grew blindingly bright in the mounting darkness.

Then the lighthouse bent down towards her, and she saw that, in fact, it was an angel, the beacon shining from behind his ineffably beautiful face. He smiled, recognising her as his own, and reached down to gather up her thrilled and terrified self in his strong arms that shone like moonlit marble. Then, her skin burning at his touch, the angel held her up to his dazzling face, from which she could not look away, perceiving there an indescribable kindness and beauty. It was with a shock that she realised her kinship to this fantastic being: it was now nearly human in shape and size, a gorgeous fair-haired man like an image in a Renaissance painting.

The angel spread his wings and flew away with her tucked

under his arm. The scent of his body was delightful, complex and evocative as the bouquet of a fine wine, and more intoxicating. She looked down at the opalescent clouds and thought, in as many words, "Wow, I'm having a genuine religious experience!"

The experience was not a purely spiritual one, however; the angel carried her away up higher into the clouds, where he made love to her, nothing but his embrace preventing her from falling to her death into the shark-infested, unnatural waters below. Yet, while it was a vastly thrilling experience, she felt completely safe at the same time.

Afterwards, they were sailing through the air over an urban landscape, low enough for her to see the swarming cars and people. Then the angel kissed her on the back of the neck—and released his hold. She hurtled down towards the pavement, narrowly avoiding being skewered by the spire or antenna of a skyscraper, before seconds later, with a great smack she hit the pavement.

Maureen gasped and woke with a much-magnified version of the jolting sensation one often has of slipping and falling on the way between waking and sleep. The knowledge that the angel had been only a dream took a few seconds to catch her, and when it did, tears formed in her eyes as she started ahead at the bare grey wall of the bedroom.

The following weekend they were having dinner with her friend Vashti, an orchestral violist, and her husband Oskar, the orchestra's conductor, in the latter's warehouse apartment. Maureen herself hardly played piano anymore; it was too depressing to feel the stiffness of her joints and reproach herself for having worked as a barista during her years at the Conservatory, so that now she suffered from a case of carpal tunnel syndrome that had grown severe enough to begin interfering with her reception work at a suburban music school. Vashti, on the other hand, had wealthy parents and thus had never needed to work during her student years. She and Oskar had no children as yet, but had been thinking about it for some time. It was distressing to Maureen that Yusuf, who was visibly bored, found no purchase in the high-toned conversation. She herself barely did.

About an hour before sunrise next morning, she found herself alone in a certain vast and palatial warehouse apartment. A feature, which had also been present at her friends', was a big Japanese screen in the middle of the floor, subdividing the living from the dining area; but this one, rather than cherry blossoms and so forth, was decorated with a dark pattern of stylised ocean waves. Maureen was preparing some kind of meal for guests who were coming to dinner, and she was there alone, knowing that it was not her home but that she was house-sitting for someone very important whose identity she could not recall. There was a sense of time passing in fast-forward; it was getting late and a feeling of panic setting in. Would the guest, who was surely none-other than the owner, arrive, and would she be ready for him if and when he did?

Then the door to the apartment, concealed by the silk screen, creaked open like something in a haunted house. Was this her mysterious guest, or an intruder? She felt her aloneness and vulnerability like a stabbing pain in the heart. The timber panelling of the roof and floor might have stretched like rubber in that moment, lengthening the prospect of the interior. Then, through the screen, she saw a light coming towards her. It was as though someone were advancing with a flickering lantern.

With exquisite regret Maureen felt that she knew her visitor from long ago, but had unaccountably and perhaps unforgivably forgotten him. That was why he would not come round to her side of the screen; she had to go to him. With trepidation she did so, and, eyes smarting, found the shining figure of a child perhaps five years old, his back turned to her in reproach.

The child was dressed in a little suit, like a page boy at a wedding. She called to him hesitantly, but he did not respond. At length, with a delicate compulsion, she went to place her hands on his shoulders, but felt as though repulsed. No, it was necessary to walk around to face him—and then she was back in the clouds of the previous dream, the same brilliance cascading from the child's eyes into hers, except that she was able to gaze back into it. The golden statue was coming to life. She went down on her knees, and he placed a hand on her head in gesture of benediction.

* * *

Maureen was riding the train home after one of her late nights at the music school. Her car was at the mechanic's, and Yusuf had the other one. It was his, after all; she was never allowed to drive the stupid thing. Sure, his workplace was slightly farther from home than hers, but she felt nonetheless that he might have shown a little more consideration, a little more concern for her welfare.

A few stops out of the city the door to the carriage opened, and several youths dressed in baggy jeans and hoodies entered, one carrying a stereo that was blaring the kind of music one would expect based on all available visual cues. Maureen tried not to over-react.

They accosted an Asian girl who was sitting alone on one of a pair of facing seats in the opposite aisle, forcing her to take her earphones out while they gestured suggestively. It was impossible to hear any words over the noise of the boom-box. The girl moved over one seat, so that one of the five youths sat down beside her and put his arm up on the seat behind her head. Maureen gathered that the girl was in distress; another of the youths was standing in front of her, his groin almost level with her face.

The carriage was something under a quarter full. Among those she could afterwards remember being present as onlookers were an old man, who looked on disapprovingly but ineffectually, and an obese woman struggling to rubber-neck around to see what was going on. There was also a young guy who obviously went to the gym, but he was listening to music on his earphones and playing on his phone, pretending that he saw nothing.

Three of the youths continued up the aisle towards Maureen. Their dark eyes had selected her without doubt, white teeth bared in predatory grins.

Then an unaccompanied child appeared suddenly in the aisle between them. He could only have been five years old, to judge by his stature, but he seemed to walk like a grown man and with an air of authority. The trio were distracted, and, as one, they refocused their gaze on the child, stopping in their tracks. "They wouldn't!" she thought fearfully at first, then angrily: "They'd better not!"

They did not. What came about then was a remarkable anti-climax which afterwards made her feel like questioning the truth of her memory.

Was it perhaps an expression of awe that she had seen on their faces, staring at the child? That she could hardly doubt, as absurd as it seemed: the way those hoodlums had retreated back the way they had come, the three turning around as one and falling in with the other two, to again plague the travellers in the preceding carriage. When the little boy turned to face Maureen, she saw that he was indeed the familiar angel-child of her dream. He was incognito to the extent that the only halo he wore was one of great beauty and radiant inner power. He was as physically real as anyone else on that train.

She glanced after him as he walked back up to the end of the aisle, turned around and came back in her direction again, his demeanour softened now that the threat had been seen off. She could not think what to say or do. When he reached her this time, the boy stopped and touched her leg, which instantly broke out in pins and needles.

"Have you got a baby in there?" he asked, nodding towards her belly and pointing, the electrically charged finger only centimetres from her abdomen.

"Yes," she whispered, wanting to feel his touch on her belly.

"Oh," he said with complete nonchalance.

It was Maureen's stop. She did not know what to do; it was as though she were both failing in a duty and missing some mysterious opportunity as, fatalistically, she disembarked. She felt troubled and, somehow, ashamed.

In the next dream there was not one child but many.

She was sitting in a lush, green field, picnic rug laid out and on it a basket full of good things. There was a sense of the galloping passage of time in the sky, whose dome went from bright to dark blue while the distant, unimpeded horizon soon began to glow with evening colours. At the same time Maureen began to feel a growing unease and coldness. She was wearing a short summer dress and had to pull it down over her legs, which were breaking out in goose pimples. It was unclear whom she was waiting for, and there was nowhere to go as the lawn spread out, seemingly infinite, in all directions. To follow the horizon with her eyes was to invite vertigo. But with the sunset, the grass, and the foliage of the solitary tree behind her began to come alive in a cool breeze that nonetheless seemed inadequate to produce such a lively effect in its foliage, whooshing with a noise like that of surf against rocks. Even the grass, not overly long, seemed to flicker like green fire. An over-large and intensely coloured butterfly landed on her pregnant belly for a second, settling its wings, only to fly off again in a moment.

No longer mentally comfortable with her back to the tree, she stood up, took a few steps, and turned to face it. In its branches there were many little pink-gold legs dangling down, blushing brightly as the sky behind them, their owners sitting still as birds of prey but relaxed as rococo cherubs. The idea then occurred to her that, since whoever it was she was waiting for was evidently not coming, she would instead share the contents of her hamper with the children. Let's see, what had she brought . . .

Her senses were assaulted by a foetid, stinking mass that looked as though it might have been dredged from the bottom of a waste bin in some alleyway. She slammed back the lid of the hamper, heart pounding in disgust.

Now, looking back up at the children, she saw that they were not as they had been a moment ago. Those legs, along with the rest of their bodies, were somehow misshapen and no longer glowing. In a moment one of the creatures, its eyes meeting hers, dropped down out of the tree like a rotten piece of fruit a couple of metres away. She jumped up and backwards in fright. The thing was naked, but partly covered in coarse dark hair. Its face was horrible: thick, ropy lips wet with slaver and avid, bulbous eyes, sloping brow, and aggressively flared nostrils that she could see were twitching at the scent from her basket. Plop, plop! A couple more followed. They were coming toward her as she backed away, convinced that the thing to do was not to appear frightened, not to run lest they chase her. But then, as she retreated warily without turning around, she realised that they were not actually interested in her. They were not beasts of prey, but scavengers, headed for the basket, which the leader of the pack had already opened and thrust his snout inside. She continued backing away as they fought and snarled over the revolting contents.

As she ran away there was a kind of temptation to turn and look back that was hard to resist. How many were there? What were they? And above all, what was at the summit of the tree? She had caught a glimpse of it before turning her back, and had to look away as from the sun itself—which made no sense, as it had sunk well down by this time . . .

* * *

Maureen went into labour at work one afternoon. She was halfway through a phone conversation when her waters broke. Her boss, who liked to be addressed as Mr Ming, was not particularly sympathetic, but he lost his mandarin composure at the sight of her abjection. It was horribly embarrassing.

Yusuf had his phone switched off and did not show up until she was well into "the zone," at which point nothing external to her own body made any difference. When they placed the baby on her breast, she felt only exhaustion.

After the birth, she slept.

Standing over her was the Angel from the first dream; opposite him the child they had conceived together. When her eyes grew accustomed to the light, she noticed that the one expression on their two faces was quite inscrutable; their eyes not quite meeting hers. For a long moment she failed to look down at what they were seeing, namely, the thing that was making that horrible sucking noise at her breast. Maureen looked down at the dark shapeless form and up again at the faces, in panic. Those hard, judgmental faces (as she now understood their looks) had no friendly advice to give, no reassurance.

At her breast, sucking in a feeding frenzy, was something like a giant leech, dark, ringed with bands of coarse black hair, its skin a khaki green that threw off other ephemeral hues like an oil slick in the light from the Angels' faces. It was the larval form of the ape-creatures from her dream—not themselves juveniles, she now realised, but rather imagos of the same ghastly species. She could see and feel the waves of her blood swelling the pulsating body, and there it was, running down to stain the white sheets. As she tugged at the parasite in ineffectual self-defence, its wiry hairs, stood on end as if in a warning sign, while it continued to drink. She was numb with horror. The only human thing about this creature was its eyes: those brown, apparently soulful eyes that contrived even now to seek out and exploit her motherly instinct. But she knew there was no soul behind them, not really. They were like the defensive eyes painted on the wings of a moth.

"Get it off me!" she tried to scream, "Please!" but found herself paralysed now, reduced to utter passivity while her life-essence was rapidly drained away. After a pause in which the pair of divine beings before her seemed to consider whether she was worthy of their help, it was the child, still held upright in the crook of its father's powerful arm, who reached out to her. Immediately the changeling relinquished her breast. She saw its contracting maw, its annular mouthparts, as it bucked and writhed; but the child now took and held it up before his face, unafraid, so that it shrunk away—literally, drying up like salted *bêche-de-mer*. Concomitantly the child's face emitted more and more light, until Maureen had to look away, knowing that whatever came next would be a miracle too great for her comprehension.

The next thing she knew, she was holding a baby in whose helpless form her saviour of a moment ago was now miraculously incarnate. Its father had vanished, for now, leaving behind a blessed assurance to protect his family from the breaking nightmare that would otherwise have overwhelmed them without remedy.

I'VE GOT SOMETHING TO SHOW YOU

"Oi! What you doin' in me yard?"

"Oh, g'day. Didn't know you was home. Just takin' out your rub—"

"Nobody asked ya! I can take me own rubbish out!"

"Right you are! Sorry. Just your car's not there, so I thought—"

"It's at the garage. What you doin' anyway, lookin' to see if me car's there or not?"

Graeme raised his hands in a gesture of innocence persecuted. "Just being a good neighbour, alright?" He then retreated fast, cheeks burning as he closed the gate behind him.

You would think that people living in a forlorn place like this would at least show a little of that fabled sense of community associated with country towns; that it might be possible to do a neighbour a good turn without getting an earful of paranoid accusations.

He should not take it to heart, he knew. Maybe the old bitch was just crazy; she was certainly reclusive enough that they had never spoken more than a greeting before, and that always initiated by him. Still, it was hard to take. He hated himself enough these days that being disliked by others hurt more than it used to. There little that he could say he had achieved in his forty-five years, nor much that he was good or gifted at. But being decent and friendly, willing to do little jobs for people like taking the bins out or even changing a washer, rehanging a sticky door—these were things he enjoyed and made a point of where he could, for the sake of what remained of his self-respect.

There was the fact that he was a dole bludger, of course. Sure, he got the odd bit of overt sympathy for being a single dad doing it tough, from the office lady at the school, from drunks at the pub . . . but the fact remained that people generally did not appreciate having you around if you lived off their taxes. And then there was the little scandal of the girls nicking things from the shops, starting to take after their mother. He had given them both a smack after the bloke who ran the general store came round and told him. Maybe there was more harm done than he had thought—especially by Tahnee, no doubt. Well, fuck his family's accusers! They should try raising three kids on their own.

It had been overwhelming to discover a year ago that his own dad had died with money. Where had it come from? As it turned out, he had made friends with another old drunk living nearby who was secretly rich and had no family, and his dad had looked after the old guy; nursed him, even, through his last illness. Graeme had cried, unable to believe his luck, just then when it was most needed, and full of gratitude as well as remorse for the years of their estrangement.

As Graeme retreated back inside the sagging old Californian bungalow he had bought with this inheritance, the rotten veranda groaned as if it would collapse any day. There were worrying cracks in the walls, and places where the eaves had separated from them, none of which he had noticed before buying the place. It was just him and the three kids here. Actually, Tahnee, the youngest, was not his, and liked to remind him of the fact, especially when he tried to discipline her. He and Wendy had been separated at the time she was conceived, she living with another man who might still be in prison for all Graeme knew, but he was for all intents and purposes the only father the girl had ever had. Graeme had his suspicions about Jack, the middle child, too. He was the only one he had insisted on naming according to his own preference, rejecting Wendy's proposal of "Jaymen." Even so, he had never been quite able to see himself in the boy.

When things had gone bad for what he hoped was the final time, it had been like a nightmare. Every night he and the kids spent in the same city as Wendy and the people she was now mixed up with had made it seem doubly unlikely that they would ever wake up.

As ever since, she had been a prostitute when they met nearly two decades ago. He was selling dope for a guy he barely knew but to whom he owed some money. The following years had been wild indeed, and he looked back on them – some of them – with a kind of nostalgia now, and pride that his family had survived, if not quite kept together. First had come Shiarna, now fifteen, and two years later Jack. But Graeme had not been there at his birth; he was in jail. Meanwhile Wendy conceived Tahnee with someone he understood to have been a very tough character indeed, who was fortunately gone by the time of Graeme's release.

But recently Wendy had got involved with a different, even rougher scene through a woman she worked with. She had always been sensible enough not to work the streets before, but now she told Graeme, "Don't worry, babe. Shaz knows some people who look after her good. Last one who fucked with 'em won't have much use for hookers again!" And she grinned in a way that was somehow new. Yes, she was turning into someone else, staying out all night and not coming home for days on end, and looking terrible when she did, like a walking skeleton. Worse, she was bringing dead-eyed, dangerous looking people into the house who did drugs in front of the kids and gave him the death stare when he objected.

If Tahnee was to be believed (and that was a big "if") these people had parties, one of which her mother had hosted while he was away working in the country. "Mum's friends got this big, like, pot or somethink full of blood, and this man come over an' he was wearin' funny clothes with feathers an' that, and he killed a chook and put its blood and stuff in there, an' everyone drunk some, except Shiarna, an' we, like, danced an' all that. It was the best fun!"

Graeme wanted to believe that it was just her imagination, but after his wife was questioned by the police over the disgustingly brutal death of another colleague he wondered, hard. They were from all over, too, these people; some of them did not even speak English. He was no racist, but at least with Aussie crims you knew pretty well what the game was.

And Wendy was obviously back on the drugs, though she denied it. She was so volatile and would go around muttering the weirdest nonsense, on and on about blood and other bodily fluids, and an increasing amount of words that were definitely not in the English language. She refused to explain what was going on, no matter what approach he took with her. He would plead with her on behalf of the kids, and she would just laugh in his face while he clenched his fists. He had never been one to hit a woman.

A while later, with some misgiving, he accepted some work laying sewage pipes at a location some three hundred kilometres away, so that he had to stay in a motel for a couple of nights. On returning, he found the kids left on their own with nothing to eat but a bit of mouldy bread in the cupboard. Tahnee was running around naked, talking gobbledygook like her mother, and Shiarna was hiding under the bed. She would go silent for days, screaming when anyone came near her. When finally she started to come around, she asked her father more than once, voice trembling and keeping her distance, "Is it really you, Daddy?" The biggest worry, though, was that Jack was apparently with his mother. He was that close to ringing Child Services . . .

When Wendy finally came home a couple of days later, totally dishevelled, looking and smelling like a corpse, he slapped her in the face. She just laughed and shouted, "You can't hurt me! No one can hurt me!" Jack, as always unruffled, simply ate in silence, ignoring Graeme's anxious questioning. Then he took a shower and went to his room to play Xbox. Subsequent enquiries were fruitless.

Graeme had gone to buy some weed from Gary, the local publican. He stayed for a couple of drinks, talking football and gossip with the handful of locals who congregated there and did not consider themselves above him. They were mostly unemployed farm labourers who would not work again till the next harvest, or else they were on some sort of pension. Gary told him not to worry about the woman next door: "You're lucky she didn't bite you like she did the district nurse! Mad as a cut snake, that one." That, in addition to four beers, was enough to turn his mood around.

Returning home, Graeme found Tahnee sitting on the veranda, dressed, as usual, like trouble in clothes bought, or more likely stolen, from the opportunity shop. Tonight it was a lime-green off-the-shoulder dress that made her look about eighteen as she dabbled her bare toes in the red dirt, having kicked off those ludicrously too-large snakeskin boots. The thought of some poor young bloke getting her pregnant in a few years' time and bearing her away was almost reassuring.

The girls were considered "weird" at school, Shiarna always so fearful and introverted that she hid indoors during lunch and recess to escape taunting, and Tahnee already smoking and teaching the little kids to swear. Jack was relatively normal and spent a lot of time with his new friends playing videogames, or riding the motorbike Graeme had bought him with his dad's money.

Tahnee stopped playing on her iPhone and called out, "Hey, Graeme! A man come here while you was out. He come inside the house, like, just standin' in the doorway, really still, before we even saw he was there. He didn't move or nothing!" She seemed more excited than afraid. Dread gripped Graeme by the bowels.

"Where's your sister?"

"In her room." Graeme hurried inside. Tahnee followed eagerly, pattering on: "At first I thought it was me real dad from when I was little, so I said 'Dad?' like that, but then Shiarna, she started screamin' like a retard, and that's when I knew it wasn't him. I reckon it was prob'ly just some paedo from 'round here," she said in an absurdly casual tone, the one intended to show how grown up she was. "But then he gone away real quick, 'cause of the screamin'."

Was Graeme right in thinking that she had rolled her eyes in describing her sister's reaction?

He tried the handle of Shiarna's door. There was a bolt on the inside which she must have drawn. A short, choking squeal came in response.

"It's okay, sweetheart, it's your dad."

Tahnee stood behind him. He could feel her smile of amusement without looking, and it irked him. She relished any kind of drama.

"Get to your room, Tahnee!" he yelled in a tone whose hostility surprised him. She seemed to take it easily enough.

"Shiarna, sweetheart?" No further response. He tried again, and again. Finally there came a feeble, distressed "Go away!" After he had continued pleading for a while, she got out of bed and clip-clopped in her inimitably awkward manner—even with bare feet—across the floorboards.

She had little to tell him other than to corroborate her sister's story, but with one alarming addition: "He wanted to know if you was home," she said, sobbing quietly. The two of them were sitting on the edge of her bed. Well, if it was "some paedo," then Graeme supposed he would have done. There was a strong smell of deodorant emanating from her.

"Tahnee said you wasn't home, and then he come closer, into the room, and he said it was okay 'cause he had somethin' to show her, and me, too." Graeme felt a frisson of mingled emotions, including a diffuse and alarming suspicion. Why the slight divergence between the two stories? What was Tahnee trying to hide?

"Then what happened? Did he . . . show you anything? Did he do anything?"

Graeme began mentally scanning the faces of all his male acquaintances. Pot-bellied, taciturn Steve whom he had had around a couple of times for a beer. Had his eyes not lingered on Tahnee in those cut-off denim shorts she wore? Then there were the blokes at the Men's Shed, an assortment of retirees and dole bludgers like himself, including one old man who, on a bad day, was possibly senile enough to wander into someone's house.

"Was it anyone you seen before?"

"I dunno. I don't think so. I just run straight in here. Tahnee said he was gone, but I didn't believe her."

"That's good, hun. You done the right thing. I'm sorry I wasn't here to protect you." He sat himself closer to his daughter, pulling her towards him with the arm that was already resting on her shoulder. But she resisted him. Did she blame him, smelling the beer on his breath? Worse, did she on some level distrust him as a man also, her recent close encounter rekindling painful memories of things that may have happened at various times in her sorry upbringing when he was not there to protect her? They had never spoken about such things, but he had his suspicions.

In a moment his nostrils solved the mystery. She had shat in her pants.

As Graeme argued at the government job agency to which he was obliged to report each month, he could not afford to spend too much time outside the house, being a full-time father in a town with no after-school care facilities. But although he spent most of his time at home, the kids, especially Tahnee, would go wandering about town whether he allowed it or not. Apart from the risk of shoplifting there seemed little danger in that. He had spoken again to both girls about the intruder incident and warned them about keeping doors locked and not talking to strangers.

At some point, though, Graeme really started to worry. He saw a car slow down in front of the house one day, its tinted windows denying him a good look at who was inside. Nissan Maxima, numberplate AQR, or possibly AGP . . . The numbers were elusive. Maybe he was becoming paranoid from boredom.

Another time Shiarna was in her bedroom, and Tahnee was at the house of a classmate she had managed to befriend. There was a knock at the door. That in itself caused Graeme's adrenaline to surge. In truth, these days he was getting to be afraid of being alone, and of the dark. It was ridiculous after everything he had been through in his life! He had been in jail, had a gun pointed at him, been bashed up, and given as good as he got. Too much weed, that must be it.

On the other side of the fly screen stood someone who might have been a salesman: that is, a salesman from some old movie, wearing an Akubra and a suit and tie despite the heat, and carrying a briefcase. He did not look like an Indian, like the only other salesman who had ever bothered them here. Apart from the intense look in his eyes, his face was normal, about Graeme's own age. The man smiled a familiar smile and opened his mouth slightly as though about to speak, but then, very strangely, did not. Time seemed frozen. Then a truck went past while his lips moved, saying something Graeme was somehow relieved not to have heard. The next thing, he reached for the handle on the fly-screen door, and Graeme, in panic, slammed the wooden door in his face and ran to check on Shiarna, who was the only one at home. She was sitting on her bed playing with her iPad. When he returned to the front door, the man was gone.

Graeme asked Gary if he knew of any "dodgy" characters around who might pose a danger to children.

"I wouldn't say so, no . . ." he said at first, characteristically abstracted, his gaze wandering off towards the TV on which a football match was playing. "But you never know. Used to be an old bloke lived out on Wickham's Road, near the tip. Few years ago now. Used to have a wife and kids. Then he hung around outside the school a bit, up to the point where they had to call Martin in." Martin Phelan was the town's police officer. "Didn't have many friends, so people was quick to judge him; didn't occur to 'em he might have just forgot his own kids didn't go to school there anymore. Problem was, though, he kept comin' back and coming back, and gettin' bloody pushy when they tried to clear him off."

Apparently, the old man was now dead, which made Graeme wonder why Gary had brought him up in answer to a request for relevant information. Of course, the anecdote had been offered as possessing thematic relevance only. That was very much the publican's style.

There was a break in the conversation as he was called upon to take an order for dinner from a group of four Chinese who had just come in.

"Seen a few of them 'round lately," Graeme remarked.

"Apparently they're here to see the stars out over the lake." Gary was referring to Lake Worrall, the vast salt pan on the edge of town whose waters were either non-existent or so far receded due to drought that Graeme had never seen them when driving past. "Sky's clearer out here than just about anywhere, they say. Guess where they're from there's so much pollution it makes a change for 'em. Yep, Chinese newspaper writes somethin' up about it, now all of a sudden we're a tourist attraction."

As the two men discussed the situation, it emerged that there was an opportunity to make some money. The stargazers had a habit of getting bogged in the sand and needing a tow out. A couple of other blokes were already out there charging up to $400 a tow. Luckily, Graeme's car was an SUV, a 2001 Subaru Forester that, although getting on in age, was still mechanically sound and could theoretically handle the terrain. Gary had said that the time to go was around midnight.

The so-called lake was only ten minutes' drive away by a road that led out into the flat lands and scrub that continued for a hundred or so kilometres before the next town. This land was covered in a low scrub of salt-tolerant plants that by daylight gave the landscape a mottled look, with alternating patches of ochre, olive green, purplish grey, and rust. There were ossified clutches of dead wood, white, grey, and burnt black, sticking up out of the low, flat ground, and the occasional Mallee gum. Graeme knew this landscape fairly well from the road, though he could see little of it at the moment. The night was dark as the Moon was new, and his headlights lit up little to either side of the road ahead.

Soon that road became dirt and came to an end. He kept on driving out onto the dry lake itself, getting a look at the native flora which was surprisingly lively by the light of his high-beams, the colours strangely far brighter than by day. Where were the cars? He would have thought the tourists would park around here on the most accessible margin. They had certainly left signs in plenty of their recent presence: chip packets and soda cans lay all around. If Graeme had felt any shame about fleecing them it was now assuaged. The thing was to keep off the salt: that was where you were likely to get bogged.

Up ahead and to the left he saw a light at ground level, so faint that he was unsure if it was real. He drove towards it. It was slow going over the salt flats, picking his way and sticking to the higher ground. Why would they drive so far out? Maybe they had calculated the exact spot, the exact meridian point, if that was the term, from which to observe whatever it was that they wanted to see up in the sky.

It was a very melancholy place, so very quiet as he wound down the windows due to the broken aircon. The air was cooler than it had been earlier; winter was on its way. Graeme began to feel very much like turning around and heading back home. The light on the horizon had a disconcerting way of receding as he drove towards it, or at least failing to get brighter as fast as it should have. He had to dip his own lights to keep it in view. This was such a huge, wide open space and, in some more than physical way, Graeme felt dangerously exposed.

The fear came out of nowhere, or perhaps simply from the darkness, as it had done when he was a child: a new-old feeling that took him by surprise, although it had been loitering in the back of his mind for some time of late. Graeme inhaled it like dizzying, cold smoke, as the engine idled while he sat here undecided whether he had it in him to press on. It seemed as though an evil, grinning face might appear at any second in his rear-view mirror, a hand be placed on his shoulder. How bloody stupid! More acutely worrying, though, was that it felt like the tyres were sinking deeper in the sand.

He had not completed the U-turn before, with a soft jolt to the left, his wheels sank further. A moment later they were spinning uselessly.

Graeme got out and stepped into what was now a decidedly cold night. He felt that he was further from home than ever before in his life—which was of course absurd. Then he looked up at the stars. Of course, the deep, dark and scintillating cavern of the sky had not been fully visible before when he was behind the wheel. Now Graeme could understand why the tourists had come so far. The wonder of it was somehow appalling, so deep that for once it was easy to believe, even to perceive, that the universe was more than just a star-studded fabric of some flat black stuff; no, it was an infinite universe, a three-dimensional maze of light and vastly predominant darkness which to look at was to get lost in, to imagine oneself an astronaut stranded alone out there in space. Of course: life on Earth was an accident, and one day it would end forever.

But there was something else yet more worrying, like a secret that was threatening to reveal itself in the sky that dizzied Graeme with vertigo and compelled him to gaze into it with such force that, to harness the power of his muscles and keep from falling onto his back, he had to resist the urge to look up at. It was like standing beneath some awesomely tall building and focusing on its summit; having to do that, compulsively, only to feel that it was tilting over, ready to crush you. Yes, the sky might fall and crush him, while the Earth seemed to shift under his feet. Was he feeling its diurnal rotation? The couple of drinks he had taken earlier afforded no explanation.

Graeme closed his eyes, which only partly allayed the spinning sensation. Behind his lids were the faces of his children. There in the middle was Shiarna with her thickset features and that familiar troubled, quizzical look. He loved the other two as well, but it was she he felt closest to; she had his eyes, nose, and hair, and so she attracted to herself a portion of his self-pity, and a tenderness that was selfless and just as deep, also. The others had their characteristic expressions which were lovable in their own way, even if they did evince the seeds of contempt for Graeme and his manifold failure in life.

There was also Wendy's face, with that disturbing alter-ego staring manically out from it. It was as though the features that he thought he had known so well were merely a mask over a darkness as deep as the sky's.

He opened his eyes. Graeme was unsure whether to rejoice or run in terror at the dark figure that he saw standing before him under the stars, just darker than the sky behind it in the horizon's fugitive glow. It was coming towards him. Those two contradictory responses of hope and fear paralysed Graeme so that all he could do was watch, straining his eyes to make out something of the figure's shape and size. Was it male or female? Young or old? Bulky or slight of build? It approached slowly from what seemed a great yet unquantifiable distance. Tough, shadowy foliage was trembling all around as the wind rose. The figure stopped and raised a hand as if hailing Graeme—but no, it was pointing upwards.

He thought of the pitiable and suspect old man Gary had mentioned, who used to live out this way. Was this his ghost? And also of the man who had come to his door, and the one who had come in his absence. In his mind a voice whispered the words, "Are you home, Graeme? I've got something to show you."

Up in the sky the stars had formed a constellation in the unmistakeable shape of a human face: eyes closed with little points of light glistening like tears caught in eyelashes, others, fast multiplying, modelling the contours of the cheeks, nose, forehead, and so forth, forming a ghostly but effective tracery not unlike a photographic negative. It was getting bigger, taking up more and more of the sky. The face was that of his son, Jack, who a couple of weeks back had gone to stay with his mother.

The problem was that Graeme's custody of the children was customary only. If pressed, it was hard to predict what the Family Court would decide, given Wendy's history of drug use and prostitution, on one hand, and Graeme's criminal record and unemployment on the other. But she was still the biological mother of all three.

How had Wendy found them? Something Graeme or one of the kids had posted on Facebook, maybe. In a way it was a lucky break that she had found only Jack at home when she came. It had been a Saturday, and the rest of the family had gone shopping to fill the cupboard for another week. Only Jack stolidly refused, which was hardly unusual. "Suit yourself then," Graeme had said, "The rest of us'll have hamburgers without you. Maybe we'll bring you back some cold chips." Perhaps he had been in on his mother's plan? Graeme had since spoken to Jack on the phone twice, and there was a delay on the line and a distant, muffled quality in the reception. Neither had much to say to each other.

The main thing to remember was that it was just a temporary visit. It could not go on past the end of the month, anyway; he had missed enough school, and if he was absent from the start of next term, there would be questions asked. Wendy had sweetly reassured him on the phone. Thank God it was her again, not the strung-out lunatic he and the children had escaped.

Jack was his son, Graeme now understood with complete certainty for the first time in his life. He struggled with a troubled heart to make out the expression on that beautiful face, to interpret it. His heart was throbbing not only with love but with fear that he would not be able to bear the sharpness of the beams that would escape as—yes, those eyelids began to open, revealing the gaze of reproach Graeme had seen, fleetingly and on a much smaller scale, so often before. But no, at the same time the child who seldom looked him in the eyes was breaking into a smile, more and more broadly as the moments elapsed, smiling beatifically, as though gently waking from a beautiful dream. Jack's eyes were opening in earnest, but the awaited beams did not shine forth. It was a slow, transfixing ordeal: Graeme wanted desperately to know if his son would be pleased to see him, would recognise him from all the way up there. But no, the eyes continued to widen further and further, revealing only more and more darkness, until a pair of empty zeroes, black holes that threatened to swallow the universe, stared Graeme down and told him what he already knew.

ANALOGUE

"Look here, I shan't give twopence for your immortality unless I'm to remain an individual"
— Schopenhauer, "Immortality, a Dialogue"

His intuitive hypothesis was that when his wife died, in that moment when she had fallen out of time and space, her unique and eternal form had been impressed, like a whole-body death mask, in the illusory substance of this world. The catch was that in the same moment it had shattered and dispersed, setting forth a labour of Hercules that he, Dylan Pierce, would only doubtfully be able to accomplish in what remained of his natural lifespan.

There was no guarantee, to put it mildly, that he would ever encounter those fragments, which might logically be on some distant planet, at the centre of the Earth, or buried beneath the Taj Mahal. For that matter, they might even be buried in the distant future, or in rock formations that for the time being remained latent beneath the Earth's crust. But he had recovered one fragment already: a dark, smooth rock, or rock-like substance, shaped exactly like a piece of her face consisting of the corner of her mouth, including the incipient lips, and about two-thirds of her uniquely dimpled chin. These details would have been enough, but in addition the slightly raised, almost heart-shaped mole about three millimetres at its widest diameter, just near the corner of her lip, had also been perfectly reproduced. It was like a three-dimensional photo negative, smooth and polished, perhaps, by the waves of the sea over long years before Cecilia's birth.

It was smooth on both sides, the edges sharp in some places, and was of the same thickness throughout, as in the case of a shard of some hollow porcelain doll. The hollowness seemed apposite, symbolic. Her spirit would come to dwell inside the reassembled figure, after all. He had tried to have the material analysed by a qualified geologist, but that would have involved being parted from it for several days, which Dylan felt was unacceptable. Instead he took it to a lapidary with no academic qualifications, who was puzzled. Obsidian was his nearest guess, but then its weight and opacity suggested agate . . . A conclusive answer could not be given.

Dylan's mental image of Celia's face, as of her body, was photographic. Of course there were actual photos, but he felt little need to look at them, so vivid were his memories where they pertained to her, and increasingly only then. He imagined gathering all the pieces together over the years it might take to find them, laying them out on a bed like pieces of a fossilised skeleton, wiring them up somehow, unless they might fuse together by magic . . . and then they would start to move, soften, grow warm, and change hue . . . And if he was not destined to succeed, why would he have found this initial piece that (not to reduce the gestalt of her beauty to its parts) immortalised the curve of a lip and the dimple of chin that were among her most distinctive features?

On the day he found this fragment, he had scoured the beach for more, not minding the cold as evening drew on and not bothering about the meals he missed, but searching until it was too dark to see. Then he returned the next day, and the day after, and the day after that. It was during the holiday he had taken soon after his wife's death to the locale of the last holiday they had taken together. He had gone back to those dunes again and again over the days that followed. He had paused over a mollusc shell stuck to another large pebble of the same black, hyaline material, but as there was no hint of the incipient contour where Celia's jaw ought to have begun, just under the shell-ear, discarded it. That reassured him: it was no case of wish-fulfilment; rather, the first puzzle-piece had presented him with an unarguable fact, and that constituted a promise, even if fulfilment was not immediately forthcoming.

But future visits to the site, which he took at every opportunity, failed to disclose anything, until his conviction grew that the remaining pieces must be elsewhere. He even retraced, at great expense, the steps they had taken as a young couple on their European tour that had been their honeymoon. But it had been nearly eight years now, and nothing further had presented itself. Then in recent months he had begun to fear, just marginally, that Cecilia was finally starting to fade in his memory, the supernatural link between them disintegrating. Had not her face behind his closed eyelids always been brighter than day? In compensation, his searching and daily meditations on her memory grew even more fervent, to the point where they almost began to interfere with his work. (That could not be allowed to happen; he needed a way to fund the extensive field trips he took during the eight weeks a year that his job afforded.)

Dylan simply had to entrust his search to fate and listen always to its promptings, meditating and then jabbing a finger, or the end of Cecilia's violin bow, at a map, with eyes closed. Overseas trips were not possible every year, but he reassured himself that whatever occult power had given him this task, it would surely not be so capricious as to place its fulfilment beyond his capabilities. As an example of the kind of torturous disappointment he faced on these expeditions, during a bushwalking trip to the Victorian Alps, he had paused a long while over a piece of a hollowed snow gum log with a whorl that might have represented an areola. But no, it was not hers, however much he wished it to be.

The only other time he had experienced a moment of subjective certainty of her presence in a physical object, or phenomenon, still troubled him two years later. He had been at home following the conclusion of an unsuccessful trip through Southeast Asia, feeling horribly depressed, and upon doing the dishes after dinner and letting out the water, had for several moments gazed into Cecilia's left eye in the swirl of the water as it drained away.

Strange to say, Dylan had never before consulted anyone claiming to possess psychic abilities, or pursued any other conventional occult avenues in his blind quest. He held no firm religious or metaphysical beliefs other than those dictated by personal experience, and had received no sign, inner or outer, that such assistance would be necessary. A stubborn man and a creature of habit, moreover, he jealously kept secret his inner life, centred around the departed love of his life, fearing somehow that to do otherwise might have the effect of grounding the circuit and dissipating the sacred charge he carried.

Harvey Krauss, MA, "psychic facilitator," as his website described him, turned out to be a paunchy middle-aged man of large stature and build. He might have been a fellow clerical worker of some kind, or possibly a high school teacher, at a guess. His appearance was slightly unkempt, as though he had just come home from work and not had time to change out of an off-white business shirt with visible wet patches under the arms. But then, he had not shaved recently, either. Dylan looked around at the cramped, sad little apartment, took a whiff of its stale air, and from the outside of his button-down pants pocket felt the sacred stone where it was secreted in a wrapping of heavy cloth to prevent those sharp edges from doing any damage that, not always involuntarily, had been known to shed his blood.

After some small talk, his host went over proceedings, offering an explanation congruent with what Dylan had gleaned from the rather unprofessional website that this "psychic facilitator" maintained. Essentially, as he understood it, he was to be hypnotised by TV static from which something in the nature of a supernatural communication might emerge. Harvey was a strong believer in Electronic Voice Phenomena as a form of communication between this world and the next.

"The volume will start low, before building up to a crescendo like the noise of a waterfall. In fact, I won't be manipulating the volume at all; it's just that you won't be hearing or seeing anything else, so the white noise will come to occupy your entire field of consciousness."

"I see. So then I start . . . hearing voices, or . . . ?"

"Perhaps," Harvey admonished with a finger. "It depends, firstly, if anyone's speaking, and secondly, how receptively you're listening. Of course, there's a roughly equal possibility that you might see something, too."

"And do either of us have to do anything, I mean, anything in particular?" Dylan was awkwardly, narrowly avoiding the question as to whether the man actually did anything for his fee besides flick a switch—not that he gave a damn about the money.

He would have paid anything if only it would yield the most vaguely encouraging result; but it occurred to Dylan that his host probably did not do this very often; by being here in this capacity he was probably feeding the other man's half-starved fantasy life.

The couch on which the two of them were seated was just as excessively soft and uncomfortable as it looked, and as dingy as the rest of the apartment's living room. There was a much more comfortable-looking armchair to the right; why could he not sit there? Based on the man's clammy and ill-kempt appearance, on sitting down Dylan had braced himself for a whiff of body odour. This turned out not to be an issue, however; it was his breath that was the trouble.

"A lot of what I'm about to say is really just common knowledge, and I don't intend to teach you to suck eggs, as the saying goes, but bear with me. If you understand the rationale behind our procedures, it may help to allay any sceptical feelings that might otherwise interfere with your receptivity. Brain processes are electro-chemical in nature: ion transfers across cell membranes aided by various chemical compounds. Do you know what that means—or, I should say, what it implies?" Dylan could only furrow his brow. "If brain processes are nothing more than electro-chemical reactions, this means that as far as human knowledge is concerned *everything* is merely a brain process—even the perceptual and conceptual data that make up our idea of a 'brain process,' do you see, which in turn means that what we refer to by that term is just a phenomenon that reveals itself to scientific investigation, while the noumenon, the *natura naturans*, if you follow, is something essentially other and unknowable, but it constitutes the one essential nature of everything, from the covalent bonds that hold the atoms in place that constitute, say, that book over there, maintaining it as a thing existing in time and space, right up to you and I with our beating hearts and firing synapses."

Harvey grinned, pleased with a verbose spiel that must have been rehearsed. Dylan was taken aback. This character reminded him a little of his precociously articulate, autistic nephew, who given the chance would lecture one endlessly about dinosaurs.

"That's very interesting. I did take some philosophy classes at uni, but it was a long time ago, I'm afraid." Dylan cast his gaze demurely downwards, noticing a probable wine stain on the edge of the beige cushion on which he was seated.

"But here's the important part for our purposes, Dylan. What happens when our bodies die and those brain processes stop?" his host continued exuberantly. "I don't claim to know exactly, but I think it's a shrewd guess that electrochemistry is translated to electromagnetism: electrons travelling freely through space—at least, and I say this again, as far as we, on our plane of pseudo-reality, are concerned. And then behind such subtle phenomena, or rather attached to them inseparably like the reverse side of a coin, experience, individuality in its barest form, continues indefinitely in a kind of limbo between phenomenon and noumenon. Schopenhauer was right about so much, but I believe this is where he got it wrong: the *principium individuationis*, the principle of identity, of individuation, doesn't just surrender its grasp. It clutches harder and harder as the core of our particular existence shrinks away to a singularity. "

"So . . . you're saying there *is* life after death? It's not just like, what would you call it? A trace, an echo we can sometimes hear? That's one theory I came across when I was researching."

Harvey paused and nodded judiciously before he spoke. "I believe there is, yes. Don't get me wrong. It's not some sort of *Divine Comedy* scenario where everyone gets their comeuppance, and world historic figures sit around and chat with guests when they're not being tortured by demons and what-have-you. No, the life-force is very primitive, stripped to its bare essence; but it's there, and it's incredibly strong: stronger than in life, I'd go so far as to say. And that does raise the question of the extent to which our own emotional attachment and attempts to communicate might play a role in sustaining the post-mortem existence of our loved ones. That's a thought that keeps me up at night, actually," he added grimly.

"Isn't there also the question of whether it might all be . . . sorry to ask; I'm not a dogmatically sceptical person—obviously, or I wouldn't be here, but it sounds like maybe—"

"We're deluding ourselves? Well, let me just say that some of the phenomena I and many other sane, rational people have seen and heard, and corroborated amongst ourselves, argue very strongly against that. I could go into details, but I'm sure you've done your own research; and in any case, the only evidence that matters will be what hopefully you'll take away from our proceedings tonight."

Dylan concurred.

"And believe me, if it were a matter of autosuggestion, I'd long ago have suggested my way out of all this." There was that tone again.

"Well, I appreciate you filling me in, Harvey. It's good to hear the theory behind it all, even if it's a bit beyond my intellect. At least I imagine I'll be more mentally receptive in front of a TV than playing with a Ouija board or something so . . . clichéd."

The man chuckled. "Oh, we really just use the television because it's easier than telepathy! Certainly, some people can receive direct communication from discarnate beings; others, myself included, find this way easier than having a receiver installed in our skulls!" Here he struck his temple and laughed, somewhat immoderately, before bending forwards and picking up a small spiral notepad from the coffee table. "So, down to business. I'll need to you to tell me as much as you can about your wife to maximise our chances of establishing contact."

In addition to more obviously significant questions about her life-trajectory, there were others that might have seemed banal were it not that for Dylan every trivial fact about Celia's life was as significant as an episode in the Gospels to a theologian.

Then came the part he had begun to dread.

"Now, of course it's a sensitive thing, and I fully appreciate that, but it might help if I were to find out some details of your intimate relationship with your late wife. Would that be acceptable?"

Dylan did not know what to say.

"I'm sorry in advance if I overstep any boundaries, but I trust you'll bear in mind that everything I ask is pertinent to our shared objective, and these sorts of details could make all the difference."

"Alright, if it'll help," he acceded with profound unease.

There were several sticky rings on the glass of the table top, where dust had densely accumulated. The only other items were a couple of paperback books, one of which, indifferently, Harvey had earlier indicated as an exemplary phenomenon of this illusory world. The title of one, in Art Nouveau script, was *The Astral Plane: Its Scenery, Inhabitants, and Phenomena.* The other had the French title *Ecartèlement.* Dylan, whose French had not progressed but only receded since high school, would have needed a dictionary to find out what that meant.

"You see, in my experience the dead can best be summoned by reminding them of the things they most enjoyed when alive, and for many people, though not all, sex is high up on the list."

Dylan clenched his teeth.

"So with that in mind, were you your wife's first lover?"

"Yes, as a matter of fact, I was. We were each other's first."

"That's very good, a very powerful thing for our purposes. Since you went on to marry, that would make your first time together a very special, memorable event for Cecilia, I dare say. And where did the event take place?"

Obvious misgivings aside, Dylan found it impossible now to turn back. He told the stranger all he wanted to know.

"Now, lastly, did you remember to bring an item associated with your beloved?"

The stone was still there in his pocket. "Yes, I—"

"No need to show or tell me anything about it," Harvey cut him off. "I find it's better for the bereaved to keep the item concealed, as I'm sure I mentioned on the phone, so it doesn't pick up any interfering radiation."

Ironic, thought Dylan blandly.

To Dylan's tremendous relief, it was now time to begin what his host termed "the induction." Thankfully, at this point he was first transferred from the dirty, uncomfortable sofa to the armchair he had eyed earlier. With the lights switched off and the curtains drawn, he stared at the silent, hypnotic swarm of black-and-white dots on the museum-piece TV's screen as it came on gradually, following the blip of the initial electron gun. Harvey droned on about how relaxed, calm, and comfortable his subject was supposedly starting to feel.

The tone of voice changed gradually as, after a long pause, Harvey began to address the departed. It increasingly lost its masculine timbre, soon becoming unnervingly high, almost a falsetto, and rather histrionic in tone. It was reminiscent of an adult speaking to a child, or to a senile adult.

"Cecilia Iniga Pierce, Celia Pierce, your name when you were a girl was Falco, remember?" He went over the names of her family members. "Remember when you were a little girl growing up in Perth, going to school and learning to play the violin . . ." Here came a list of friends' names and incidents involving them that stretched back to early childhood. Harvey had been attentive, for example noticing and mimicking the way Dylan would alternate between his wife's full name and its slight abbreviation. This was followed in essence by an account of her primary and secondary education, mentioning competitions and academic awards, the family's relocation to Melbourne, and so forth. Hearing his own eidetic account being recited back to him at such length, Dylan stopped listening and returned to the imaginary scenes themselves, until his own name came up for the first time. ". . . And then in Year Ten a new boy joined your class. His name was Dylan, Dylan Pierce—remember him, Cecilia? Celia, remember your husband, Dylan . . . ? You fell in love and got married later on." Here came a detailed account of their courtship. "Come here, Cecilia, come here, into the light, and talk to us; come out of the dark to where you can see again; come here where it's light and warm, and there are sights and sounds and things to taste and smell and touch and hear; come back where there's life . . . Yes, oh yes, that's a good girl . . . It's been a long time, hasn't it, Celia, Cecilia? Oh, I know, I know it has . . ."

The speaker kept pausing as if he were listening for something. Dylan strained his ears, but the rush of white noise divulged nothing. Had Harvey been speaking only at conversational volume, hearing him might have been difficult.

"Remember all the things you loved? Remember music, Celia, remember playing the violin? Remember Mozart, Haydn, Boccherini . . . ? They were your favourites, and you played them on your violin at home, for yourself and for your husband

Dylan, and for your friends and family. You wanted to be a concert violinist when you were young, remember? You almost made it, too." (The account of her eventual disappointment was omitted, along with anything else that Harvey deemed "liable to arrest her progress" by its unpleasantness.) I bet you want to come back and hear music and play again, don't you Cecilia . . . ? Oh, yes, I can tell you do. And remember all those other good things? Remember the home-made *capocollo* your parents used to give to you and Dylan when you'd visit each other? Remember wine? Your favourite was red, a nice cabernet or a shiraz; you had a glass every night with dinner after work, listening to music with your husband or sometimes just watching TV, and falling asleep in his arms. Celia, Cecilia, remember chocolate? Remember ice-cream? Remember sunshine? Remember holidays, like the one you and Dylan took to Europe . . . ? It was your honeymoon, your real one, even though you'd been married for five years by then. How you went to hear the Berlin Philharmonic, you saw the Forum and Saint Peter's and the little town of Schito in Lazio, your grandparents' town, and so many other beautiful things, and you wanted to stay forever . . . And then there was your last holiday, that little trip down the east coast of Tasmania the year before it all went dark? Oh yes, Celia, yes I know, I know . . . It's a long way back, and it's hard to find your way. Just follow my voice, Cecilia, just follow my voice. I'm here to help you come back to your husband, back to your life . . .

It was hard not to be impressed by Harvey's performance, its fluency, degree of detail, and intensity. It was something like an episode of *Here is Your Life* narrated by Vincent Price. Thus far the narration had been chronological, but now, as promised, came the anticipated divagation into the couple's intimate history.

"Celia, you married Dylan, you married your husband when you were twenty-one. He was your boyfriend before that, in high school in Blackburn . . . You lost your virginity to him one night in his car, the white station wagon, in the back, with the seats folded down, remember . . . ? It was cold that night, remember, at the park a few streets over from your parents' house.

It was so cold you wore his smelly gym clothes to keep warm because you had to stay the night, and you'd told your parents you were staying with your friend—remember your friend Hannah? Hannah Martin . . . ? You were close to her all your life. Oh, remember when you lost your virginity to the man who became your husband, Cecilia? You liked to be on top so he could kiss your breasts—your "*boobs*," you called them, remember, just like that first night in the car . . . ? Remember your body, Cecilia, how sometimes you loved it and sometimes you hated it? You'd think you were getting fat, and Dylan would come and kiss the parts you hated and make you love them again . . . Yes, Dylan Pierce, your husband, whose hair was so fair and wavy and nice to touch: Dylan Pierce, the man you married at your parents' home when you were twenty-one, and he was one year older, with all your friends and family there to see . . . Oh yes, oh, I know! Yes, it's really your old husband Dylan from when you were alive! Say hello, hmm . . . ? That's it, yes, nice and loud so he can hear you! Good, Celia, that's good. If you keep talking like that he's bound to hear!"

There was no mistaking that the self-described facilitator did in fact either believe, or wish Dylan to believe, that she was speaking to him. He glanced off to one side, but the TV had got brighter so that when he did, he found it had so affected his eyesight in the dark that he could see nothing.

"You and he wanted to have children, Celia, remember, a boy and a girl. The girl was going to be named after your grandmother, Rosa, who died when you were little; the boy was going to be called Robert, after Dylan's father. Your husband hasn't forgotten, Celia; he still wants to have those children with you . . . Yes, that's right, yes. Come back to him now, Cecilia, Cecilia Pierce, come back . . ."

It occurred to him that if this strange man really was communicating with his wife, he must be hoping to actually reincarnate her; otherwise this would be too cruel.

He watched the screen eagerly, though bemusedly, seeing nothing as yet and beginning to wish that voice would stop addressing his wife as though she were an idiot. Dylan smirked to himself, juxtaposing his memory of his wife earnestly expounding on Haydn's contrapuntal crisis of the 1770s with the patronising tone in which her ghost was now being addressed.

She was not here anyway, he felt, not that he could blame her. Nothing but static and white noise. There was something to that part of the experience, though, that was unexpectedly disconcerting, like being immolated in a cold fire of nothingness. But then Dylan began to feel his sceptical attitude slipping away. Was this hypnosis taking hold at last? The voice had finally either stopped speaking or had sunk beneath the noise. Perhaps the wonder was that he did not hallucinate more spectacularly; all he saw, and arguably at that, was a series of blotches that slowly spread over the convex surface. They seemed to occur wherever his eyes rested too long in one place: a common enough optical illusion. But now, was it a human, and perhaps a female, form that he saw advancing through the storm, a concentration of white static particles hazily limned with slightly darker patches? Yes, it was surely there. The figure kept advancing, gracefully, with the attitude of Botticelli's *Primavera*. As she approached farther it was as though she were battling against a storm threatening to blow her off her feet. Details were absent, just as though Dylan were watching a black-and-white TV show with the fuzziest of reception—which, of course, he probably was. He could sense the woman's exertion and almost feel those gale-force winds on his own face (though that made no sense, as they would logically have been behind him!).

Still no figure stepped forth from the ground in the auditory sphere.

The screen was now almost completely white. Dylan felt a familiar and profound sense of loss as the idea suggested itself that the woman, whose figure had indeed begun definitely to suggest Cecilia's, had been fatally buried in a snow drift.

But then, as his eyes again adjusted to the brightness, Dylan found he could discern more tonal variation in the swarming light particles. A pattern of blotches began to appear and darken, just as they had before. This time, however, they did not coalesce into a human figure; no, the image was only schematic: one . . . two blotches in opposing upper quadrants of the rectangle . . .

one right in the middle . . . and now a big one at the bottom that expanded into a highly irregular shape—yes, a mouth. It seemed that they were being drawn by erasure, as if by the unskilled finger of a child, as he watched. A poignant memory of drawing and writing in foggy school bus windows occurred to him as a point of comparison. The mouth now grew bigger and bigger, those invisible fingers getting the outline wrong and so widening it repeatedly, until finally it actually erased the "face" along with the static covering the rest of the screen.

After this the screen stayed dark until, a little stupefied, Dylan realised that the TV had actually been switched off. Then the medium, facilitator, or whatever he called himself, planted that big, ugly face in his. He jolted and clasped a hand to his pants pocket, as though to his heart.

"Hello Dylan? Wakey-wakey . . . There you are!" He smiled. "I gather you must have heard, or possibly seen, something?"

"Why? Did you?" Dylan asked in a daze, rubbing his eyes.

"No, but I wasn't looking," Harvey answered. "I must say, though, that was one of the strongest EVPs I've ever heard, and I've been doing this for, oh . . . a long time now!"

It suddenly occurred to Dylan that this was in all probability part of the act. As much as one could see faces in the proverbial clouds while they were there in the sky above, it was probably easier still to convince someone of something they had already "seen" upon retiring the matrix of illusion.

"Do you mind if I ask . . . ?"

The question and the importunate tone of its asking seemed to Dylan like something approximating a breach of professional ethics. He had managed to wake up sufficiently to put the man's honesty to the test.

"Yes . . . I heard her say"—here, the white noise echoing in his brain, he just had time to think—"'I'll see you in the next world.' It was really clear. Definitely Celia's voice." Henry, Harry . . . whatever his name was, smiled, apparently relieved that his client had proven himself so suggestible. The man said nothing else, just continued smiling like a tom cat as he paced the room, arching his back, rotating his neck and shaking his wrists and smoothing his clothes in what seemed an exaggerated and unduly prolonged routine. Was it some kind of ritual? Dylan sat up in the recliner.

"I suppose I should have asked her something," he continued, giving in and speaking to fill the space between them, "but . . ." he trailed off in the midst of his subterfuge, mind suddenly vacant of words and concepts.

Things seemed to have slowed down; Dylan's perception of time subtly deranged by a suggestion of eternities opening up behind each momentary perception, between each particle of sound still crackling in his eardrums. Where moments ago he had felt relatively alert and canny, he now felt dizzy.

"No, no, don't worry about that. Language is less important to communication than we imagine, especially communication of this very special kind."

"Oh I know, but still . . . if I'd asked her a question only she could answer . . . that would prove . . . what, that it wasn't some other ghost getting in on the act, I suppose." The air-conditioning was blasting a simoom through the room, awakening nondescript, unpleasant odours, and Dylan knew that he had reached the limit of his gift for subterfuge.

Something terribly restless had taken hold of the spiritualist (damn it, what was his name again!). He was now pacing in earnest, and rubbing his hands together. Dylan got out of the chair and stood watching him, hands clenched in his pockets.

The man sighed deeply. "You know, Dylan, I pity the dead. They're so eager to speak to us. And as much as we sometimes want desperately to hear from them, we can be so fearful and selfish that we're unwilling to hear what they really have to say, what they need to say even if, ultimately, there's nothing that can be done . . . So many people just want reassurance, something to assuage their guilt so they can, you know, 'move on.'" He grimaced and made contemptuous little quote marks with his fingers. "Just where do they think they're moving on to, eh?"

There was a sharp twist at the corner of the man's lower lip that, at least insofar as a burn mark on a tortilla might be said to resemble the Virgin Mary, startled Dylan with its resemblance to Celia's expression when she would fight against laughter.

"I feel that way about Celia sometimes," Dylan confessed,

candidness breaking through defences whose purpose he was starting to forget. "I feel she's waiting for me to save her, as though, I don't know . . . she's shipwrecked somewhere. If there's anything in the world I can do for her, I'll do it! But I just . . . don't know! I don't know what to do." He felt tears brewing.

Harvey nodded. "You're very sensitive, Dylan, I can tell. I like to think I am too, but you know, I use the word without any connotation of some actual, qualitative gift. If people like you and I are different from the majority it's probably just the strength of our emotional ties to those no longer in this world. Look here, stay a while till you come back to yourself. It does take a bit of time, and I can see you're not ready to drive yet. Take a seat while I put on the kettle!" He said this and went about it with such alacrity that it was impossible to refuse.

Dylan remained standing and looked around. Dust lay on everything, thick in the crevasses between the carpet and the skirting; books were piled up on the floor between the chairs and under the table, and on top of the two bookcases on opposite walls. On the other two walls a stopped clock twitched, facing a Canaletto print he now recognised as the one of those that had been on Celia's parents' walls. They had not known who the artist was but were impressed that their daughter's boyfriend did. The recollection of twenty years past was vivid as though the event had occurred earlier that day. He continued to stare. The feeling of unnatural stillness behind the movement of the figures in the gondolas and the flouncily rendered ripples drew Dylan momentarily into the ambient world of the picture. It must have been about eight o'clock now, and it had been a long day . . . a long week . . . the best part of a decade without her . . .

When after a few minutes his host returned, Dylan found himself speechless, now that it was apparently his turn.

"Admiring the artwork?"

"This painting . . ." he began. "I . . . sorry, still recovering my wits!" He scratched his head, and the man chuckled. Blushing, Dylan came and sat down on the musty sofa where the man was waiting. He hated it when people's names slipped his mind. (The memory that retained the dearest relics of his life in such perfect condition was not always completely reliable in day-to-day things.)

"Oh, you didn't have to go to such—"

"I think tea is something that should be done properly. This was my mother's tea set, and I hardly get the chance to use it anymore." He turned the floral teapot clockwise twice and counter-clockwise once in preparation to pour it into the matching little cups. The set looked like it might indeed have been an old lady's best china. All the accoutrements were there, including a little plate on which rested a couple of fruit digestives.

"Well, thank you. So, have you been doing this sort of . . . work . . . for long?" he managed.

"Long enough that it's changed me, and not for the better, I have to say."

After pouring and placing the cup and saucer in his guest's hands, Harvey continued speaking in a surprisingly heavy tone. "I've heard enough EVPs to know what they all boil down to. The dead—I don't like to say this, and I wish it weren't so, but . . ." He was evidently choosing his words carefully. "I know you didn't come here for reassurance in lieu of truth, Dylan, so I'm going to give you the truth as I've come to know it through years of experience. And personally, even though I know what's waiting for me now, I'm glad I know, I'm glad!" He said this with such decisiveness, that his tea sloshed over the side of his cup as he set it down on the low table. "If it were just me, and someone, some clairvoyant, were to tell me that, for example, I'm destined to die of cancer, I wouldn't want to know. I've often thought that the only reason we get up on any given morning is because we don't know what the day's going to bring; if we did, well, life would be a very different proposition. You can extrapolate as much as you like from that!" He smiled wryly.

Dylan was barely following him. The tinnitus was getting worse.

"But it's not just me; I'm not—none of us are—alone ultimately, though it feels that way often enough, so despite everything it makes me feel closer, more connected to all of them—to all of us—as if I could say a prayer, and they might hear it, or give them a drop of water to slake their thirst down there . . . I think of it as 'down' . . . I think of how a trapped miner must feel when he hears the sound of the rescue team getting closer, even if he never makes it out alive . . . Maybe someone will talk to me when I'm gone. I'm not sure who, though! Maybe it'll be you, Dylan!" He grinned unpleasantly.

"What are you . . . ? So you're saying the dead are in Hell?"

He would have felt offended on Cecilia's behalf if the idea had not struck him as absurd. He wanted to leave immediately, but remembered that a service of sorts had been performed, and that it must presumably be paid for, which was a difficult topic to raise just at the moment, with the eccentric maundering in full swing.

The man sighed. "Yes, let's see: Buddha, Mother Theresa, Gandhi, John Lennon, Jesus, Martin Luther King . . . have I left anyone out of the saints' parade?" he counted them off on his fingers, grinning subversively over the conventional litany. The names sounded inexplicably strange to Dylan. "Actually, there may be exceptions. That would certainly be the traditional view, and I hope it's the correct one; but as I say, I speak only of what I know empirically. Hell, maybe the Calvinists are right, eh? And there are other possibilities. Our loved ones' torment might not be literally endless; perhaps oblivion awaits them in the end, or some of them may eventually return to be born again and again until they've learned their lesson, whatever it might be; that's another traditional doctrine, as I'm sure you've heard. Maybe time is cyclical. But for now, what I hear and see tells me that they're all essentially trapped in the dark, in solitary confinement. And for them, where they are, a moment feels like a century. Or more accurately, like an eternity, since time is only measured by its effects on sensory phenomena: the clock ticking, the leaf yellowing . . . and where they are, there simply aren't any such things.

"And we can't hear anything they say, not really, despite what I might have led you to believe. Maybe you thought you heard your wife speaking to you before, and maybe not." The speaker was grinning again, knowingly. "Maybe she did speak. I'm not denying it, you understand. But those words you attributed to her were yours, that's for sure. And yet . . . no, you could say I do hear a little of what they really say, in their language, so to speak, and . . . I can tell you, it's enough. More than enough. It's more like hearing someone cry, or laugh, I suppose, in a way, or an animal—" Dylan's face must have darkened; he had certainly heard enough now. "Well, that's what I hear, anyway, and in the nature of things I suppose I can never be sure that it's not my own imputation."

"Well, these are certainly . . . weighty considerations," Dylan said, hoping that it would be enough. Then he took another sip of tea, thanked his host, pled tiredness, and asked what he owed. It had not come up previously either on the phone or this evening, and perhaps not surprisingly given the man's conduct and attitude, he insisted that no payment was due. Dylan did not wrangle but thanked him, and shook his hand before leaving with only a partial sense of relief.

On the way home he found himself in such a reverie that he lost his way in what seemed a maze of residential streets, even though home was only a couple of suburbs away, and he knew the area well. Retracing his way proved impossible, and it was with some embarrassment that he finally pulled over and resorted to the GPS.

That night, predictably enough, he had a peculiar dream. He was at the beach where the sacred stone had given itself up, that one fragmentary piece of the puzzle that had seemed so promising. It was a secluded place, a calm bay with white sand and heaps of granite boulders covered in lichen of variegated colours down on the shoreline.

The region behind the dunes rose high and was overgrown not only with samphire and other low-growing plants, but lushly with trees and ferns of various species that made a sheltered track, a kind of lovers' walk, extending for what seemed miles. It was the sort of place where children would both love and fear to wander, in which even an adult might feel unnerved despite the unlikelihood of crime, walking alone by twilight and knowing that at any moment, around the next corner, one might meet a stranger who could be anyone at all, perhaps the Devil himself.

In his dream Dylan was taking this lovers' walk by himself, just as he had more than once on that first holiday subsequent to Cecilia's death, feeling, he now knew (and as he had less overtly felt in real life), that he was almost sure to encounter his beloved around the next bend in the path. The thick shrubbery to the side farthest from the beach rustled, and he stopped, halfway between joy and panic. By this point an embankment had risen to his left, and kept rising rapidly until it stood taller than him. Among the tufty grasses and ground-covers there opened up a tunnel. It was the lair of an animal, clearly, its circumference moulded smooth by the body of its inhabitant. The entrance appeared to open like a dark flower, larger and larger, tangled roots hanging down like a tattered curtain over it.

The combination of dread and curiosity he felt switched to something more urgent as he heard a noise that might have been a human cry. He listened intently through the wind in the leaves, and the crickets starting to sing, focusing on what was now definitely a sobbing noise coming from deep in the burrow. It was a child who had crawled in and got lost, he was sure; in fact, it could only be Celia herself as a little girl, before he had even known her, in so pristine a state of innocence that it wracked him with a compassion that exceeded even his need to be redeemed from her absence.

Dylan began to crawl inside the burrow. The outer noises ceased as his own breath and heartbeat formed the accompaniment to the sobbing noise he was moving towards. But then as he came closer, it started to intensify in a disturbing way, until the sobs, amplified perhaps by the acoustics of the tunnel, were those of one so distraught that they have difficulty drawing breath.

There was a torch in his hand, which he now lit. The beam was very bright and hot, quite like a miniature sun. He understood somehow, in the vague and contradictory manner of dreams, that it was a torch of fire, and that it would also serve as a weapon in case he had to fight some monster for the sake of Celia's safety and freedom.

"It's alright, Celia! I'm coming! I'm coming!"

Then he saw that is was not her he was coming for; it was

something very different. Despite the intense disappointment and repugnance the revelation inspired, he felt an equally intense pity for the creature. Its face was not human, though it tried to be. Its features were dark spots, holes, or indentations in the weirdly inchoate substance of its body, which seemed only a kind of thickening of the air.

It possessed only a simplified face, rendered crudely as though by the fingers of a child in a lump of dough, and Dylan remembered having seen something similar in the recent past (just where, he could not have said). He understood that it was choking on itself, on the doomed inadequacy of this attempt at physical manifestation. How it might hurt him was as unclear, but it looked sinister enough, like a kind of pseudo-human larva, with more than a little of the spider and centipede about it. Its flesh, so to speak, was mottled, of indeterminate hue like a painter's palette thoroughly smeared over in the process of being cleaned, so that all tended towards greyness. What appendages the thing had was hard to say. They seemed to emerge from and retire into its body as though newly created and destroyed in each painful, chaotic movement.

It crept towards the light of the torch, the nothingness of its eyes and mouth growing darker, larger, and rounder, swirling with centripetal motion as its grey pseudo-flesh fell under the light.

Then suddenly it lunged at him, shrieking, and burnt itself as Dylan warded it off with the torch. Now it hung back, whimpering and cowering horribly against the wall of the cavern. Ominously, though, it failed to retreat down the tunnel from whence it had come, its eyes and mouth still betraying a look of terrible hunger. He knew that the moment he turned his back, it would lunge again. The only other choices were either to put out the torch and surrender himself, or go on the attack. Dylan could do neither. He was trapped. And while he was considering this, the torchlight started to dim.

The resolution came in the transition from sleeping to waking. Now with a kind of sorrowful, lukewarm relief he realised that the situation was unreal, just a show, a horror movie he was watching on an old analogue TV whose reception was failing and resolving into grey static as he slouched towards wakefulness.

It was a crash that woke him decisively, though one muffled by the white noise in his ears that seemed to contain all the monstrous noises of his dream, and many more. His awareness was cast into the void of that noise: part animate, part the howling of wind, and part electronic fuzz, and of the strangely peaceful swarm of particles before his eyes that would not quite coalesce into substantial form. It was like a storm of confetti, or of tiny falling leaves, except that he could not make out the trace of any colour by the moonlight that snuck in from behind the blinds and the open door, vaguely delineating the contents of his bedroom. Also, the light was flickering.

Everything was moving as though thrashing about in that storm, but Dylan could feel nothing but a kind of electric chill that radiated out from inside him. He lay there for some time, concentrating on the noise in his ears and watching as the light fitting swung on its cord and the blinds clattered and broke themselves without disturbing his reverie. At length he made out something within the maelstrom that was somewhat like a human voice, though it spoke no words he had ever heard before. Perhaps the best translation of what it said would be the single word "Please!" screamed with such urgency, such an attitude of ravenous hunger that it should by rights have alarmed him. It echoed and was renewed repeatedly.

Now, looking over at the nightstand, Dylan saw that the petrified fragment of his wife's face was gone. This gave him his cue to leap out of bed and commence stumbling through the house towards the source of the loudest crashing. It was coming from the kitchen. Everything along the way had been upended, furniture knocked over and torn apart, eviscerated; books strewn across the living room floor, their pages fluttering or flying like confused birds just as the curtains, only one of which was still on its rod, swirled frantically in a wind that might have been something within rather than without them. The windows were broken, and a piece of glass whizzed past Dylan's face as he fought his way through the storm, not feeling any cold or fear.

Celia was here! He called her name. Why had she not come straight to him? He understood: she had wanted first to clothe herself in any material form possible, but especially she had sought throughout the house for those things that had belonged most to her. Her clothes were there, flapping about amidst the couch stuffing and the broken furniture from which her new limbs had been improvised. He understood—telepathically perhaps, since it was hard, and growing harder, to make anything out by sight—that his wife was trying to put on her favourite dress, the fitted one of that violet, satiny fabric that she had worn on special occasions, and was tearing it in the effort; likewise, she had broken her violin in the act of trying to play it—poor darling!—it was there just below the chin of her death mask, the neck broken but still attached by the strings. Its case formed the centre of her body amidst all the swirling debris, each piece of which sought its own proper niche, seldom finding it. Despite all the chaos and utterly passionate urgency in the air, everything in the room seemed to be swimming through a grey atmosphere of asphodel meadows.

As Dylan Pierce stood facing his wife, too overcome to do or say anything, he noticed that it was rapidly growing darker.

Did she see him? Was she shy? Embarrassed about her appearance, as if that mattered! Or was it that she had found no eyes as yet, or none among those glimmering lightbulbs that would serve? He called to her (unable now to hear himself over her voice that was a host of natural, unnatural, human, animal, and fallen angelic noises, crying as one from inside and outside his ears). The air was thickening, and the strobing light broke time into a succession of moments, light, dark, light, dark, with the latter gaining on the former. It was like an old film reel running slowly down. But they found each other, he weeping and crying as much as he could yet remember of his wife's earthly name in tones of hysterical relief and welcome. She embraced him as he did her, and ten digits composed of shards of glass and the contents of the knife block entered his flesh as she pulled him into her.

LIONS

After almost a month, Callum still cowered whenever the Mercedes pulled up outside his family's imposing new home in Glen Orchid, one of the city's leafy green, old-money suburbs. In his imagination they were not essentially different to real lions, although being made of stone might make them all the more implacable. Their blind white eyeballs were the worst, because you could never tell if they were looking down at you, ready to spring as you passed between them; and every time the boy passed between them he closed his eyes, with a sensation of being swept inexorably in their direction like a dead leaf on an autumn wind—or more accurately, in terms of his imagination, like a miniature little boy in an enormous bath, towards a plug hole.

All of his five, going on six years he had been living in a city apartment that was big in its own right, but nothing compared to this place; then one day after school Jade, his *au pair*, took him here and made him understand that his old home was his no more. He could not understand why she seemed excited about it, or why his parents had done this to them. Callum was not a baby anymore; he could follow cause and effect, and he had seen the boxes and the walls and floors getting barer as they piled up, and he had overheard his parents' conversations. But still he had started crying and struggling against his seatbelt as soon as he understood. When the lions came into view for the first time he had actually stopped, too afraid to move or make a sound.

Separating the yard from the street was a very high cypress hedge, with a remote-operated gate in the old-fashioned wrought iron style. The tessellated surface of the driveway was long and still full of dead weeds that the gardener, who came a couple of days a week, had recently poisoned. The yard was lush with diverse foliage and flowers. Callum imagined that he was living in the midst of a mysterious forest in which hungry predators stalked.

This afternoon Jade had to carry him, patting him on the back and shushing him like a baby from the carport onto the sandstone terrace from which the edifice loomed; otherwise he would have been pulling at her dress and crying. It was lucky the boy was so small for his age. He thought that the lions must have been, in some possibly paraphysical sense, on their trail, and that they would be lucky to make it inside. It was odd, he almost knew: even as he looked back down the driveway he did not expect to actually see the lions. They would never bound into view just like that.

Now it was, "Don't worry, sweetie pie, we'll be safe inside," and then, "Whoops-a-daisy!" Jade dropped her key, smiling again as she put him down to pick it up. "You're getting such a big boy!" she panted, while Callum clutched at her leg to keep from being sucked down the drive, and she patted his wispy head, ever-patient.

It was a great relief to be inside—except for those massive bay windows and all the little arched ones that ran all along the front wall of the ground floor. Through their stained panels the garden outside seemed a kaleidoscopic nightmare, hot and dark like the embers that might have been seen in the house's various fireplaces, if ever they were used. Later, when it grew nearly dark, Callum would see his own reflection superimposed upon the shadowy lions' habitat. Glass would be no match for stone, he knew, when the time came. Also, if he looked too long into those funhouse mirrors, it quickly became difficult to tell what was outside and what was in.

But Jade soon cheered him up. They played, watched TV, and had dinner, and by eight o'clock Callum was lying in bed, somewhere between sleep and waking. He was alone because his mother had told Jade she was not allowed to sleep with him anymore; he had to grow out of needing her there all the time. She had stayed to sing him to sleep, but now he had woken up. The pussycat face of his night light looked evil, and it cast just enough light for him to wonder what was hiding in the shadows. He could hear the crickets in the garden, and it sounded like the breathing of some great, inhuman beast. Callum missed the traffic noises of the city.

Then suddenly he heard a roar—yes, a roar! He could not

breathe, let alone run and hide.

Then came footsteps inside the house, and the distant tapping of what might (but only might) have been shoes on the shiny wood, soon muffled by carpet as ineluctably they came up the stairs. The house was still a vast, mysterious entity to Callum, and when the lights went out it became a hellish maze in which you could potentially get lost forever in a world of night. If this reinstituted trial bedtime separation from Jade had proven a partial success, it was due solely to the boy's fear of the house, now become a lion's den, which had kept him from screaming out or running to her room, even if it was just next door.

Of course, it was probably just one his parents, but how could he know for sure? All he knew at this moment was that someone or something was coming up the stairs towards him. It sounded like a person, but then, it was easy to imagine a lion walking upright on two legs; in fact, that idea was the most frightening of all. Those steps had hit the downstairs floorboards heavily like stone.

Now, as whatever-it-was neared his bedroom door, Callum could hold back no longer. He screamed and screamed until a light came on outside his open door and something or someone was upon him while he struggled, screaming still.

* * *

Lyndon Holman woke, still exhausted. Once Callum had got over his alarm at whatever-it-was-this-time, there been no more noise; even so, he found he could not get back to sleep immediately, despite the pills. Where was Jade? He would have gone and tucked the boy in himself, but felt literally too tired to move, paralysed by the succubus of work, which he had only recently and belatedly come to perceive in her true, hideous form.

But still he drifted on the hither side of unconsciousness. What was wrong with the boy, still incontinent, still speaking like an infant just learning to string his words together, and so spindly and sick-looking? The doctors had said . . . what exactly? Lyndon had to admit he had not been paying attention, at least not after the first couple of visits, but in essence he understood that they were stumped.

No, Jade was alright—better, she was devoted, had studied so that she could be Callum's integration aide as well as his *au pair* by the time he started school. To be honest, she was also more or less their housemaid, notwithstanding the woman who came twice a week. (Lyndon would have done something about that, but Kathy insisted he leave it be.) A pretty girl, too, with her fine, fair complexion and those articulate, pixie-like features and the green eyes that suited her name; possibly a good figure, too; but then she was always so conservatively dressed, like a real-life Mary Poppins, that it was hard to be sure. It was a new style of alternative fashion, he gathered, and not without its appeal. You never heard about any boyfriends, or friends for that matter. Lyndon had begun to notice such things more intently of late, since he and Kathy had stopped having sex. And did Jade not look at him in a certain way, occasionally, and increasingly take more than a polite interest in his work? That night last week when they had sat in front of the TV together, sharing the sofa that he could only wish had been smaller, Callum asleep in her lap . . . He would never do anything about it, but still it was nice, a vestige of the simple joy that had otherwise completely evaporated from his life.

Actually, was he dreaming, or had she come and knocked on his bedroom door earlier, sometime after he had come home in the early evening and headed straight for bed for a nap? Probably just telling him dinner was ready. Lyndon's thoughts trailed off as the pills resumed their efficacy. Soon he dreamt of a satisfactory resolution to his marital difficulties: an improbable one involving both of the women of his household. It made a pleasant change from dreaming about work.

If Kathy had come home last night, she had not come to bed. Nothing unusual in that; she often went to sleep in the living room, in front of the TV or the laptop screen, after coming home late from work. It was an old habit. Now that they had the space, she had made up the guest bed, arguing that they both needed their sleep, and that his snoring drove her to it. He loved her, she knew it, and he knew that she knew. It had always been that way, and in consequence there had always been a sort of Eleatic distance between them that now was only expanding.

Looking out the back window through a screen of golden birch leaves, he sipped his coffee. The doctor said that he should give it up if he wanted to sleep naturally, but there was no way that was going to happen. He felt surprisingly cheerful. At least they owned this place outright, having subdivided and traded in a couple of investment properties, as well as cashing in some intangible assets, in order to buy the grand home that they both, but particularly Kathy, had always dreamed of. He admired the gleam of the stainless-steel finish and the marble-topped benches—sorry, "task stations"—as he leant on one. The outdated kitchen had been the one drawback, according to her, when they were considering the place, so they had had a new one installed. Of course, his wife seldom cooked anything.

Now he heard someone coming downstairs. Jade, no doubt; Kathy would be downstairs. But when she appeared in the doorway, it turned out to be Kathy after all. She was wearing her dressing gown, but it did not look as though she had showered. She had panda eyes, messy hair, and a foul expression on her face. Callum was with her, held by the hand.

"Oh, good morning, both of you. I thought . . ." said Lyndon cheerfully, feeling absurdly like one caught doing something he should not.

She stared at him without smiling, for a long moment. "Morning." The boy said nothing, as usual, mouth hanging open as though daddy had horns growing out of his head. Kathy sat Callum down at the table, went straight for the cupboard, and took down the cereal, before turning to the fridge. She was stomping around, hostility emanating from her like an almost-visible aura. Lyndon had subtly to get out of her way, trying not to cringe.

"Hey honey, I was thinking, why don't we go out for breakfast this morning? It's a beautiful day."

She scoffed. "Not today, Lyndon," she said, and refused him even a glance as she shook the cornflakes into Callum's bowl.

Often at times like these Lyndon remembered the song lyric, "If you want to be happy for the rest of your life, don't make a pretty woman your wife." Kathy's proud, graceful carriage, that cold awareness of her own beauty, was in everything she did, he reflected, watching her as she pulled out her chair and sat down, flicking her hair, back to him. He found himself becoming angry. She should be more supportive during the difficult time he was going through professionally; though of course he did understand how the uncertainty of it affected her as well. But if their marriage had been in any decent shape, the audit should have brought them closer together, rather than driven them apart.

"Too much work to do, on a Saturday, to spend time with your family? Fine. I suppose I should have booked in with you in advance; it just seems like we don't spend any time together lately. I mean, fair go, I'm not asking where you were last night—"

"I told you, Lyndon! My sister was in town." She did not bother to turn around.

He cursed himself. Recriminations would be counterproductive, but he could not resist. It was the way she put him on the defensive.

"Of course. Sorry, I forgot, what with all that's . . . Look, Kathy," he sighed, "sometimes it feels like everything's just . . . *work*." Damn, he had apologized. No recovering from that.

But she managed to misunderstand him, turning her chair to a miserly degree in his direction. "Honestly Lyndon, with this audit hanging over our heads I don't know how you can think of anything else. I certainly can't until I know where we stand, financially—*legally*." She was looking squarely at him now. "And soon I might be the only person here with a salary coming in, so excuse me if I'm prioritising my career at the moment. We can talk about this later. Callum doesn't need to hear about our problems."

The boy just sat there quietly, mouth hanging open, blinking. It disturbed Lyndon that he had so little fatherly feeling towards Callum, deep down.

Kathy was alluding to the fact that Lyndon, as CFO at Morgenstern Piper Escrow, was under pressure from an independent audit investigating various allegations of fraud in his department. The situation had the potential to embroil both him and the company both in very costly legal trouble, which in turn would naturally affect investor confidence. That his position was at stake was only the start; his career might actually be over, and then there were the fines and even the technical possibility of jail time. Just now the latter did not seem too bad.

"Very classy, Kathy. Take a stab at me, then hide behind our boy." She gave him daggers, but he went on, "I'll never understand how you can talk to me like that when I've supported you to get to where you are today. You owe me—" Lyndon now found himself saying. He was going to say "consideration" or "appreciation," but was not allowed to finish.

She stood up roughly now and leant over the bench towards him, enraged. "Supported me—really! How much do I owe you? Go on, tell me, and I'll pay you out!" It was true that they had always maintained separate bank accounts, besides the shared one into which they both paid equally for household expenses. But Kathy's earnings even now as HR manager were well below his, and it was true that she had not yet obtained her Master's degree when she first started at the company and they had met, over a decade ago, though she had insisted on paying him back for the tuition fees which he had been happy to cover up-front. Her husband's position at the firm probably had not hurt her career, either.

"Kathy, please. That's not what I meant. I really have no idea why we're arguing like this. I only wanted to take you and Callum out to breakfast, for God's sake!" He hesitated to say, "and Jade too," though her presence would at least have ensured some level of decorum.

Rather than sign the proffered truce, Kathy decided to open up a new front. "Fine then. Callum, drop your spoon, and get up." He in fact held nothing in his hand, only staring ahead in distress. "Daddy wants to take you out for a babycino."

"Kathy!"

"When I came home last night he was crying out in panic and you were fast asleep with your earplugs in. I had to—I stayed in there with him all night, and neither of us slept a wink. I told you I was going to be home late; you knew it was up to you to look after him!"

She knew nothing of the sleeping pills; Lyndon regarded

them as shameful, a womanish vice. "But Jade . . ."

"She had the night off, remember? You were supposed to be on duty, and Callum wasn't supposed to know! God, if I hadn't come home when I did our son would probably still be lying up there with his bedding soaked through!"

At this Callum, unnoticed, commenced quietly weeping.

When did Jade start taking nights off? Lyndon tried to recalibrate his emotions. "So you're pissed off with me because you had to spend some time comforting your child while his permanent babysitter was away for the first time this year?"

Just then, coincidentally, they heard her enter via the front door: a Godsend! The clock on the microwave made it only 8:46.

It was often like this between them, though seldom as bad. Forced to take his stand, Lyndon found himself reproaching Kathy by rote, as if she were subliminally feeding him his lines. He had to leave.

Having greeted Jade with a tense, though grateful smile on the way out, Lyndon was now strolling down the driveway. He attempted to reassure himself by admiring his fair domain. The garden was lovely in the morning sunlight, and the air was warm. It was annoying about the dead weeds everywhere, though; when was the gardener coming back for them? He was around often enough but seemed to get little done. Lyndon could hear birds together with the trickling of the fountain and traffic noises that were far enough away to cause no mental disturbance. The street was a quiet one despite its proximity to the suburb's main shopping strip (chiefly restaurants and antique shops, like the one at which he had bought that mahogany dining table that had been "the wrong shape for the room," according to his wife).

What alerted him to the missing lion statue was the piece of it that remained on the footpath, the spattering of marble chips and dust. He looked up; the Sun was in his eyes, so he crossed to the other footpath to get a proper look at the lofty pedestals above the gate. The lion on the left was entirely gone.

His dignity already shaken by the exchange with Kathy, the vandalism struck Lyndon as a grave personal affront. Rage grew within his bosom as the anonymous insult sunk home. To think that it could happen here, in the millionaire's row section of Glen Orchid! He would call the police immediately. He would call the council and demand that they install some speed bumps in place of those pathetic rumble strips, too. His day was ruined. It was an omen: he was going to lose his career and his marriage. It would happen in slow motion, step-by-step, but the end result would be as senseless as this overnight act of vandalism. "Bastard!" he yelled, kicking the gatepost as hard as he could. Lyndon surprised himself. Then he bellowed again as the pain of a fractured toe rewarded his effort.

Kathy had felt for a long while like a somewhat green twig flexing under pressure, not quite ready to snap. But she would not wait until she was all dried up; the time for decision had now arrived. She understood Lyndon's thinking about the move: mistaking the symbol for reality, he had thought that investing in a substantial home would solidify their shaky marriage bond. And that poky little apartment had certainly contributed to the friction between them. So what the hell, she had thought, nothing to lose, and possibly something to gain.

Her solicitor thought there was a chance that she could get the house, or at least the best part of the sale proceeds. Done right, the thing could be kept out of court, anyway. From talking to friends who had been through similar situations, she gathered that some men would sign away anything to avoid painful legal proceedings and, who knows, to impress their ex-wife with their magnanimity. Kathy thought she knew Lyndon's character. It was a strange thing, she reflected, that a man at the top of the business hierarchy could be so weak.

But she and her solicitor were concerned about the audit of Lyndon's department, should it result in legal costs and fines, or should his assets be frozen. As a result, it would be best to act sooner rather than later. She was thirty-six now, and it really seemed as though she were facing her last ultimatum: settle for what she had here, or take a last shot at happiness. Morgenstern Piper was a sinking ship, too, for that matter, but there were opportunities opening up to her all around the world.

She had met Keir Sweeney at a conference in London last

year. He was speaking on strategies for optimising workflow, but had managed to make it really funny and entertaining in such an irreverent way, while at the same time showing that he could talk Six Sigma and all the rest in his sleep. Technically it would be a big step down from Lyndon, but money was far from the only thing in life; she had never been as materialistic as he accused her of (just because buying her things was all he knew how to do!). Anyway, Keir was a highly successful productivity consultant who ran his own business. He fascinated her: on one hand it was as if work, and life in general, were nothing serious at all; but then you also go the impression that really he was very efficient and had a gift for focusing on the essential—unlike Lyndon, who wore his responsibilities like a lead-lined cape. Keir had got her attention, along with everyone else's, when his presentation began with a challenge for anyone who was just there because their boss told them to be, to leave. "Don't worry, I won't tell on you," he had said, and turned his mischievous smile directly on Kathy.

Callum was acting yet more strangely than usual since the vandalism of the statue, having deduced a confirmation of his lion fantasy from its disappearance. Now and again he even claimed sightings outside the window, behind trees and shrubberies, and so on. Then he would cry hopelessly, certain that someone, himself or another member of the household, was sure to be eaten sooner or later.

"Where's the lion now, do you think? Where's he hiding?" Jade asked one afternoon after school. They were in the midst of making a cake, one of the boy's favourite activities.

"I don't know," he said, pausing from licking the spoon in his hand. Then he pointed to the window above the kitchen sink that looked out on the back garden. "There."

"So he moved from the front and now he lives in the back?"

The little boy nodded his little-old-man head. He was thin yet jowly, and his white hair always looked as if it were thinning. But Jade had faith he would grow up some day into a strapping man, just like his father. She really could not see his mother in him; but then, that was probably just her bias: she admitted to herself that she did not like Kathy. And it was not just jealousy; the woman could be quite cold and unpleasant, besides being, frankly, a bad mother. Since a childhood car accident had robbed Jade of the prospect of having children of her own, she had come to feel that working with other people's children was her calling, and the arrangement she had with the Holmans was ideal. It seemed unlikely that they would ever be separated while Callum remained a child.

"Callum, you know, lions don't really like to eat people."

"Yes they do!" He said with great conviction.

"How do you know?"

He thought about it. A child of few words, his only answer was a pained look that combined equal parts of fear and confusion.

"Did I ever tell you, when I was a little girl I fell into the lions' cage at the zoo, and a big scary lion came up to me and sniffed me all over? I had a lolly in my pocket, and I gave it to him so he wouldn't eat me, and he didn't."

"Did he eat the lolly?" he asked breathlessly. Good, she had him. She was the only person in the world with whom Callum could have a conversation like this; with anyone else he was more than halfway towards mutism.

"Yes, and then he licked me on the cheek to say thank you."

"No he didn't. Lions don't eat lollies. They eat people." Jade liked that stubborn streak; it meant he had inner strength somewhere, deep down.

"Let's see then. Maybe we can make friends with this lion like I did with the one at the zoo. We'll leave him something, like maybe a piece of this cake when it's ready, and if he takes it we'll know we don't have to be afraid."

He protested, but then just before sunset Callum finally allowed Jade to lead him outside, where they placed a slice of the cake on a stone bordering an overgrown garden bed right up the back of the yard. He held her hand tightly; there were the dark cypresses and other trees, and the nasty-looking old garden shed, too.

The following morning the plate was empty and a note was left underneath written all shaky in capitals ("It's hard for lions to write because they don't have hands," Jade explained):

> DEAR CALLUM,
> THANK YOU FOR THE CAKE. YOU ARE A GOOD BOY.
> I PROMISE I WON'T HURT YOU.
> LOVE, THE LION XXXOOO

Shortly afterwards, Kathy and Lyndon had the argument that would end their marriage.

Lyndon had had to face the audit panel that day and found their questions difficult to answer. He was then summarily informed of their decision to suspend him, albeit, for the time being, on full pay. When Kathy came home he was sitting in the downstairs living room closest to the front entrance, where she could not avoid encountering him. He was halfway through his second bottle of wine since coming home mid-afternoon. He had begun disburdening as soon as she walked into the room, just as if he were certain of a sympathetic ear despite the fact that she had not even bothered even to text him "good luck" or "how did it go?" all day. His turpitude was embarrassing and damaging to her own reputation in the company, she knew; people would stop talking when she walked into a room. And now he was acting like a maudlin idiot.

"I just don't know what I'm going to do from here, Kathy."

"Well, you knew it was coming. At least they're still paying you."

"I'm sorry! Did you say 'they're' or 'we're'?"

"What?"

"Whatever you said, I know what you meant. You can't just turf me out, you know—much as I know you'd like to!"

"What are you talking about, Lyndon?" Had he got wind of her plans to divorce him?

"You may be the head of HR, but you're not on the Board!"

Kathy rolled her eyes, regaining her mental balance. "Have another drink, Lyndon. That'll make it better."

This was doubly maddening as he seldom drank at all. When was the last time he had had more than a couple in one sitting? Lyndon already had the bottle raised to top up his glass; but rather than follow her instruction, he stood up and said firmly, "No. Fuck this. Fuck you. I'm leaving." He had meant merely for fresh air, but now his heart thrilled to the possibility of misconstrual. Perhaps he could regain his wife's respect just by staying in a hotel for a night or two?

Kathy was about to reply, but intuition told her no. A drunk-driving conviction might be a useful reference point in the near future.

Lyndon blundered about for a while, up and downstairs in that stiff, uncoordinated way he had developed since hurting his toe, grunting irritably as he searched for his keys. Kathy listened from the spare room that had become her bedroom, and could not help smiling to herself. Where did the fool think he was going?

He did not return. Presumably he had come back during the following day to pack the suitcase that was missing from his cupboard. Jade had not seen him. Well, this was a surprise, especially since the fight had only been minor, really. To be sure, it was more as if he had packed for a short trip than for a permanent move.

Callum interpreted his father's disappearance along predictable lines. "You said! You said!" was all he could say to Jade. And when three days later his mother did not come home from work either, he was inconsolable. It was less the fact of her absence, or his father's, that set the boy so much on edge, as the fear that the lion might come for him and Jade, too. So they slept together that night in the way they had every night before his mother had insisted on separating them.

The next morning was a fine day, and Jade said that it was too nice for school, which was welcome news to Callum. He was not settling in very well and had still not made any real friends, though at least the other children refrained from picking on him. (That was because Jade was so well-liked; all the little girls and boys made a special effort to be nice to Callum because they wanted to impress her.)

After breakfast, the two of them went outside to hang washing on the line. Jade was very happy and excited, Callum thought. Talking about everything, games they could play and nice things they could eat and drink, and places they could go, like Adventure Park and the zoo. It scared him in a way; she was so excited—and afraid, too. Normally Jade would hang the clothes on the end of the line that was closest to the house, and use the pulley; but this time the two of them were up the other end, in the shade of a big ash tree near a quaint little garden shed placed amidst a flower bed.

Over the song of the birds, suddenly he heard a clattering and a bumping noise coming from the little shed. Both he and Jade looked in that direction, as Callum had already noticed she had been doing a lot. She stopped talking for a minute, and then told him it was time for a game of hide-and-seek. He was "it" and must close his eyes and count to a hundred so that she could find a really great hiding place. Panic seized Callum, and he thought about running inside; but he knew he had to be wherever Jade was, so he pretended to do what she said, but followed her with his eyes through his fingers. Instead of hurrying to hide, she had wandered off slowly, uncertainly just a few metres away to the little old shed that jutted out from the Cyprus hedge that fenced the property on that side. There was more noise like before, but also a horrible one like someone coughing very hard into something that muffled it.

Then Callum saw the lion's face in the window, and he screamed.

Jade turned around and ran to him, got down on her knees and took him by the shoulders. She told him to remember how the lion was their friend and how he would only hurt bad people, and then that the two of them were really lions too. The lion in the shed could be his new daddy; in fact, he had been his real daddy all along. All Callum could understand was that Jade was really, really scared. Her pupils were very big, she was squeezing him hard, and the words kept pouring forth in that high, shaky voice.

In a moment the shed door opened and the lion stepped out, revealing that big, horrible head that the boy had more than once glimpsed before with its wild, dirty mane and cruel features. Jade stopped talking, stood up, and spun around.

The lion was angry. He roared, calling Jade a horrible name that Callum did not understand, except that he was so angry he might actually eat her right then and there. And then he came forward, slamming the door behind him so hard that it bounced back open. Callum broke away as the lion grabbed Jade and hit her in the face, and she fell down, his big red paws staining the white of her jumper as they pulled her back up to her feet.

"I'm sorry!" she kept on saying in a tiny little girl voice, "I'm sorry!"

The lion told her to take Callum back inside and wait, so she picked him up where he stood to one side, rigid with panic, picked him up and threw him over her shoulder like a baby, then ran back up the path to the house. She was talking more about how the lion would never hurt them, not really, whatever he might say, and how they were all going to be a family together somewhere far away. But Callum was not listening. He could not stop screaming, having caught a glimpse of what and who was inside the shed.

EMPATHY

> Moloch the loveless! Mental Moloch! Moloch the heavy judger of men!
>
> —Allen Ginsberg, "Howl."

It was only with the utmost reluctance that Jenna agreed to attend the workshop with Ted. He was hovering around while she and her friend Dina, who was heavily involved with a campus group calling itself "The Nonviolent Alliance," discussed who each of them were going to bring this week; and surely in the eyes of outrageous fortune it was meant to be, since a vagary of the breaks roster had brought the three of them together that day. Ted, both girls were well aware, belonged to that peculiar species of dork combining traits of social awkwardness and extroversion. Apparently it was a combination that served him reasonably well in this customer service job, although it could only fail him in efforts of establish relationships with normal people.

They were in the lunch room at Brightsparks, the energy retailer in whose contact centre Jenna and Dina worked part-time while studying for their respective Arts degrees. Jenna helped herself to a pear from the table that bore a sign saying, "ONE piece of fruit only per employee ONLY!" bit into it, and made a face as she set it aside on the bench. "I just don't know who I'd bring . . ." She had so far managed to avoid attending the group's workshops. "I just feel like it's kind of . . ." she tried to avoid saying "embarrassing," knowing how important these workshops had become to her friend after the latter's unpleasant experience the previous year, when she had been raped by some guy she half-knew in the aftermath of a house party.

"Don't know who you'd bring to what?" Ted's presumptuous interjection saved her from finishing the sentence. "For you, I could always see what's in my diary." He looked her up and down in his habitual, shameless fashion.

Then Dina explained a little about the group, how they stood for eliminating all violence against women by teaching men how to empathise in one-on-one workshopped scenarios, and how their leader, Professor Alana Goldberg, drew inspiration and methods from Eastern spiritual traditions. Ted nodded.

"Yeah, cool bananas, sounds great! I ever tell you about the time I stayed in a Buddhist Ashram in India? We really smoked up the ganja in there, tell you what. Fun times! And I'm totally down with feminism and stopping violence against women and all that, too. Reminds me of my mate's sister. Sad story. She dated this guy once who was no good for her, you know? My mate called the cops, but of course they wouldn't do anything, so him and me, we went 'round to *talk it over* with the guy, know what I mean?" Ted's hand gestures were amusing in a grotesque way, whether he was smoking an imaginary joint or putting up his dukes. He was unable to stand still; it was the same when he was on the phones, always standing up and gesticulating. The two girls exchanged glances; he was known as "Energizer Teddy," a name he embraced. "Of course, it was hard to get through to the bloke, Ted continued, "because, you know, in Muslim culture they've got different ideas about how to treat women."

Jenna thought Ted would be in for it with that comment. Dina normally had zero tolerance for any form of racism or bigotry; instead, though, she just kept smiling and ignored the provocation. "That's excellent!" Dina interrupted. "We'd be so happy to have you along. Hey, I've got to get back on the floor now, but I hope you can make it. I'll email the deets."

Jenna was left rather nonplussed, having to listen to more of Ted's self-aggrandising talk. It seemed that his white-knight intervention had been a success without any need for violence, after all. Furthermore, he claimed to have been involved in many progressive political campaigns in his time (he was several years older than Jenna; in fact, who the hell knew *how* old he was?) and wanted her to appreciate what a highly socially conscious and compassionate individual he was, with passionate convictions, prominently concerning "gay marriage" and "the environment."

It was wasted effort on Ted's part, in more ways than one. Besides the misguided approach and the narrow shoulders, pot belly, and dandruff problem, Jenna was not really into any of that activist stuff. If fact it was a closely-guarded secret that she was interested in rather little of anything, though she lived in the expectation of finding something, perhaps via the true love she would meet one day, in which she could fully believe, and that would give an ultimate meaning to her life. For now it was just Godard films, the novels of Milan Kundera, vintage clothes . . . that sort of thing. She was a self-identified "boho" girl. Meanwhile, the direction of Ted's gaze told her where probably he perceived his life purpose to lie.

The workshop was regularly held upstairs in the Student Union building in a big, empty space known as "The Ballroom" that was sometimes used for yoga classes, and for book and poster sales. It was on a Sunday evening, oddly enough, when no one was around on campus; which perhaps made sense, as it was invitation only. Jenna might have felt a little unsafe had it not still been light when she arrived; it would be necessary to leave together with Dina and maybe Ted, or preferably some other guy, later on. Jenna walked up the stairs from the food court to the floor that housed the food co-operative and desks of the Union office holders. Although a student at the campus herself, this was not a place Jenna had ever frequented. In the Womyn's Officer's window, she noticed a motley of posters and placards so profuse it looked as though an effort had been made to barricade the door with them. She passed under a wall-to-wall banner overhead proclaimed: "Refugees are welcome! Racists are not!"

Outside the designated space, Jenna hesitated, seeing no sign anywhere to confirm that she was in the right place. The double doors were closed, but voices could be heard from inside.

Self-consciously, Jenna opened the door with a creak and peeked in. There was a ring of cushions and beanbags, not chairs, on the floor, with a portable whiteboard at the farthest point. A table had been set up with an urn and some tea and coffee things to one side in the only other sign of hospitality on display. There were about a dozen people, roughly equal numbers of men and women. Ted was there already—of course he was.

He was talking to a short, dark, voluptuous woman in early middle age with a full-bodied head of curls. This would be Alana (everyone called her by her first name, apparently). Her presence was large, and her voice sonorous though somewhat nasal. There was no sign of Dina.

Jenna's presence has been noticed immediately, Alana glancing in her direction. In a moment the Professor excused herself from Ted, saying "Well, it's wonderful to have you here tonight!" and approached the newcomer, striding so purposefully across the polished floorboards that Jenna had to check herself from turning and running. Ted, who now saw her, waved from where he stood.

"Hi, can I help you?" She asked with an ambiguous smile, eyes magnified behind a conspicuous pair of glasses.

"I'm Jenna, Dina's friend."

"Oh! That's wonderful! I've wanted to meet you for so long, I'm sure Dina's told you," she exclaimed, taking her hand and squeezing, rather than shaking it. Her palm was incredibly warm. Dina had. "I'm Alana. I've just been talking with your friend Ted," she said in a knowing tone that made it unnecessary for Jenna to chafe at any possibility of her relationship with Ted being misunderstood. "He's quite chatty, isn't he?" The rapport was established.

The small talk that followed confirmed it. Jenna was afraid that she would have to prove her feminist *bona fides*, her intelligence, or both; but Alana just asked her a series of questions about her life that got her talking and put her at ease. She seemed genuine enough.

The next greeting shook Jenna, however. It was Mark Rufus, a guy she had dated a couple of months ago, just arrived with Dina, who stood there practically smirking at the joke she was evidently playing on them both. Dina knew their history well. Jenna noticed that Mark was wearing the same leather jacket that had looked so good when he had worn it on their first date, but which now appeared a bit try-hard to her.

"Hey . . . !" She found herself trailing off as though unable to remember his name. "What are you doing here, Mark?" He looked embarrassed. "I mean—sorry, I didn't mean it to sound like that. It's really great to see you! Deen, you didn't tell me . . ."

"Well, I was on campus yesterday. I'm teaching now, you see, in the Arc and Design faculty." Jenna could see that he was trying not to brag too obviously, but wanted to tell her that as well as being a high-flying young architect he was now also in demand as a university teacher. "You know, just a couple of days a week. It's great fun. Anyway, I ran into Dina in the quad, and we got talking, and here I am," Mark threw his forearms out to either side in a restrainedly expansive gesture, "doing my bit on behalf of mankind, I guess!"

It was not as though Mark and Dina were friends. Jenna knew that she was always on the lookout for male workshop participants, to the point that now she would sometimes even hang out in bars and ask the guys who hit on her. The rule, apparently, was that there had to be equal numbers of men and women, and bringing the same guy along more than once was not the done thing. False modesty aside, clearly Mark had an ulterior motive for being there, and Dina was happy to exploit it. Jenna glanced at her friend, who gave her a mischievous look that confirmed her suspicion.

Thankfully it was not long before things got started. "You know," Alana began, assuming her post in the midst of the circle after everyone had taken their seats on the floor, "I've done these workshops in workplaces, schools, and prisons: places where attendance is compulsory; but when I do them on campuses all around the world it never ceases to amaze me how many men there are like yourselves who volunteer, week after week, to support and participate in what we're doing, which is nothing less than to help create a better, more equal, and more peaceful world for all of us: women, men, children, transgender, queer, straight, and everyone else under the Sun! So first of all, I need to say a big welcome and a big well-done to you all just for being here." This was followed by female-led applause. "And well done all you women, too. I'm so impressed at the effort you make every week to spread the word, and how seriously you all take our work here. I couldn't do it without you! We truly are changing the world, one workshop at a time!" There was another round of applause, and big smiles all round.

The preliminaries were shortly over, with Alana stating that they had "a lot to get through."

First came sentence-completion exercises. The men had to finish the sentence, "I like being a man because . . ." the women then doing the same with reference to their own gender. Jenna was terrified as they went around the circle, not knowing what to say. It was just like in tutorials. When the moment came she just said something tautological about being herself, and blushed.

Next the sexes segregated and were told to stand in concentric circles, taking turns to say what they thought about rape in the space of five minutes—yes, a whole five minutes each! Mercifully, Alanah clarified that there was no requirement to work with the guy they had each brought along, so, no doubt much to Ted's disappointment, Dina, rather than Jenna, took up a position opposite him, while Jenna's eyes met Mark's. She felt decidedly flustered.

"Well, what do you say about a topic like *rape*? It's quite a big . . . can of worms, huh? I mean, not that I'm saying it's—or that it should be controversial *per se*; that's not what I mean at all . . ." he waffled, playing with his jacket zipper. "I guess, if I'm honest, the only time I think about it normally is when there's something in the media, like that poor woman recently who . . . what was her name, the waitress walking home late . . . ? You know, out west, in one of those dodgy suburbs? Isn't that terrible? I can't even remember her name. But look, I know that's just a case that made the news; it's not always, like, 'stranger danger.'" Mark made quotation marks with his fingers. "What is it they say, that statistic? One in three women? It seems incredible, but I don't doubt it's true. And then they talk about how much more likely is it to be a date, or a family member . . . I don't know these statistics very well, obviously, But I guess when someone throws a figure out there like 'one in three' it kind of puts you on the defensive as a man, and you feel like you have to distance yourself from all this rape and sexual violence that's going on all the time but without, uh, protesting too much, if you know what I mean. We, us men, I don't think we should be defensive about it. We need to listen more, you know, to what women are saying, and hear what it's like for *them* . . ."

He was blushing like a little boy, but it produced repugnance more than tenderness in Jenna. Images of Mark and her in bed flashed through her mind, of his worshipful lovemaking, and that look in his eyes that was still there before her; then of those eyes filled with tears . . . And how poorly this stumbling, cowed individual before her compared to the suave persona she half-remembered, incredulously, from the early days of their acquaintance.

"It's okay, Mark. I appreciate what you're trying to say, honestly I do, but to tell you the truth I'm just here to support Dina. I know you're a caring person and I don't think all men are rapists or anything like that; I don't even think I'm a feminist, really. Sure, I believe in equality and stuff, like everyone else, but—God this is . . . so weird! It's actually kind of creepy, I think. Maybe I just don't get it because I've never had, like, a really bad experience."

Recovering his balance, Mark made bold to touch her forearm. "You're a good friend to her, I can tell." She managed not to flinch. They spent the next few minutes just talking about Dina, her hardship, and the way she had dealt with it, which after all was perfectly apposite.

"Okay everyone, I overheard some great discussions there, some really open exchanges, and that's great." Overheard? Jenna shuddered. Were those dark orbs glancing her way? "Now if everyone could face this way for the next exercise."

It was just as dry as what preceded it: a group brainstorm on the causes of rape, the general consensus being that the answer was "structural inequality," "patriarchy," "intersectional oppression," and suchlike. Jenna volunteered nothing, but sat watching the clock, praying that she would not be called upon. It was irksome to hear the men repeating after the women the things that the latter had already said, and looking to them for approval. But then, sure enough, Alana addressed her by name: "Jenna, do you have anything to add?" All the acceptable answers were already on the board. She should just have said, "No, I think it's all been covered," but in her confusion the best she could do was say, "I guess maybe some men feel . . . frustration when they think women are, I don't know, giving off signals . . . and they don't understand the difference, or something." There were some quizzical looks, but thankfully no overt hostility.

A truly awful moment came afterward, however, when Ted started talking about his friend's sister, and about Muslims and different cultures that don't respect women or the laws of a liberal society. It was like he had no understanding that he was uttering heresy. Before long he was quite brutally shut down by a several women and men working in concert, one practically shouting that "Western civilisation *is* rape!" Jenna disliked the look on Dina's face while this was happening, and the way Alana allowed it, smiling beatifically over the pecking party as though she were an impartial moderator. She herself did not necessarily agree with Ted, but she had no love of hearing people shouted down. And then again, she did recall what it had been like walking down Edgeware Road and through Hyde Park alone during her sojourn in London . . .

This, thankfully the final talking activity, was followed by what Alana called "a deepening of approach." What really differentiated her program from other anti-rape workshops, she explained, recapitulating what Jenna already knew, was how they used various meditation techniques deriving from yoga and Buddhism that were designed to "expand consciousness and enable us to identify with the other, and ultimately with all sentient beings." She told the group that it was unnecessary for them to share in any religious or metaphysical presuppositions; she herself was a Jew (a "buju" she joked: a Buddhist Jew), and if one followed another religion or was an atheist, no matter: the practices they were about to engage in were compatible with any belief system that valued peace, love, compassion, and above all *empathy*.

"I can promise you it will be rewarding if you stick with it until the end; but of course if anything makes you feel uncomfortable in any way, you're perfectly free to exit yourself from the activity, and I'm more than happy to discuss any concerns afterwards, and just generally debrief, because it can certainly be an emotional experience."

It began with a breathing meditation, guided by Alana's, sonorous yet slightly goose-like voice. It was hard not to be affected by a certain prophetic quality in her diction, however. So far there was nothing spooky, just fairly pleasant relaxation. Actually, after a while the relaxation was intense, and even quite wonderful, like a hot bath.

At some point the breathing meditation developed into visualisation. After it was all over, Jenna had a sense of having seen things very vividly which it was hard to believe were wholly imagined, even though the memories were all very disjointed. There were strange shapes and colours still floating around in her consciousness, and things that Alana's commentary made clear were personifications of emotions, some peaceful and others violent. She could not remember, either, if she had felt disturbed by any of it: the many sets of waving arms, the huge demonic faces with mouths like savage animals, and the other, compliant beings they trod down or chewed and swallowed with their many mouths, and many other things that she would catch a glimpse of now and again for days and nights afterward. There was a sense of awe, certainly, and fascination; and throughout the sound of Alana's voice which Jenna began to feel was somehow her own, emanating from some deep part of her from whence the fantastic entities also came.

Lastly, rocked gently awake by Alana's enigmatic tones, the participants formed male-female pairs again. Jenna again found herself opposite Mark, and surprised herself by taking his hand. They were supposed to visualise the scenarios to be narrated by Alana. This time they were back on planet Earth, on the physical plane, and the situations were things like being whistled at in the street, being pestered for dates or sex, etc., right up to actually being assaulted and raped. Jenna found it emotionally intense in a strange way; she marvelled at how vivid it all was in her mind. Jenna thought she had a pretty good imagination, but normally were she to close her eyes what she saw would look blurry and shifting; whereas this was more like watching a movie, even if, from the next day's point of view, it was more like one of Godard's later films that were just a little bit too weird.

And it was paired up with a breathing exercise that she

would have imagined it difficult for a beginner to execute, even on its own; but as it turned out, nothing could have been easier for her at that moment than to pair it with these complex mental operations.

After spending some time under instruction to build up an emotional response (which was never faint or long in coming), Jenna was instructed to open her eyes and look at Mark. It was as though she alone was being spoken to, and there were no other couples present. She would be instructed to take a deep breath of pure, cleansing light—and this Jenna could actually see as if it were part of the physical reality surrounding her, illuminating only her immediate surroundings in the strangely darkened room. Then she would breathe out coal-black smoke, black against the dimly lit air. Alana said that the smoke represented all that horror and fear and loathing she, the being who was and was not Jenna Davies, had generated via the visualised scenario. At the same time Mark would open up and breathe in that darkness—she saw him suck it in—then, on the outbreath, convert it to pure white light and restart the cycle.

Nor was Jenna actually upset by those intense feelings she was generating. It was a phenomenologically alien experience in which she played the role of a crucible filled with emotions that were like white hot metal: rage, hatred, humiliation, despair, and so on. But for the time being at least, she was made of a substance with a far higher melting point. She was now one of those ferocious deities she had visualised earlier with their many eyes, their various animal heads, up to and including that of a lobster, adorned with a necklace of human skulls.

Despite how personal to her they seemed, as best Jenna could remember, Alana's commentary and instructions had all been in the third person: "*Pundasa* stares at *Svamini*, his eyes seeking out and lingering on the sacred zones of her body . . . *Svamini* exhales the black smoke of her pain; *Pundasa* inhales and accepts it into the core of himself . . ." and so on. Those names, or something like them, stood out among the many strange syllables Jenna half-remembered as they slowly dissipated from her mind over the days that followed.

Meanwhile something else happened, besides what Jenna

was strictly being told to feel and do. In those long moments when she was looking into Mark's eyes, while his gaze answered hers, she saw clearly that he loved her, and knew that for him, right then and there, his whole reason for existing was to love her. At first, she felt not too bad about it at all, as she had in real life both with him and the various other guys she had had to let down; there was no sense of guilt at all. As with the other emotions there was a certain excess of clarity and detachment that somehow detracted nothing from their intensity.

And yet her equanimity was incomplete. Jenna noticed something about Mark's eyes that she didn't like, and that grew upon her, supervening over all the turbulence, until she was feeling a constant, unambiguous hatred for that stupid, besotted look on his face, and especially in those creepy, glistening eyes that dared to extend that hungry, importunate look as though he wanted to crawl all over her like a big disgusting slug. In dreams afterwards those eyes still came at her like a pair of feelers.

And then Alana was telling her to return to her body, to feel the sensation in this part and that, to stretch and open her eyes. Jenna looked at the clock. It had been three straight hours, and no-one had complained!

As for getting home, it turned out not to matter about the details. She wandered off on her own while Dina stood around talking with her girlfriends from the group. Her safety on campus after dark seemed hardly an issue to Jenna, nor had either of her admirers tried to stop her. It was like no one else was there. Which meant that she in turn felt invisible—a great relief.

Three weeks later, Ted won the Employee of the Month award, on the basis of an abrupt surge in his KPAs. There was no ceremony associated with this, as more than half of the staff worked odd part-time hours; announcements were made by email, and there was hell to pay by the employee who missed or failed to respond to one, despite the fact that no time was allocated for this. Teamleader Tamika (head of "Team Voltron," to which both Jenna and Ted belonged) said in her email that besides his high call-resolution statistics, what was so good about Ted's approach was his "use of empathy." He received the customary Subway voucher as a reward.

Later that week he burnt his hand rather badly in removing a super-heated bowl of soup from the microwave in the staff room. Jenna was there when it happened; their breaks continuing to overlap on the unpredictable roster. He no longer hassled her, though, and when he caught her looking curiously in his direction, would look quickly away. Ted and his soup. It was another thing to wrinkle one's nose and laugh at him, another reason to suspect he might be a bit autistic or something. Ted always ate the same thing for lunch, the same brand of ready-made microwave soup, in different varieties. His cupboards at home must have been stacked with it. Jenna overheard a conversation once in which he had argued the point with an unwilling colleague about whose soup was best, whether it was worthwhile cooking for oneself in the present day and age. She smiled to herself, remembering how Ted had practically shouted, "Here, you don't believe me? Taste it, taste it!"

The strange thing when he burned himself was that he did not seem to be in any pain, so she doubted what she had just seen.

It was not until later, when they were back on the floor, that Jenna noticed a huge blister in Ted's palm, swollen literally to the size of a kiwi fruit. He was standing up, talking with his hands as had always been his wont, but his voice was softer nowadays, almost feminine.

She finished the call she was on and then put her phone in "not ready" mode.

"I think Ted's hurt," she explained to Tamika after calling her over. "Look at his hand!"

The teamleader glanced at Ted, who was advising someone complaining about their bill, "Well, I certainly hope this payment plan will help you to get on your feet while your husband recovers. I just wish there was more we could do for you. Let me see, I could email you a copy of our Energy Shortcuts Cheat sheet, if you'd like, but of course I can just imagine what it's like with the kids on holidays, turning things on and then wandering off all the time! Can't let them out of your sight, can you?"

Tamika walked around to Ted's side of the divider and in a

moment looked back up at Jenna with the same expression she could feel on her own face. She let him finish the call, then said, "Ted, I want you to go in *not ready*."

"Sure thing, Tamika. Have I done something wrong?"

"What's wrong with your hand?"

He held up the uninjured one, and stared at it.

"No, the other one, there! Oh my God, Ted! You better get yourself to the medical centre. That looks terrible!"

"Oh, yes!" he agreed, "Terrible! I see what you mean, my mistake. I'll just sort that out for you right away." Then he got up and walked out directly, leaving his jacket on the back of his chair.

Jenna had been haunted by the image of Mark's eyes upon her ever since the workshop. She was lying in bed trying to get to sleep, and there they were again, mirroring back something in herself that she absolutely did not want to see.

She had asked Dina what the idea had been, bringing Mark, and her friend had disclaimed any mysterious intentions. They had just happened to bump into each other, nothing more. The two girls had talked very little about the strangeness of all that had happened—or more likely, not actually happened. When Jenna had brought it up and tried to describe her impressions, Dina gave a vague explanation that, yes, some people did experience that, essentially going into a lucid dream state during the meditation practice. She invited her back, to talk it over with Alana if she wanted, but Jenna reacted with a revulsion at the idea that she was unable to conceal. She began to feel that the two of them had grown apart.

And still Mark's eyes refused to leave her alone. In reality, deep down, she knew that she was no one special. She understood that if it were not for her above-average looks, a guy like Mark, so brilliantly accomplished that in theory he should have been out of her league, would never have looked at her, an undergraduate call centre worker, like a goddess come to Earth to make his life complete.

Her feelings towards him, she knew, had never made any sense. Objectively Mark was a good catch, as her incredulous friends had all pointed out without being able to make Jenna waver in her decision to end things with him. He had a great job and great prospects, too, and she knew that, if they had felt like she did, some of her friends would have strung him along to take advantage of his great apartment, free meals, and swish restaurants, etc.; maybe even used him as a point of introduction to other guys who might be more to her liking in whatever indefinable respect Mark was lacking. But Jenna was not like that. She supposed that she was just flighty, like so many girls her age. Experience and the right man would someday overcome what was probably just a self-thwarting instinct, a yen for a bohemian lifestyle of self-absorbed, glamorous unhappiness (with parents stepping in to pay the bills semi-regularly). It was a pattern with her. At a certain point she would just lose interest in a guy she was dating, without being able to explain it, and then she would feel empty and confused.

It was as if those eyes in her head were mocking her. How could Mark really think she was worth gazing at with such devotion? Could he really be that stupid; or was he playing a joke on her, making fun of her insignificance by putting her on an undeserved pedestal? No, that was ridiculous, but the irrational suspicion lingered. She felt a lot of emotions related to but lacking the clarity of those she had channelled in the workshop.

She was not exactly sure why she went to see Mark in the end, given that she would have done almost anything to avoid seeing that look in his eyes again, but thinking about what had happened to Ted gave her some idea.

Jenna still had the swipe card to his flat at home in her dresser drawer. The proof of the professional triumphs Mark boasted of in self-deprecating style was there in the form of his luxurious and perfectly situated apartment. He told her how within a couple of years of graduation he had made himself indispensable at the firm where he had done an internship, and how it gave him such an "amazing sense of purpose." His enthusiasm had caught her imagination and made her like him more. It was on the third floor in a laneway in the middle of the city, looking out over a chic little alleyway that housed a couple of bars and a Japanese restaurant. She had gone there with him on their first date, and he had gloated a little to reveal where he lived right at the end, having made her promise to go there with him if he told her.

Not wanting to create an aura of suspense around her entrance, Jenna left the intercom alone and took the liberty of swiping herself into the building, a convenient curtain of hair between her face and the security camera. The huge pneumatic door, like that of a bank vault or an industrial freezer, clicked open. "We're here!" Mark had said with a cocky look that night, what was it, six months ago? She could hear his voice, and it made her feel sad. He had seemed like a cool guy back then, not the puppy-dog, or worse, that she remembered from Alana's workshop. Yes, she hated what seemed to come over all guys a month or two into a relationship. She hated that word, "relationship"!

There was no one in the foyer, and Mark, of course, might not be at home. He was a busy guy, after all. It was not as if she had gone so far out of her way; it was more or less on her way home from work. She would take the elevator. There was a little spasm in her belly when the doors opened. No, it was empty. She reached the third floor, walked down the hall, and pressed the intercom, nervous because she knew that he would be able to see her grainy picture from inside the flat with those eyes of his that would not leave her alone. Perhaps he would weep for joy. She shuddered.

Jenna still was not sure exactly what she wanted to say, but something told that her words would be unnecessary. Her explicitly formulated plan was just to return the swipe card, a gesture he could hardly take the wrong way, as long as she made a swift exit afterwards. Even that was going to be completely awkward. Imagine his disappointment, the hurt look in his eyes—ugh, the very thought!

The smell of freshly cleaned carpet brought back that blurry night, and the subsequent ones, of which there had, after all, been only a few. That particular node of her limbic system being stimulated, she also recalled Mark's aftershave, and the smell and feel of his leather jacket. He had been so sexy at first! An unexpected flower of nostalgia opened up under her diaphragm, as she heard him saying with a kind of ironic smugness, "Welcome to my pad. Make yourself at home!"

She felt that he was home, and irrationally, became only more certain of it when he did not answer. He was unable to take action, and she was in control; a not entirely pleasant feeling.

She was right: there he was, standing at the far end of the living room, by the drawing table over by the big window looking out over the evening skyline. The room was lit dimly, standard lamps casting their light upwards on the ceiling. Mark was facing the wrong way, feeling the wall beside the desk with his hands like a sleepwalker. He was naked from the waist down, wearing a business shirt that just covered his groin. The place stank as though the rubbish had not been taken out in a long while. In hindsight, Jenna thought she knew already what she was about to see. After a few moments of hesitation and dread, she called his name, and Mark turned to face her. On his blood-streaked face there were two clotted red pits where his eyes should have been, but the expression of sickening devotion remained unmistakable.

THE HORRIBLE THING

Okay. I'm recording this just for myself, to get it all straight in my mind. I know it's probably just schizophrenia taking hold, or stress. But I have to admit that part of me believes in these memories. They're so clear I can't really deny them—except rationally, of course. But, worst-case scenario, this recording will be for someone else to make sense of, after.

When I turned fourteen my parents bought me my own TV for my birthday. I'm thirty now. It was exciting because we'd just also got a pay TV subscription, and suddenly there was a lot more to watch than *The Simpsons* and *Dawson's Creek* and that stuff. There were all kinds of movies, including foreign ones like *Betty Blue* that made me feel grown up and excited, and I remember discovering *Twin Peaks*, as well. Sport I couldn't care less about, then or now.

I used to stay up every night watching just whatever: old horror movies, Japanese cartoons . . . so I was probably sleep deprived when I saw the thing I'm going to be talking about. I'd also probably eaten something nightmare-inducing, like maybe cheese toasties. Yes, I can remember making those often. I had an amazing metabolism back then; could eat anything and didn't have to worry about my weight, or my complexion, either.

Deep breath . . . I'm just going to call what I saw on the screen that night, and again more recently *the horrible thing*. And if the first time I saw it was a dream, then maybe it was stored away in my subconscious afterwards, ready to resurface when I saw something that reminded me of it at a time when I was emotionally and physically vulnerable. Anyway, it's because I want to rationally explain the horrible thing that I'm writing this. So I'm going to put it in context before I actually get round to describing it. Maybe that'll help me remember some detail that makes sense of the whole thing, whatever that might be . . . or maybe I'm just putting off the description because I can't write it without wanting to scream.

There was a boy I was kind of "going out" with then, Pete Hickey. Perfect name for a teenage heart-throb, right? I suppose you could say "going out"; I mean we did, literally, a couple of times: went to the movies, held hands, and kissed in the back row. When I got my TV he asked me right away if I could get any adult channels, "You know, porno stuff," he said. I didn't know, and I hadn't thought about it, but I started to after that. And I felt guilty about it because of course—double standard—girls aren't supposed to be interested in porn, are they?

Pete said you could unscramble the signal; he said you just needed a universal remote, which I'd never heard of, but he said you could make one out of a regular remote just by unscrewing the back to expose the circuit board; then you'd get a coin and rub it back and forth to . . . I don't know, de-magnetise it or something. It sounded like bull, on the level of smoking banana peel to get high, which we tried, but what did I know?

I wasn't about to tell Pete I was interested in what he was saying. He would have thought I was a slut and told the whole school, even though he and I never actually went all the way. But I took note of what he said, and I decided to give it a try.

So there I was late one night, sitting on the edge of my Little Mermaid doona cover, heart in my mouth, trying to catch a glimpse of people fucking. I imagined that if my parents found out they'd disown me, even though, thinking back, they probably would have hardly minded. In the white noise and fuzz I'd occasionally pick up on something and try to tune in, but it was hopeless. I don't know how long I kept trying; a fair while, I think. I remember thinking I'd already lost my innocence in principle, so with any luck I might as well enjoy what I'd sacrificed it for.

Then, snap! The picture became really clear, though kind of washed out like security camera footage, almost black and white but with just enough colour not to be. At the same time, there were a few details standing out, saturated in colour, like the main actress's red lips. There was an interior, a woman standing in a kitchen over the stove. She looked like she was about to head out for a night on the town. So why was she cooking dinner? No, she must be having someone around, someone she wanted to look hot for, because she was wearing a top that showed a lot of cleavage. I remember glancing down at mine and pushing it together, to see if I could get it to look like hers. She was also wearing this really slutty skirt, really short, and the way it glistened it was made of leather or vinyl. So I thought I might just have found what I was looking for!

But she just kept on making that sauce, sautéing the onions, then taking them off the heat and disappearing off to one side to add the meat, or another vegetable, a shake of salt or seasoning, etc. She wasn't an expert cook, that was for sure; very inefficient in her movements and getting through a lot of wine in the process. It was weird: there was no music that I could hear; the only sound was the sizzling of the frying pan, but this woman was moving around, almost dancing, and boogieing more and more until it was kind of absurd, kind of grotesque, what she was doing. She must have been drunk. The way it was shot, it was like there were a few different cameras around the room recording her simultaneously. This was going on way too long to be anything but badly edited reality TV. I probably thought I was watching footage from a slow night of *Big Brother Uncut,* if that existed yet, I forget . . .

Behind her must have been the door to the rest of the house, because when the doorbell rang she spun around so sharply I nearly screamed; it was such an awful, mechanical snarl, that doorbell, and the woman looked so frightened.

She put down the knife she was using to finely chop, chop, and re-chop some garlic, and turned around but didn't do anything right away. I guessed that whoever she was expecting must have had a key; like maybe it was her husband or her live-in boyfriend, and so he never used the bell. Then there was a loud knocking, followed by another ring. The camera showed her face in profile, then from the front. So frightened: her expression was so intense, larger than life, and the camera picked up the tiny wrinkles that appeared on the smooth skin of her face. She was a little bit older that I'd thought at first. Then slowly, like she was afraid of stepping on a squeaky board, she crept through the next room, which was the living room, and towards the front door. First she looked though the peep-hole, then pressed her ear to the door. The camera showed a close-up of her red lips, open and trembling.

Then, God, there was this . . . voice. It was like—I'll see if I can do it: "Puh-lease, dere be a accident out he-yah. I need use your phon, okay?" It was a high-pitched, nasal, a little boy's voice. And obviously he was, you know, ESL. Then it was like the woman was miming the fact that she was thinking about it, putting a finger-tip in her mouth and furrowing her brow even more. She even scratched her head and made a chin rest with her fingers, like as if she was a children's TV presenter or something. I wanted to scream "No, don't be stupid, don't let him in!" because somehow despite how theatrical it was in one way, I really felt that I was watching something unfolding that very moment in real life somewhere.

"Puh-lease, dere blood ev'ywhe-yah. My mum-ma and my da-da—" I remember he said it like that, but so calmly and not actually sounding *that* young, more like a teenage boy pretending to be a little kid. I was on the edge of my seat. "My mam-ma and da-da, dey bad hurt, they bleedin' so much out he-yah. You help, please you help . . ."

This was in the days before everyone had a mobile, so I guess there was some believability about needing to knock on someone's door to use the phone. Still, it did occur to me that the woman could offer to call an ambulance for them instead. Anyway, it was completely obvious that there was no way she should open that door; but while this went on, the voice pleading and the woman procrastinating, it was like I started falling under the spell myself. I started to understand where the woman was coming from, hesitating: what if there really was an accident? Could she live with herself if she didn't help them?

"Okay, I'll let you in," she said, slowly, in this incredibly earnest tone of voice.

The door creaked. Sure enough, it was an older child—actually more like a teenager. He stood in the doorway, arms by his sides, perfectly still. He was wearing baggy street clothes, including a hoodie that hid his face, and casting a long shadow into the room. He stepped inside, and the woman stepped back, kind of cringing like she couldn't stand the light. Then the others followed, and uh-uh, they definitely weren't children. Two, three, four men came into the living room, and the last one turned around and closed the door.

Well, if it was a porno I was watching, it should have been banned, because what happened then was definitely not consensual, even though the woman was pretty well limp and didn't put up a fight. The camera angle was high, almost a bird's eye view at this point, so at first you couldn't make out the rapists' faces; they were wearing hoodies and baggy tracksuits just like you'd expect, I guess—I mean, if they were going for anonymity.

Well, they raped that poor woman again and again on the floor, over the sofa, dragged her here and there by the hair. They slapped her around. One of them spat in her face; another pulled out a knife and cut her skirt off her, drawing blood from her thigh, then cut her on the cheek as well. Even the teenage boy who'd tricked her had his turn while the others cheered him on. At first she was begging them to leave her alone, then later on just whimpering, crying, not actually saying any words. And they were joking around with each other at the same time, laughing horribly and talking in their language which sounded very strange to me at the time, full of tongue clicks and other noises you don't get in English. They weren't in any hurry; even helped themselves to food from the kitchen while they were waiting their turn. I can't believe I sat and watched it all, but I did. God, does that mean I enjoyed it . . . ?

Next thing, the door behind them opened. "Knock, knock!" It was the husband or boyfriend calling out playfully as he pushed it open. Then, "Oh . . . my . . . *Gaahd*!" he gasped just like that, in an American accent and kind of a stylised, high-pitched, sing-songy way. He dropped the bunch of flowers in his hand and just stood there while the rapists all turned to face him, except the one who was . . . doing his thing. Forcing her face into the corner of the settee, he was; from the guy's viewpoint you could see that. Then the camera focused on the husband's, or the boyfriend's, face. His cheeks were a little too pink, I noticed (one of those over-colourful details I mentioned, and his eyes were very blue). He was good-looking, I guess: tall, blonde, and well-built, and wearing a suit. But with those rosy cheeks and the bright, darting blue eyes he looked more like a doll than a man. Then after a long moment of standing, watching, looking like he was going to fall over backwards, he turned around and ran the hell out of there, slamming the door behind him while the rapists laughed.

So, alright, maybe he was going for help. That would have made sense. Even though his instinct might have told him to stay and fight, that way could only end badly, for sure. It made more rational sense to go and alert the neighbours. And that could have been what he was doing; I mean, I guess it must have been. But then the signal cut out, so I was left in suspense.

Then again, sometimes, especially now, I do wonder if it was actually something in me that cut out the memory of what happened next. And maybe what I saw planted a seed in my mind that might explain . . . God, no, I can't bear—!

Well, that's the end of the first part of this story. I stopped watching late-night TV for a while after that, or any TV at all that I could help. What I'd seen that night kept coming back to haunt my dreams for a long time after; like, I'm not sure I ever completely got over it. The worst thing was I couldn't even talk to anyone. Sure, I didn't have to admit to looking for porn, but even so I'd watched it and not turned it off right away, so what did that say about me? I felt dirty. And what was to be gained by telling anyone? How could they have reassured me?

Anyway, I eventually sort-of forgot about it, lived my life, finished high school, went to uni, travelled, went back to uni and got a second degree in information management, which led to getting a job as a community librarian. Not much different to the customer service jobs I did while I was studying, to be honest, but at least the money's better, and it's a bit more meaningful. You meet people, all kinds, and sometimes you hear their stories. It's really eye-opening where some of them have come from, and it makes you appreciate what you have and want to share it with others who haven't had the same privileges.

I never dated a patron before, but this guy I've been seeing, John, I met at the service desk. He told me his real name, his tribal name, and there was just no way on Earth I could pronounce it. I still can't. I mean, I deal with people from diverse backgrounds all the time; it's not like I wasn't willing to have a go, but he was making sounds with his mouth, his throat, his nose, that there was no way I could reproduce. Then he laughed in this crazy way and said, "Call me John."

The thing that attracted me at first was that he's got the most charming smile. Never stopped smiling, even when on our first date he told me about how his people had been kicked out of their homeland and massacred in some kind of horrible witch hunt. It sounded like what happened in Rwanda in the '90s. Anyway, the thing was, it was happening in several countries all at once because his people are spread out between a lot of different places in Africa, and they don't have a country of their own. They're called different names in different places, and they're pretty obscure, so it was like the Western media never connected the dots.

I've dated a lot of guys—I shouldn't admit that, but it's true—and the ones I really liked all broke my heart. I wasn't even thirty, and I felt like damaged goods, like I'd never meet anyone who was good for me; and then John shows up at the loans desk with his big smile, and he just says, "I like you," like that. Can you believe it! "I like you. Please, you come, we eat." Well, I was on the rebound, so I thought, "What the hell?"

He works stacking supermarket shelves and lives with his family in a Commission flat. When I ask him about them all he says is "many, many, many!" smiling and rolling his eyes and making a funny whistling noise through his nose. I've never seen where he lives; figured he was embarrassed so I never pushed him. Things have moved really fast, and we've been spending lots of time together, almost like a married couple. It's not what I would have expected with a non-Western guy; I would have assumed he'd be more traditional; but then, I thought, maybe he's just really down-to-Earth after everything he's been through, what with surviving massacres and everything.

To tell the truth it's only been like a month since we met, but almost straight away I started feeling more and more like we were soul-mates. It's totally bizarre, I know, and I swear I've never been like this with anyone before. We hardly talk; John doesn't speak much English, and I can't even seem to learn one word of his language, but that's how it is. Now, I don't know. I kind of want to go to him and see . . . maybe I'm wrong and he can make it alright . . .

So it was all going weirdly great until last Friday night. We were watching TV when I nodded off on John's shoulder after a hell of a week. When I woke up he was asleep, head back, mouth and eyes open—yep, sleeps with his eyes open, that's normal for him!—and snoring in this funny way he has, similar to the whistling noise he makes through his nose when he laughs.

And what do you think came on the screen?

There was a sexily-dressed woman making dinner. It took a while for me to recognise it, all the details I'd half-forgotten but that were so familiar: her face, her lips, her blonde hair, the over-the-top mime-show of the way she was moving. I was frozen, totally paralysed like in a dream; never thought to switch it off. So there you go, must've been a dream, right? But maybe I was asleep too, and it was just a dream . . .

It all unfolded just like the first time I'd seen it with the violation and the violence, total déjà vu. But that wasn't all. I think it was worse this time than when I was a kid because I was about to see what I'd missed the first time, or what I'd repressed.

The rapists were black, which I'd noticed the first time but without reading anything into it, of course. I mean they were, like, really dark-skinned Africans, and they had those ritual scars on their foreheads like the Sudanese do, only bigger and higher up, like . . . I'll get to that. So, black on black . . . plus the hoods, plus the way the camera angle was mostly high and distant, taking everything in that was happening all at once, while everything was going on . . . anyway, like I say, maybe I just repressed certain details the first time, I honestly don't know.

Then as the final rapist, uh . . . finished the job, he threw his head back, laughed and made a horrible whistling noise like a kettle. And I couldn't believe my eyes. I couldn't believe *his* eyes! There was a crown of them like a tiara on his bald head, like black pearls, blacker even than his skin, but shining just like dewdrops, and they winked open when his two eyes, his human eyes, closed!

They just walked out when they were done, and closed the door behind them. And straight after the partner guy came back in, like he'd just been waiting outside. I mean, the rapists must have passed him on their way out! So he shut the door and stared at his wife or girlfriend or whoever, bleeding, lying there with her knickers around her ankles, and he dropped to his knees like some kind of ham actor, and ripped his shirt open without saying a word.

What came next was totally surreal—I mean, even more so. You could see that time was passing in fast-forward. The light from outside got darker, and the shadows inside got heavier. It had gone from evening to night, so the room was only lit by a standard lamp in the corner. It was mood-lighting; you could hardly see a thing. Then it started getting a bit brighter, and I saw that the man and woman had moved a little. It was like watching the hands of a clock move, it was so slow. Hypnotic. I thought of Japanese Noh theatre (which I studied at uni) and how the actors do that: move really, really slowly, making every tiny gesture take on this, like, amazing intensity.

After a while the man had walked a way towards the woman on his knees, one hand over his heart, the other reaching out for her. She'd got up and was crouched in the corner of the settee, covering her face, and she was holding an arm out towards him with a gesture like, "No, I don't want to hear it—get away from me!"

Days kept passing faster and faster, measured by the pulsing of the light through the blinds and the shadows' waxing and waning. The camera angle changed from time to time and focused on some detail, then went back to the whole scene. Now I saw his hair growing (hers was probably growing too, but it was already long, so it was less obvious). Fingernails too.

And while they were posed there like that, well, they weren't eating, so I guess that explained how they were wasting away. It was so disturbing: you saw the skull under the skin coming out while their eyes didn't blink at all, just got wider and rounder. The woman slowly uncovered her face, and it was almost the worst thing I'd seen yet; slowly, bit by bit revealing the horror of what she felt until I felt her pain like it had happened to me. And his wasn't any better. God! Mouths hanging open like they were screaming in agony, but no sound. The whole thing was totally silent except for a little faint city noise from outside.

At first I thought the redness was from the silent screaming and the blood smear, but then I saw that the woman's skin was coming out in an awful rash that got worse and worse, like an extreme case of chickenpox or something. I wondered if it had to do with the cut on her cheek from the rapist's knife; then I wondered if she'd got some STD. It took days, maybe weeks, I don't know; I was in a trance, just staring—but eventually her whole body that you could see was just totally covered in these big, scabby looking boils about the size of a twenty-cent piece. It was horrible.

Then her skin started—God, deep breath, deep breath!—it started twitching. You could see that there was something inside those boils that was trying to break out.

The two of them had started to slump. I realised it had been happening for a while before I noticed it. The camera focused on her cheek, where she'd been cut and the cut had scabbed over the top of a couple of those disgusting lumps. So, the scab opened up like—ugh!—like a broken zipper, and this *thing* crawled out. It looked like a spider crossed with a man—with a baby, I mean, like, it had four legs instead of eight. That was at first. Then more legs popped out of its sides, long, thin ones, unfolding. I guessed they would have been its ribs, or curled up where its ribs would have been if it was human. It was an impostor, a parasite. Half-man, half spider.

Yes, half spider, because it had those eyes that went all the way up onto the crown of its bald head, just like the rapist had. I saw them wink open like it was slowly waking up. Then it crawled down her face, and out of the camera frame super-fast, so much so that I had a feeling that it might scurry out of the TV and onto the carpet in front of me. In front of me and John.

I jolted back in my seat. It was the first movement I think I made except for probably breathing and blinking, the whole time.

God, then she just exploded as they all come out, like that first one had given the signal. All the rest of those little things under her skin burst out at once, they swarmed the man and almost totally covered him up. I watched as they ate him alive—yes, you could tell; they were crawling across his eyeballs, and you could see those huge glistening pupils darting around—and into his open mouth: everywhere; and then afterwards they were crawling in his eye sockets. He stayed paralysed, couldn't make a sound. But you could hear all of those little jaws working together, tearing away while he was melting like a bloody candle. Meanwhile, she—she was like, fuck, like one of those banksia pods after the seeds have fallen out. So horrible, there just—I just—oh God, hang on . . . !

Sorry, back again. That was me actually being sick. I don't want to think about what it means.

Finally, the screen went blue, and I remembered fully where I was, and who I was with. I felt him move a little bit, saw him out of the corner of my eye lift his head, and the whistling of his snoring which I'd just blanked out completely had stopped. I turned around and faced him, and by the light of the TV it was like we'd been zapped into the world of that place on the screen, colours kind of washed out but everything really sharp.

I screamed. His human eyes were closed, where before they'd been open, like I said. And his spider eyes for the first time ever were shining open at me; and then there was his smile! It wasn't charming any more.

Well, I ran out of there and I've been staying at my mother's for the last week, feeling sick: feverish, losing weight, vomiting what little I can eat, and just lying low, trying to understand what the hell's going on in my life. And the thing is, I'm coming out in this rash . . .

THE SLEEPING BEAUTY

They were walking past a Fernwood gym one day while out shopping when Shannon uncharacteristically sighed, "I've put on so much weight this year. If only I had time to get to the gym!"

Nick responded by getting overly excited: "Hey, why not? Maybe we could go together."

"Together? You do know that's a women-only gym!"

"Oh, sure. But I mean, we could go somewhere else. You could do your cardio, and I could do my weight training—or whatever . . ." He trailed off, knowing that it had been a *faux pas* to sound as though he were prescribing a specific course of exercise. He always said too much when nervous.

She gave him a suspicious look before apparently thinking better of it. "I could never go to the gym with you, sweetie. No offence, it's just I'd be too embarrassed, you know, sweating and . . . bending over and everything, not to mention with all those strange men around! Other women would be bad enough!"

So Fernwood it was. When some weeks later he presented her with the membership voucher on her birthday, her face went grey with shock.

"Thanks." Was all she said, so faintly it seemed as though she had been winded.

"I remembered what you said, you know, the other day, when we were walking past the gym, you know, about wanting to get—wanting to join . . ."

They had agreed to wait until after the working day was over in order to celebrate Shannon's turning twenty-five, and had met up in the city at a favoured eatery. She had said she wanted something to look forward to during the day. Now they were in a Vietnamese restaurant, and just at that moment their meals arrived.

The silence continued some moments longer. "Right," she muttered as though to herself, "I see." Then she dropped the cardboard slip on the table with trembling hands, stood up, and, very awkwardly, commenced to extricate herself from the booth where she was so tightly wedged in, all without so much as looking at Nick. It was warm in the restaurant, and she was as usual overdressed, but she definitely had not been so red a minute before.

"Shanny, are you alright?" He began to reach out towards her, then withdrew his superfluous hand.

She did not answer, but lost her balance slightly, standing back up after remembering to turn around and retrieve her bag. She twisted around in the narrow space, her flank, garbed in a colourful abstract print beneath her cardigan's hem, pressing into the table's edge and causing ripples to appear in her steaming bowl of *phở* soup as Nick watched in dismay.

She managed to get out without either spilling her soup or looking him in the face, then left the restaurant. Fortunately, when he got up to follow he was not waylaid by any of the busy wait staff. Shannon was not immediately to be seen out in the street. He felt panic.

Nick wandered up the street and back, unable for some time to focus his mind on any notion of probability or proportion. At length he found her in the driver's seat where they had parked across the road from the train station. A billboard interposed a black rectangle of nothingness between them and the nearest streetlight. At least she had not driven off without him; but then this was not a safe area, and Shannon would have known better than to invite a carjacking had she returned to her right mind as yet. There she sat, staring ahead, tears running down her pretty, pudgy face, smearing the tasteful makeup she was wearing for the occasion.

He tried verbal and physical blandishments. "Just don't!" she snapped, pushing him away as he pawed at her frigid form, loathing himself. At length she turned to face him and asked, "Why would you do something like that? I mean just how fucking insensitive are you!"

Again, he reminded her of their conversation of a month ago.

"Well obviously you thought it was a great idea!"

"Honestly, Shan, I thought you'd like it; I just went off what you said that day on Green Street."

"I can't believe you, Nick. You obviously don't know anything about me! Sure, you were listening when I said I wanted to lose weight, but you sure as hell weren't listening when I told you about what happened to me at school, for my sixteenth birthday . . ." Here fresh tears burst forth, and sobs took over. In fact, Nick knew very well what she was referring to. A group of girls—none other than the "cool" ones—had pitched in and bought her an exercise DVD, a suit of workout clothes two sizes too big, and a box of meal replacement shake powders. Shannon had been naïve enough to take their prior efforts to befriend her at face value. The worst part, apparently, was their insistence that the gesture truly had been one of friendship, and that she was simply ungrateful.

"I never want to eat again! I hate this body, it's disgusting!" She cried, beating her broad chest with those dainty little hands.

Still, Nick felt in his bowels that something must be done. And there was nothing he could do but attempt to vindicate himself with a return to the "lead by example" approach he had tried in the past. Unfortunately, this was complicated by the fact that he himself was naturally skinny, so presumably the example would have to be taken on a fairly abstract level. "You're so lucky, you can eat what you want," Shannon would regularly say. "You eat what you want anyway," Nick would think in reply.

She always maintained that she had tried every kind of physical exercise known to man and that all had failed. He had never known her to do much, however, although she had once gone through a phase of daily jogging paired with conventionally healthy eating, to no discernible effect. Nick wondered if secret junk food binges might not be the problem.

So he went ahead and worked out three to four times a week, over several weeks, increasing his calorie intake accordingly. Unfortunately, his hope that Shannon would follow his lead in the intended respect was frustrated, while she followed it readily enough in the other.

In terms of his own fitness, the results were coming along; he felt stronger and more confident, even if no one would yet mistake him for a body builder. He had even begun to toy with the idea of speaking frankly to her, perhaps even presenting an ultimatum. Meanwhile, she began to nag. He left his clothes in the bathroom; he was late home and failed to tell her; and worst of all, he tempted her with food she "shouldn't be eating."

She seemed so glum, staring at her fully trimmed baked potato one night and sighing, that he had to ask what was wrong.

"I've put on . . . I've gained so much weight lately!" There were tears in her eyes. Shannon never used numbers when talking about her weight. "Just about every night now you come home from the gym, and we have a big, rich meal like this, and I can't help myself, even though I know I shouldn't be eating like this."

"Sweetheart . . ." he commiserated, holding back.

"I know it's my fault. I should have more self-control," she added unexpectedly and with emotion. Ordinarily Nick would have interpreted this admission as a dangerous lure, but tonight seemed somehow a likely candidate for a significant occasion, a turning point in their relationship on which their much-improved future selves might look back fondly someday.

"Shanny, I didn't realise you were feeling this way." He took her hand across the table. It was limp and clammy with resentment and distrust, as well as self-recrimination. Still, he carried on. "Maybe you and I have different needs."

"What do you mean?" She flinched, and stared him in the face with prosecutorial intensity.

"What are you saying, Nick?"

He took a deep breath. "I'm just saying that carbs, like that potato there . . . I mean, if you want to lose weight—and that's your choice entirely, which I respect either way. But if you do, maybe you need to be on a different diet to me. I'm not saying go hungry, right? Just maybe base your diet on foods that lower blood-sugar and fill you up, like meat and non-starchy veg. You know the thing about carbs and insulin?" It was a topic he had been reading up on with great avidity.

"Well it's nice to know how you really feel about me, what you think our relationship should be based on! Here!" she stood up, "You might as well have my dinner too, since it's no good for me. I hope it makes you big and strong so you can leave me and find someone you're more attracted to some fucking gym bunny with a gap between her thighs!"

He could not eat another bite, as it happened. And his attendance at the gym began to suffer permanently after he skipped it to come home early with a tub of ice cream and a bunch of flowers the following day.

It was a month or two later that Shannon decided suddenly to return to university. Following a chance meeting, she proceeded to properly catch up with an old friend whom she had not seen for years, and who was now doing a PhD in gender studies. "Milly's out there learning and doing stuff she believes in, and what have I done since then except get my degree and stay in the same crappy job I've been doing for the last five years?" she exclaimed in the course of a debrief with Nick.

Got fatter, he thought lethargically.

She toyed with a few options. Her first degree had been in media and public relations, a field in which she had never worked (or, for that matter, really wanted to), instead winding up in her current job performing data entry for an importer-exporter. There was an option of going part-time in this role, however, and as it was Nick's job as a mid-ranking student services officer at Barton University that paid the majority of their bills, the impact on their standard of living would be minimal. While Shannon was deliberating over a range of vocationally unfocused options, from philosophy to visual art, she was also seeing more of her friend Milly and being introduced to the latter's circle.

Thus Shannon's eventual choice was to undertake a Graduate Diploma in Gender Studies.

She really took to her studies. Mounds of books piled up around the house, and on the credit card. She bought new, unflattering clothes and began to wear her reading glasses, which she exchanged for pink rimmed ones, as a fashion statement. (Nick awaited with trepidation the day when she would dye her hair some unnatural colour.) He saw less of her, and most of their time together was spent in front of the television, eating takeout dinners, after which she would retire to the office to study until late.

She was also getting bigger, though the data provided by Nick's eyes was hard to quantify, given both her continuing reticence on the subject and her habit of snipping the size tags off her clothes (which led him to suspect that, after all, she was less "body positive" than she made out).

One evening they were having Thai when Shannon snorted and spat a half-chewed noodle that landed on his knee.

"Can you believe that!" She was referring to a Weight Watchers' commercial in which a newly slender woman proclaimed: "I didn't just do it for me; I did it for all of us," meaning her family, among whom she was pictured smiling, kissing her husband, playing with her children, etc. "Anyone who doesn't recognise fat phobia as a form of acquiescence in patriarchal norms should just fucking watch this! Disgusting!"

He made sure her eyes remained focused on the set before flicking away the noodle. Little outbursts like this—and not so little—were becoming commonplace in their relationship. The plan had long been to start a family as soon as they could afford it; presumably it had now been superseded.

Once their social isolation had been shared, but now Shannon was deeply involved in her friends' and comrades' subculture. There was nothing secret about it, though; from the start Shannon wanted to draw him in, even as merely an inert prop. He got to know "the girls" and their assorted male and female partners in a largely observational capacity. At first these social occasions took place in coffee shops and bars around the locale of his workplace and Shannon's place of study, which were unfortunately the same.

It did not take long for his further induction to the group to proceed.

It appeared after all that there might be some truth in her assertion that "fat" people (as she had begun to identify herself) were as capable as anyone else of leading full, active lives. The evidence took the form of a flyer for a sort of theatrical show that Nick would have given much not to attend. "It's something some of my friends are starting up. Wanna come?"

FAT BURLESQUE

Come see Cellulite Cindy, Morgane the Man-Eater, Miley Walrus, and friends perform their inimitable and subversively arousing hits, including "You Look Good to Me," "Big Sunflower," "A Chocolate Affair," and "Feeding Time at the Zoo."

Join us for a decadent evening of body love and fat acceptance! Skinny folk are welcome, but in the event of a full house, be advised that you may be asked to sit in some lovely lady's ample lap!

The letters of the title were pink and shaped like fleshy clouds or cushions. The pictured performers tended to confirm Nick's worst apprehensions.

A fat woman tried to put a corset on an even fatter one, and both fell over in a pile. There was a type of pole-dancing which gave the impression that the pole was a necessary aid to the performer's standing up. Wearing an appropriate headdress, Morgane the Man-Eater sang an ode to her quite spectacular stretch marks entitled "My Tiger Stripes," at the culmination of which she performed some bestial actions with a male audience participant. Thank God it was someone else! Food, especially viscous dairy and chocolate, were frequent props, and indeed most of the show resembled more closely an eating contest than anything else Nick could think of.

Then there was the Miley Cyrus pastiche. The image of "Miley Walrus's" twerking buttocks would stay with him for a long time after. It was amazing what the woman was capable of making her flesh do; that big white, puckered rear looked like some obscene jellyfish or undiscovered deep-sea creature propelling itself through the ocean's depths.

After the show it was late. They were in a group of ten or so, mostly female, heading on to another bar or perhaps to a takeaway. That was the topic of conversation when someone whistled from the other side of the street. Because Nick always assumed people were looking and judging, he leapt to that assumption before steadying himself. It was probably nothing.

"More cushion for the pushin', eh boys!" More whistling.

"Come here and say that!" yelled Shannon, of all people. Nick experienced an attack of physical fear in addition to that of shame which he was already reeling from.

"Nah, you might eat me!" replied the drunken smart-aleck.

He took her by the hand, afraid that she would run across the street to attack.

Instead, someone whose name he had missed replied to the taunters with a beckoning gesture she had used in the show, "Don't be shy, honey, come on over here, and you can eat me!"

He had been to previous occasions such as this, but this was the first where the speaker was male. The title of the bearded hipster's paper was: "All Fat is the Lord's: A Comparative Study in Affective Labour and the Labile Materiality of Fat." In addition to the beard, the PhD candidate in question wore a side-part and large plugs in his distended ear lobes. Under a pink cardigan, his T-shirt displayed the slogan: "PIZZA ROLLS NOT GENDER ROLES."

". . . In contrast to the Western-Aristotelian discourse, in which fat is identified with hypertrophic excess in violation of the golden mean, so-called primitive peoples, such as the San of southern Africa, have constructed the fat body as a paradigmatic object of desire; similarly, other pre-modern and non-Western cultures have exulted fat itself as a signifier of abundance, health, and fertility, a fact underscoring the urgent need, as identified by Jomo-Gbomo and Levine, among others, to decolonise the health sciences . . ."

They were upstairs in the union building at the main campus in a large, carpeted room full of uncomfortable metal and plastic folding chairs. Some of the attendees used these, but most were empty, the heavier women sitting on bean bags or cushions on the floor that, he knew, had been brought along specially. The room stank of heterogeneous food aromas, and there was a constant accompaniment of chewing, swallowing, and slurping noises.

". . . The lability, indeed the volatility of fat, solid one moment and liquid or even gaseous the next, may to some extent explain the ambivalence in which it has long been held in Western culture . . ." Nick looked at Shannon, who appeared slightly clammy despite the fact that it was winter, and there was no, or from his point of view inadequate, heating. Nearby sat another woman whose eyeliner was running while her greasy pores struggled to breathe.

". . . A growing number of feminists, male, female, and non-binary, are now exploring the possibilities of a new frontier in affective labour and liberatory praxis in their personal relationships and communities. Many heterosexual, cisgender males now identify as 'fat admirers,' an orientation which, for all its rootedness in the human experiences of diverse peoples throughout multiple histories (and her-stories), is queered in mainstream discourse by reference to the dominant paradigm of female beauty in affluent, late capitalist society . . ."

Nick was horrified at the intimations of just what this "liberatory praxis" entailed. By the end of the paper, he was fully engrossed in the retrospective dissection of his life and the choices that had led him to be seated in this room, among these people, at this point in time.

After the talk came the Q&A. A woman with short, spiky hair, still reclining on her beanbag, spoke with the aid of dismissive hand gestures that caused her upper arms to wobble disgustingly. "I'd like to raise an issue with this anti-woman subculture you seem intent on sanitising and rebranding as some kind of feminism. I'm talking about these men who call themselves "fat admirers" and "feeders." In reality it's a lifestyle centred around the physical dependence of women on men, and the appropriation of the fat female body as yet another object of male desire and aggression. Obviously it's just another guise of patriarchy, just an exacerbation of the oppressive violence of the gender binary of active and passive roles. What have you got to say to that?"

The speaker was apparently timorous when not reading aloud an essay. He was obviously upset by the woman's aggressive tone, and his response sought to placate her by disavowing any sympathy for the undoubtedly dreadful, sexist, and exploitative practices she had in mind (although it was unclear to Nick, at least, just what the point of difference was supposed to be).

Then someone else spoke up: "I don't see it that way, Michelle. I'd argue that to interpret consensual feeder/feedee relationships as a form of 'violence' or 'oppression' buys into essentialist thinking and the valorisation of the medical gaze which construes the fat body as somehow inherently grotesque or deformed. Moreover, there's a vast intersectional literature, based on people's lived experiences, in support of the contention that these relationships can actually overturn the traditional gender binary in which, of course, the woman is scripted as exclusive nurturer and caregiver."

"Yes," someone else piped up, "and as a queer woman I'd like to add that I see value in the shift away from heteronormative genital sexuality in the eroticisation of the oral zone implied by feederism. And I'd just like to say, Michelle, that some people like myself find it really offensive when people like you presume to question our agency. We're actually adults who can make our own decisions!"

"Well *I* find it really offensive when people like you masquerade as feminists with these porno-chic burlesque shows of yours!"

It was on then. The room was quickly polarised between the radical feminists and the "Fat Burlesque" crowd, who were in the majority. The males, including the speaker, remained out of it, and Shannon as a novice member of the latter group allowed the more voluble and confident to speak for her.

Afterwards, in response to her enquiry, Shannon allowed Nick to get away with saying only that it had been "interesting."

They were returning from a dinner party at the home of one of "their" new friends.

"You were very quiet tonight."

"Aren't I always?"

There was an uneasy silence as they travelled through the night lit by fluorescent signs and occasional street lights that thinned out as they made their way home through the formerly industrial Western suburbs. The radio was chattering on low volume, providing half an excuse for silence, until Shannon switched it off.

"Ari and Sonia seem so in love," she reflected fondly.

"Yeah, they sure do." Ari had been feeding Sonia all night, teasing her with tidbits that got smeared across her face in the course of their game, and wiping her mouth with a napkin afterwards. Self-disgust at the life he had passively chosen overwhelmed Nick so that he almost forgot to stop at the traffic lights, hitting the brake suddenly so that they jolted forwards in their seats.

"Geez," Shannon exclaimed, "careful!"

"Yeah, the way he was shovelling that cake into her. Jesus Christ!" Nick said, heart pounding as the words found their own way out past the censor, hissing and crackling in his consciousness and hers, like oil poured into an overheated pan.

"What do you mean?"

"I don't know . . . Actually yes I do. I mean where is that guy's self-respect?" He smacked his palms against the wheel and stared straight ahead, gritting his teeth and tensing his bowels.

There was a shocked pause before Shannon replied. He could feel her eyes on him. "Oh my God, Nick! That's a horrible thing to say!" It was as if she were genuinely shocked to the core of her moral being, offended not just personally, as before on those rare occasions when he had overstepped the mark in coaxing her towards self-care, but on behalf of humanity itself.

"I hope you don't mean what I think you mean!" she added.

"I don't know what you think or where you get your ideas from any more, Shannon," he replied with more dignity and coherence than he would have thought possible (even though, of course, he knew far more than he wanted to).

"Well I don't know how you can be so prejudiced, so downright hostile towards our friends, when by now you should understand enough about fat phobia and the harm it causes. Or maybe you still don't understand. Maybe you never will."

"Yeah, maybe not."

Finding her still frigid towards him almost twenty-four hours later, he predictably truckled and, to make it up to her, bought a tub of her favourite rocky road ice cream. He was relieved to find that a verbal recantation and lengthy reassurance was not required. Her confidence really had grown of late.

Towards the end of the academic year, a certain doyenne of Fat Studies from the US, Professor Jaz Huffington, had come at the group's invitation to speak to and dine with them in the course of her tour to promote her latest book, a popularising tome entitled *The Fat Feminist Cookbook: A Recipe for Equality and World Peace!* It had received much coverage in the mainstream media, drawing endorsements from the likes of Rebel Wilson and Gabourey Sidibe, and doing more than anyone since Linda Bacon's *Health At Every Size* to further the agenda of politicised gluttony. Shannon admitted she was star-struck, though that did not stop her from participating in the discussion while he just sat there, for all intents and purposes alone with his thoughts. Despite looking to Nick very much like a heavily pregnant bulldog, thirty-two-year-old Huffington moonlighted as a plus-sized model, and the cover of her book showed her being hand-fed a chocolate-covered strawberry by her very much in-shape, negro husband.

Nobody minded about Nick's silence; by now they knew him as well as they ever would. There had been jokes bandied about representing him as an "ornamental" or "trophy" man, he knew, and was only grateful to be exempt from having to endlessly agree with the absurdities that were passed around the circle like an electric current waiting to be lethally grounded should he ever succumb to the temptation to open his mouth and speak his mind. He was also grateful not to have to hand feed Shannon on this occasion, except for the odd token mouthful from his own plate, if only because the copious food was for once not the main focus of her attention.

Huffington was holding forth: ". . . The problem with HAES, as constructive as it's been, is the latent essentialism in this notion of a 'set-point weight.' What I argue is that we need to distance ourselves from *any* discourse of biological determinism whatsoever, so that we come to view the pathologisation of fat on a level with phrenology and racist pseudo-science . . ." Those around her, including Shannon, listened, agreed, and amplified her pronouncements.

Nick looked around him at the couples at the banquet table. No order was being observed between courses. They had been eating for an hour or so, and some were onto dessert, while others were still filling up on pizza and pasta, or carving up steaks and schnitzels. And all the while talking with their mouths open.

It was small comfort that there were couples more grotesque than he and Shannon in attendance. Looking at her profile he noticed with anguish the beginnings of a web of broken capillaries starting to appear in between her crows' feet and triple chin. She had started ageing, fast.

Nick was feeling crazy, like he was about to do or say something unadvisable. He excused himself and went to the toilet, where the nauseating smells of food were suddenly overridden by lilac-scented air freshener. Here he locked himself in a stall, and tears began to flow, silently at first, then audibly. He could not go on like this, he whispered to himself. But knew this to be untrue. He could and he would, despite everything and despite himself. He noticed that he was feeling quite dizzy. It was not alcohol: he had always been a teetotaller.

Shannon had never been perfect, but under the fat rolls she was a pretty girl. She could even have been striking, with those black Irish looks of hers, and what in its natural state would surely have been a good figure. On some level, though his discomfort had grown steadily (more or less apace with her actual weight gain) in the course of the relationship, he had always felt fortunate to be with her, and thus responsible for correcting this one great shortcoming that was, after all, a kind of judgement upon him as well.

When he emerged, conversations were of course continuing in that pseudo-intellectual gibberish of theirs. But as he staggered towards the big table, surprisingly, the sounds grew no clearer: now not a single English word or phoneme was isolable in the noise coming out of their mouths. It was as though here was in an aviary full of flightless birds—or giant, bird-voiced slugs—twittering, cawing, and screeching at each other through vocal chords of a completely alien type.

The waiters were still human, though, and could not help

staring in dismay at the menagerie that had invaded their workplace and was likely to riot when the food inevitably ran out. As invisible as Nick felt to the erstwhile women around him and the weird little insectoid symbionts they carried in tow, he felt the embarrassment of being stared at by those normal humans who numbered him among the aliens. He had felt it before—always felt it when they were out in public, to some degree—but now it was excruciating. A lovely girl of about twenty in her whites stood under a picture of the Leaning Tower of Pisa in the alcove that led to the kitchen, thinking she was out of sight and furtively texting her romantically normal boyfriend the gruesome details of the sight before her. He could hear her thoughts as she composed the message in her mind. "OMFG u shd see this! Sooo sorry i got mad when u teased me bout my luvhandles . . ."

The room itself was unchanged; there were still the same eclectic postcard pictures—the Leaning Tower, a villa in Tuscany or somewhere, the New York skyline, the Rat Pack, some guy who in a different context might have been comically fat shovelling pasta into his mouth in a black-and-white movie still. But around the long table everything was evaporating into something suggestive of smoke curling from a couple dozen giant, invisible cigarettes. There was a smell of something impure, like dried dung or plastic, burning.

The wisps of smoke coalesced in the shape of grotesquely obese bodies. And Nick noticed with shock that the plume rising nearest him was perhaps the fattest of them all. He had believed the opposite; even taken some kind of pride in the knowledge that at least his case was not the saddest of all, that there were other couples more depraved. It made sense now. That time she had fallen over and not been able to get up; the way he would invariably wake up on top of her in their king-sized bed; those times (increasingly rare) when they had gone outside together by day, and her shadow had seemed too big for her, and people had stared and stared.

He squinted into the smoky shape beside him as it grew increasingly translucent like a vessel of blown glass, simultaneously starting to reveal something inside: something big and dark, of ambiguous outline. It seemed to be moving in a complex, self-propelled way, almost filling the glassy bulb of Shannon's body. The tendrils were dark and glistening.

Shannon's translucent face swung around. He could make out her expressive brows, whitely pencilled-in, it seemed, enabling him to answer her monstrous gaze with his own. "Nick, what's the matter? Why are you staring like that? You look sick!" He understood that this was the meaning of the noises she—or perhaps *it*—made with its alien voice box. When she reached out what was supposed to be a hand to his face, he flinched violently and fell over backwards.

When he woke up, Nick could understand more or less every word Shannon said, the first of which were, "Oh Nicky, there you are! Poor baby!" He was looking up at the ceiling of the restaurant, and Shannon was looking down at him, human concern and even love apparent in her face. She looked just like the wheelchair bound hundred-odd kilo woman she ostensibly was. In reality, he knew, she was much larger.

He had fainted, that was all, and been unconscious for about five minutes. The ambulance arrived, but Nick insisted that he felt fine. He would go for a check-up the next day, which revealed no cause for concern.

Still, over the days that followed there were some residual echoes of what he had seen at the restaurant, not a moment of which had he forgotten. If he cleared his mind of preconceptions, he could see, in spectral outline like a soap bubble surrounding her, the outline of Shannon's true body, just catching the light at times. And perhaps as a result of this perceptual breakthrough, what was more horrible, he could touch her true flesh, feel its clammy, pillowy unwholesomeness like an aura around her false form. What did others see, he wondered? He tried not to flinch at her touch.

"Nick, can you give me my painkillers? It's really sore tonight; can you give me three instead of two?"

Shannon had been prescribed oxycodone for the pain in her leg. In addition, Nick had got himself prescribed Xanax for the sleeping problems he described in his check-up at the doctor following the episode at the restaurant. How much would be necessary was hard to know, given his uncertainty both about Shannon's true size—not to mention how much of that bulk was indeed hers.

He crushed two more of the opioids together with two of the other and put them in the bottom of a bowl-sized cup. He then added chocolate buds, sugar, cinnamon, chili, and a pinch of salt. It tasted slightly bitter so he added more sugar and confirmed that he had achieved the right balance with another tiny sip. He then served the drink to her in bed.

"Oh, Nicky, what did you put in this? It's so good!"

"Just three, like you said."

She gulped it down.

"I'm so tired," said Nick. "It's been a hell of a week."

"I know." She reached over to stroke his forehead, and he did his best not to flinch. Soon she was fast asleep, snoring like a grampus.

The obvious approach was simply to leave her where she lay and prevent her from getting out.

When he heard her snoring, Nick prodded, shoved, and shook her to make sure. Then he got up and removed Shannon's wheelchair to the living room. That was the main thing; she had no other means of unassisted mobility. There were two possible exits: door and window. The window fronted onto the backyard, so with the high fence no one would be able to see her distress. All things considered, though, he was going to have to monitor her just about constantly. Fortunately, he had a couple of weeks leave owing at work which he had been urged to take as soon as possible. One week was probably the limit before people started getting suspicious, however.

Surely she was fast asleep, but still his heart pounded as he contemplated what she would think, say, or do, should his efforts wake her up. He had bought a hog-tie device from a sex shop that was easy to fasten without the need for any skill in tying knots. He held his breath through the nerve-wracking process of turning her over, arms behind her back, and legs bent up. If she woke up her assumption would be that he was trying to make love to her (though he had not initiated sex in a long time). He panicked for a moment when it sounded as though she were mumbling something; it was when he handled her sore leg. But no, she slept on.

He made sure her head was tilted to one side, and lovingly gagged her with a strip torn from one of the bed sheets. She would thank him, he knew, if she survived.

It was almost noon. Pacing up and down the hallway on his tiptoes, Nick worried about the absence of any noise from the bedroom. Maybe he had given one too many painkillers? He opened the door slowly so as not to disturb her.

"Shannon . . . ?"

There was no reply. Her face was just as he had so vividly imagined it, half-buried in bedclothes, but the eye was closed. Was she breathing? Images of her leaving in a body bag and him in police custody flashed through his mind again. He approached and took a closer look at her face. Her eyes were closed. They were closed *tight*.

"Shannon . . . you're awake."

Then the eye opened. He tried to give the speech he had intended, that would explain and justify his actions, but in seconds she was screaming with all her might into the gag. She was outraged, and he could feel it vividly as if their roles were reversed. She was calling him unintelligible names. Struggling. Threatening. But after all, no one would hear, and she could hardly get very far, even if she managed to roll onto the floor.

"Careful, you'll hurt yourself if you fall." Having backed off a couple of steps, he now advanced and sat down next to her on the bed as either her energy ran out, or she realised the truth of his warning.

"Shannon, I've seen what's inside you, and you just have to trust me. It's up to me to help you, since you can't see the problem yourself; but you must feel it, deep down."

No response. Just the frightened, accusing eye. Perhaps she did know?

Nick had never felt so in control. Bit by bit, emboldened as he went on, he took advantage of the situation to unburden himself, telling her all that he had wanted to for so long. After a while the tears started, and he thought that they might even have been tears of contrition. But it would have been yielding too much to remove the gag on the first day.

She became more pliable as time went on, and although she had abused him the first time he took the gag out, the second time she instantly began begging for food, in addition to the water he had brought. It did not take long for pathos to set in; she was a recovering addict, after all. "Please, Nicky, I can feel my stomach digesting itself . . . !" Her voice was so weak and pathetic Nick could hardly bear it. "Don't do this to me, Nicky! I love you, don't you love me?" He patiently explained that even a person of normal weight could last up to a month with no food. Her eyes bulged in terror.

"Please Nicky, Please! I'll go on any diet you want. I'll try the Atkins again, go to the gym—"

"No, Shannon. I'm sorry. The creature that's inside you wouldn't allow it. We have to kill that parasite so that you can live."

Her hysteria was such that he had to put the gag back in. Interestingly, if he read her response aright, she had not actually seemed *surprised* at his statement. Did her lack of explicit denial mean that she knew?

It was hard to stay firm, though, when changing her diaper and washing her backside as he had to do for the first few days, uncuffing one hand in order to turn her on her side so that he could reach the baby wipes into her crevices with gloved hands. She was compliant at these times, but would plead unceasingly for freedom, for something to eat, until he had to put the gag back in so as not to weaken. Then her tears would plead silently. For her comfort, he would turn her onto one side or the other from time to time, releasing either her feet or her hands from the hog tie, but never both at once.

After five days she became incoherent and began singing catches of songs in a high, tuneless voice. It was still enough to wake him from his light sleep in the living room on the fold-out. He wanted as far as possible and practicable to suffer with her, the woman he loved. He had taken to sitting in a kitchen chair at her bedside throughout most of the day.

The next development was that she started to complain of something which she referred to only as "it," "eating her inside."

Inside Shannon was a dark, tangled forest. The branches of blood and nerves were there, of course, and the internal organs pertaining to her own proper organism; but then, coiled among them like a serpent was something that, he feared, might not possess independent corporeal existence and so not respond to the starvation treatment. Its wriggling behaviour was like that of a worm; a hookworm perhaps, that Nick was aware could grow to an enormous size and devour as much food as a normal human. But then, he reflected, people thus afflicted did not gain weight; they grew emaciated. The implications terrified him . . .

And her family and friends were messaging her on her phone and on social media. He replied, but it would only be so long before they would need to hear her voice.

He looked up on the Internet ways of luring parasites out of the body. He tried leaving a steak in her diaper, then, when that failed, with greater trepidation he tried the other end of her digestive tract. He had to pin Shannon down to keep her from biting at the meat; she was salivating uncontrollably, choking on it, but too weak to struggle. He tried bread and cake as well, without success.

He sat beside her, staring for hours on end, trying to renew and deepen his first insight, to see through to her insides as clearly as he had done back in the restaurant. Meanwhile, probably the opiates she was taking on an empty stomach were contributing to her incoherence. The last non-delirious thing she had said was a day ago: "Please, I'm so hungry . . ." Now only inarticulate sounds escaped her as she lay staring back at him in a trance beyond hunger. They reminded him of the horrible twittering of the creature he had seen back then. His intention was not to sedate it, though, but to drive it out. That meant unfortunately that Shannon would have to do without any more pain relief, too.

He had tried worming tablets, then more worming tablets, then more again. They only made a mess and augmented her pain—though he could see the worm writhing as well. It got so bad that he had to reinstate her gag, long after he had thought her too weak to scream.

Then, on day nine, an intelligence seemed to take hold of her. Nick was woken by a wheedling voice that chilled him utterly, it seemed so unlikely now after eight days and nights of steady decline in his captive's articulacy. "Nick . . . Nick . . . please can you come here for a minute? I need to talk with you. I'm willing to be reasonable."

He came, stopping by the kitchen to collect a heavy frying pan with trembling hand, not knowing what might be awaiting him behind that bedroom door.

But no, it was Shannon as he had grown used to seeing her, on her side, bound as before, hair tangled in sweaty black strands that criss-crossed her beautiful yet still chubby face. Her voice was thin and pained but clear as she called out to him once again, just as he began cautiously opening the door on the dark bedroom. The bluish light of the nearly full moon found its way in around the edges of the blinds that were pulled down over both windows. It reflected off the water glass beside the bed and the pallor of the bed sheets.

"Nick, you've done enough. You've tried everything you can, unless you're actually going to starve me to death." She stopped, breathing heavily. "I know you think there's something inside me, some parasite that's taken me over. I don't know, maybe you're right. But if it's true, can't you see I'm its victim? You don't want to punish me anymore, do you? Look, how about we stop this, and you take me to hospital so they can run some tests? If there's some kind of parasite, they'll find it, right?"

Nick slowly shook his head, making no effort to conceal the frying pan that he held against his thigh. "No." he whispered, decisively. It was not her speaking, he understood.

"I'm sorry," he said, and went to close the door.

"Nicky, if you don't take me to the hospital I'll die. I haven't eaten for over a week!" Her voice was straining to stay calm, human. As he withdrew, no-longer repressed emotion flooded into her voice. "You can't keep me here like this forever! I know my mother's been calling; by now she knows something's happened to me!"

It was true, and he knew that the Facebook message about going camping out of phone range was a thin one. He updated it with another message about having had a bag containing both their phones stolen. It was lucky that Shannon's parents lived several hours away, in the country, and were not particularly nosy. In case anyone came snooping around, though, he had parked the car in another street.

"Look, I know I was wrong about all that fat acceptance stuff! You were right to put a stop to it, Nick. It was just rationalisation, and I was being selfish expecting you accept me being so fat I couldn't even walk. I understand why you've done this, and I want to change, Nicky, for both of us! I'm sorry, I'm sorry . . ." She started crying. "I'll try paleo properly this time; no cheating, I swear!"

The next morning Shannon did not wake up at the usual time. She might almost have been dead but for a scarcely perceptible oscillation of the chest.

Inside her was quartered the parasite whose dark shape Nick could once more see as her body dematerialised under his famished gaze. Instead of a worm, he now perceived it as something more like a centipede: one of those long-legged ones he sometimes found in the bath; except that the legs themselves had legs, and these in turn had legs . . . In other words, the thing had a root system! All black, blue, crimson, and purple it was, in the X-ray light of his supernatural vision. As he had feared without daring to fully articulate it to himself, Nick now saw that the parasite was completely intertwined with Shannon's own nervous and vascular systems. She was like a tree infested with mistletoe; so much so that it was impossible to tell who was actually breathing right now. Shannon might be dead already, or soon to die.

There was his sleeping beauty, pale lips parted, her broad chest and broader abdomen rising and falling so peacefully. Had she lost weight? Some, no doubt, though any dramatic contrast was lost on him, keeping watch on her day by day. Could she die of starvation while remaining overweight? Surely not; but at the same time, this could not go on forever. Nick guessed at the danger to himself; he had seen *The Exorcist*; but he would gladly have sacrificed himself if it came to that.

He placed the sugared tea and the shortbread on the nightstand, then dipped the teaspoon into the cup and withdrew it, pregnant with opalescent liquid. This he carried to Shannon's mouth in his trembling hand which somehow did not spill a drop until the tip of the spoon reached her bottom lip. Yes, he was sure.

A gasp. A moan. A pair of wide open eyes. Was this some kind of trap? they seemed to ask. But now that she had tasted it, how she wanted more! Her neck craned up from the pillow and her tongue popped out, desperately seeking another taste. As so often, there were tears in her eyes. "It's okay, sweetheart. There's plenty more. You've suffered enough, Shanny." He gave her spoonful after spoonful until she calmed down, and the apparent suspicion in her eyes subsided before they closed. Nourishment was the only thing on her mind.

Then he dipped the biscuit in the remainder of the tea until it almost dissolved, and gave it to her. This time she looked at him as though all conflict between them were forgotten. Yes, she loved him no less than he her.

"Here you go. A special treat."

In that moment she bore him no ill will for the torture inflicted on her. She was a baby at its mother's teat. And in that state, she fell into a deep sleep: the deepest since the start of her confinement.

Nick wiped away his tears, knowing that the beautiful moment was now past.

It was up to him to discover whether Shannon and the creature that had at some point taken possession of her body and mind were truly inextricable, or not. So he thought, holding in his trembling hand the scalpel that would be his equivalent of the Prince Charming's sword to commence cutting through the malignant forest to the clearing where, he prayed, his love lay waiting.

I Say!

The presenter's name tag identified her as a Marie. Yes, she was that type: Mediterranean extraction, a little brashly spoken, and wearing a not displeasingly tight skirt and blouse. Probably in the midst of planning an expensive wedding followed by a Grecian honeymoon with her well-to-do tradesman fiancé. Her eyes met his, and Linus glanced down at the paper she had given him. From each pair, choose the word that describes you best. At least this place was better than the last job agency he had been allocated. There, his case worker had really got on his case, threatening him with a tele-sales job and showing little sympathy when he had brought up his documented history of depression and anxiety. The man's suggestion that he needed to "get over himself" had given Linus the excuse he needed to call Centrelink and complain of discrimination.

"Excuse me, what's this word? I never seen it before."

"Which word, hon? Oh, you mean 'neutral'?"

"Does it mean, like, 'new'? It sounds like 'new.'" The girl in the front row said in tones that suggested she might have a hearing impairment. Marie gave her a few moments of one-on-one help, while her pupil exclaimed like a dull child who wants to be the teacher's pet, "Oh, I see" (with a lisp: "Oh, I thee!") and "Thank you!" repeatedly.

He had not noticed her before: those ample blond locks that fell loosely over her pink-gold shoulders resembled nothing so much as threads of silk. (Linus was proud of his talent for literary description, but had to acknowledge that sometimes the cliché was available for a reason.) He had noticed her from the first, though without having got a proper look at before she seated herself in front of him, partially obscured by someone's obese back. But now he caught a glimpse of a profile too gorgeous to belong in a place like this.

With girls like that, seen from behind at the traffic lights or in the next corral at the library, fleetingly or not full-face, Linus always wished that they would not turn out on closer inspection to be as desirable as they appeared. Yes, the hair was perfect, the sweep of the figure promising, but what about the face, the bust . . . ? So much could go wrong with only a handful of variables. And it was a relief to find out that the girl with gorgeous rear view had a witch's nose, a flat chest, etc. Otherwise he would have to accuse himself of letting his destiny walk away at least once every day.

"You . . . f-find . . . it . . . e-asy to . . . i-int . . ." The object of his interest was hunched over her test, shoulders bunched up next to her ears in a caricature of awkward application, raw silk strands sweeping the undeserving desk as she repeatedly, ineffectually tucked them behind an exquisite ear. Linus could just make out her profile at this acute angle, and it was very promising. But seriously, was she playing some kind of joke, talking like a retard? Of course, being semi-illiterate had not implied a mental handicap historically, but what excuse was there these days? The managerial state had a lot to answer for, not the least of which was teaching everyone with an IQ above 70 how to read.

He was now quite lathered up. To himself, out loud but under his breath, Linus exclaimed as he often did when registering female beauty: "I say!" It was an old-fashioned Anglicism that he had privately adopted from somewhere or other; and then, because he was haphazardly studying Greek in his spare time when not working on his novel, he translated to himself, "*lego*!" from there preceding to contemplate that mysterious, catch-all metaphysical term that was its cognate. Yes, physically here was the very *logos* of womanhood. She was the divine word alright; but then, once more, she opened her mouth.

"Excuse me, teacher," she said, one syllable at a time, to the leathery looking woman beside her ("Eth-cooth me"), "Can you please tell me what this word is? I'm not very good at reading!"

"In-tro-duce. It says you find it very easy to introduce yourself to others."

"Oh!" she said, as if these words had been a revelation. "Thank you!"

"You can call me Fi-fi," said the girl to her neighbour in that dull, deaf-sounding voice of hers, "That's what my friends call me. Some people think it's short for something but it's not; it's just Fi-fi. What's your name?"

"Lisa," the woman next to her answered in the husky voice of a heavy smoker. "See?" she added, presumably pointing to the adhesive strip on which she, along with everyone else, had written her name on arrival. "You've got one too!"

"Oh, it's got your name there!" She laughed, a surprisingly pretty sound. "Sorry Lisa, I got no nous!" And she laughed like a donkey.

No *nous* indeed! The kind of thing a grandparent might say when scolding a child . . . Intelligence, good looks, and grace usually went together, both in Linus' personal experience and in theory, since evolutionary theory predicts that the most successful men would reproduce with the most physically attractive women, given the typical mating preferences of each gender. (Most people were incapable of thinking frankly about such things, he knew, and he took pride in the fact that he was an exception.) Nor, incidentally, was Linus a supporter of the counterfactual "dumb blonde" trope.

But notwithstanding these considerations, if the girl was not mentally retarded, she must be both autistic and dyslexic, or something of that type.

Predictably enough, as the results to the personality test came in, it turned out that the room was full of "creatives." For example, the woman who had charitably assisted Fi-fi turned out to be quite garrulous, talking at some length about her punk-inspired clothing design business, "Rusty Blade Couture."

"Excuse me," Fi-fi interrupted, raising her hand like a schoolgirl and addressing the presenter. Linus gulped at the perfect globe of the breast thus revealed, ". . . But I just want to get a waitress job. I got experience," she added, as though having been coached to do so, "and everybody says I'm a real people-person. I did a practice thing, like, what do you call where, like, you work but you don't get paid? At Café Ba . . . Ba-cio, you know?" She giggled at her difficulty, a little more delicately than before. "But they didn't let me have a job. So, like, is there any waitress jobs you know that I can have?"

Linus knew the dive Fi-fi mentioned, Café Bacio. They served tomato paste, cheese, and mystery meat on under-cooked gluten disks, as well as alcohol, and they were open all night. It was unheard-of to eat or drink anything there unless everywhere else was closed and you were very drunk.

Marie took a moment to compose herself. "Well, I'm sure there'd be somewhere you could get a job waitressing, Fi-fi. Have you had a look on the job search websites? I can show you—"

"Can you please look at my résumé, please? I brung it to show you!" She waved a sheet of paper.

Fi-fi engrossed the presenter's time for a few minutes, while the others looked at the time and realised that their hour's detention had been served, then began slipping off in silence. Linus stuck around, pretending to look at the crinkled, week-old newspaper on a table nearby, his heart pounding as he stole repeated glances at the girl; glances that overwhelmingly confirmed and magnified his impression of her pulchritude.

"Listen, it was lovely to meet you but I've got to go," said Marie, shouldering her bag and gripping Fi-fi's forearm patronisingly to wish her a "good luck, hon."

"Thank you, uh, what was your name again . . . ? Oh, right. I hope you have a really great day, Marie! I hope I see you again, 'cause you're nice!" she said before bending down to pick up her own bag, angling her rear end advantageously from Linus' point of view, who both to optimise his angle of view and to look busy, had made his way over to the computer bench that ran along the side of the room and turned on one of the wheezing, grunting machines. The noise got her attention, and their eyes met. She smiled every bit as ingenuously as he might have hoped.

It was the first full-face view he had got, and it was like staring into the Sun. Her skin was perfect: fair, yet lightly tanned to a delicate, even glaze, as though basted with honey. She was plump in the best, non-euphemistic sense of the word, and her mammary endowment was nothing short of extraordinary: under the hot pink singlet top she was wearing it was plentifully apparent that she wore no bra, and had no need of one. She looked somewhere around eighteen or twenty.

His heart was beating tremulously. She looked like a porn addict's distorted recollection of the woman who, in his self-pitying moments, Linus still credited with having ruined his life just over a year ago. He suffered from a kind of sentimental superstition that every woman he had been with had taken, permanently, a little of his personal essence away, and given only temporary pleasure in return. He was like a toothpaste tube that had been slowly rolled up from the bottom, a little more used up with each memorable night.

But this one seemed to require so little investment; she was the very incarnation of fun, of *jouissance* (in a sense owing nothing to the charlatan Lacan, of course).

Linus made up his mind and called after her as nonchalantly as he could manage, "Hey there, Fi-fi!"

She turned, a slightly startled but unsuspicious look on her face.

Linus smiled as reassuringly as possible. "So, I couldn't help overhearing. You want to work in hospitality?"

She looked confused.

"I mean waitressing. You want to be a waitress?"

"Oh yes! Have you got a job for me?"

Oh yes, he certainly did. He could see the pinkish brown at the edge of an areola peeking out the top of her décolletage. Linus forced his gaze upwards, taking the cigarette from behind his ear that he had already rolled, eager to light up and assuage his nerves once they were outside. He tried not to look shifty as his eyes darted around to ascertain if anyone was watching with disapproval.

"You got a minute? Or is someone waiting for you?"

"Oh no, I'm by myself," she said candidly.

"Come on then, let's walk and talk, Fi-fi." They headed down one flight of fire stairs past the broken elevator and out onto the street. Linus deflected her eagerness to talk about jobs by mentioning that she reminded him of someone; did she know him? Had they ever met? Where had she gone to school? (The latter question was craftily designed to gauge whether she had noticed the difference in their ages.) She claimed not to have gone to school at all. "That's why I can't read good!" she giggled.

Even to his smoke-damaged sinuses she smelled like ripe fruit and flowers, and moreover like ripe girl-flesh. It was intoxicating.

"Don't be so hard on yourself. There are different kinds of intelligence: verbal, spatial, mathematical, practical . . ." he waffled dizzily.

"Wow, you know lots of big words." It was about the truest comment anyone had ever made about him. "You shouldn't smoke, it's bad for you," she added with pantomime sternness.

"So you don't want one then? Everyone smokes in hospitality, don't you know?"

"Really?"

"Oh yeah, it's like a requirement for the job. I used to wait tables myself, still do on occasion." Careful, careful, must demonstrate high value! "Then I was a bartender. You can take it from me, it comes with the territory." He gave her what he hoped was a winning smile.

"Comes with the . . . ?"

"Smoking. You have to smoke if you want to be a waitress. It's that simple. If they ask you in the interview do you smoke, you'd better say yes."

"Really?"

"Uh-huh."

"Okay . . ." Fi-fi took the cigarette, and her baffled expression resolved into a smile. Linus lit his and held out the flame. She responded by holding it out towards him, apparently not understanding that it was necessary to put the other end in her mouth and inhale at the same time as it was lit. His fingers tingled as he touched her hand in the process of setting her straight, gaze fixed on those glistening lolly-lips that hung slightly open, so trusting, so silly in every sense.

She coughed, bending forwards violently from the waist. When her beautiful face came up again it was cherry red, and its expression was that of a scolded, uncomprehending child. He put a hand on her shoulder. Static electricity from her top, or perhaps another kind, zapped all the way through his body, but he did not withdraw it.

"Are you okay?" he grunted huskily.

"I don't like it," she whimpered, finally, as her breath returned. Fi-fi handed the cigarette back to him as if it would bite her. "I can't do it. I tried, but I can't do it! Can I still have a job, though, please?" She might have been close to tears.

"Of course you can Fi-fi! I was just joking about you having to smoke." Linus exclaimed with unfeigned compassion, and rubbing her back.

"You're mean!"

"I know. But I promise I'll be nice from here on. Shake hands?"

Wow, still tingling.

My friend owns a café. I'm sure he'll give you a job on my recommendation. You may have heard of the place? It's called Four Walls."

"That's a funny name!" She literally laughed. "No, where is it?"

"Well I could just give you directions, but it's tricky to find. Are you doing anything right now? I think my friend's hiring at the moment." As he said this Linus realized he could just as easily have made himself the owner.

"No, I'm not doing anything. Can we go there right now? I don't want him to get someone else to be a waitress!"

"No problem. Let's go."

They started walking. A moment later she turned to him and said, "Excuse me but what's your name?"

"Oh that's right, I haven't said. I'm Gerrard. Gerry." Yes, he was going to lie, having had the foresight to have removed the name tag earlier on. He had not known with certainty that he would do so, however, until the false name was out of his mouth, the image of his old philosophy lecturer, Gerry Nicholson (a firm proponent of hard determinism), flitting across his mind.

"I'm Fi-fi," she said despite the fact he had already addressed her by name, and her name tag was still in place. Then she asked, "Is black your favourite colour?"

"Pardon?"

"Pink's my favourite colour. That's why I got this pink top on. You like my pink top?" Whoops! He had been staring. "I just bought it at this shop. Oh, I can't remember what it was called, but there was lots of pretty clothes. When I get a job I'm gonna buy lots and lots of pretty clothes and things that's pink."

"You must have read my mind, Fi-fi: I love it," he said a little too enthusiastically, perhaps; but then, were the usual courtship rules in any sense applicable where favourite colours were a topic of discussion?

"Well, black's my favourite colour because I'm a pretentious intellectual."

"What's that?"

"Someone who wears black all the time and isn't a goth or a biker." She looked confused. "Don't worry."

"You're funny!" she giggled as the thought lines dissipated. "I think you must be smart, Gerry, cause you talk big words, and you make jokes I don't understand. I like you."

God, why could not every interaction with a woman be so ingenuous, so full of joy and promise?

"Oh, thank you . . . what's your name again? Sometimes I don't remember good."

Perhaps she had suffered a traumatic head injury? Not that he could talk: one of the ways Linus habitually and unintentionally demonstrated his disinterest in boring people was by forgetting their names. He hoped that was not the reason for Fi-fi's forgetfulness. "That's okay. Gerry. Short for Gerrard. You'll have to work on remembering names when you're waiting tables!"

She laughed. "I got that joke; that was a funny one, Gerry! Sometimes I say stuff without thinking about it first." She paused, then added: "You're a nice person, Gerry. I'm so glad I met you. When we first met, I knew you was going to help me!" She beamed, hanging onto his sleeve, her breast almost touching his arm.

He smiled. "It's just over the street and a few blocks—"

Then, to Linus's astonishment, she took his hand. "You should hold my hand, Gerry, so I don't get run over."

His blood effervesced.

Four Walls was a place he used to frequent when he was making enough, between the scholarship and the tuition, to afford an overpriced beer or two and a shot at picking up. One of many little nightspots that would under no circumstances be open at three in the afternoon. But his silly darling would not know that. As they walked the couple of blocks together up the busy thoroughfare, he felt all eyes on them; he could taste the jealousy, the incomprehension. Why Fi-fi wanted to waitress was beyond him; she could have a soft-core website and retire by the age of twenty-five—maybe he could be her manager. Or perhaps there was someone she knew and looked up to who did that.

"Oh no, it's closed!" Linus exclaimed. "I thought we could have a drink, and I'd introduce you to my friend, the owner."

"Oh, no!" Fi-fi echoed, her mouth hanging slightly open in what looked like a pantomime of dismay.

"Well, what are you doing now? Are you busy? I think they open in a couple of hours, so maybe—"

"Hey Gerry, I got an idea: let's go to my house!" Fi-fi exclaimed, recovering her spirits.

Her place, eh? Linus was about to suggest his. But did she live with her parents? With someone, at any rate, who looked after her and took a dim view of saturnine would-be sexual exploiters of whom there had probably been quite a few already? He almost asked if she lived alone, but thought better of it. She might yet conceivably be capable of being spooked.

Fi-fi explained that she lived in an upstairs apartment just ahead on North Road, the same long thoroughfare they were currently travelling. It was a dingily inner-suburban shopping strip that grew dingier and more Middle-Eastern in the direction they were headed. He had once rented a bedsit around here from an elderly Italian lady who evidently had had no notion of the contemporary value of real estate. This provided some fuel for conversation, though Linus was unable to prompt Fi-fi to divulge anything further about her living arrangements.

The place, when they reached it, was a familiar sight: he had walked or trammed past it innumerable times, and it was paradigmatic of the forlorn, ghostly little shopfronts of this area. Behind the dusty windows, bearing old Coke signs and rendered with hand-painted renditions of pizza, giros, and hamburger, lay all the appurtenances of a disused takeaway bar.

To Linus's semi-surprise, Fi-fi inserted the key into the front door and entered that way. To one side of the counter, whose dust coating trumped that of the windows, there was a corridor leading past what was probably the store room and a toilet to a staircase, carpeted in something so badly worn out it resembled hessian. The place was frowsty. Linus hung back, getting an eyeful as Fi-fi went up ahead of him. She was wearing a tight, black and pink striped skirt that from this angle just about revealed the parting of her buttocks as her hips jolted from side to side like a well-freighted hull on a stormy sea—but oh, it was watertight. Yes, Linus had noticed before that her manner of walking was like her manner of talking: endearingly, temptingly gauche and unselfconscious.

The apartment was a total mess: a combination of mouldy, toilet and compost smells—really quite unpleasant, though if he stood close by his hostess the effect was ameliorated. Linus could hear and see flies buzzing around, especially in the kitchen but also in the living room, where there were several dirty plates, bowls, and mugs on the coffee table, along with some glossy magazines and unopened letters. Linus had known girls like that before, who smelled like roses and looked immaculate but lived in squalor. It was something that tended to happen in share houses. It was a thought that gave him pause. The stereo was pumping out some chintzy rubbish at moderate volume.

"Uncle John's coming tomorrow. He helps me with stuff, like with shopping and money and that, 'cause I don't know the value of money, and one time I spent, like, lots and lots of money on this pretty necklace." She giggled. "He was so cross with me, but I cried, and he didn't make me take it back."

The necklace was obviously plastic, besides adding nothing to the view.

There was a large poster of the singer Pink and a couple of others of artists Linus could not immediately identify. He asked his hostess' taste in music and got the same effusive, incoherent answer he would have expected from his sister, an extroverted thirteen-year-old whose tastes were the same. The kitchen, bathroom, and bedroom were all separate, which was unexpected given the apparent smallness of the shop front.

While Fi-fi was enthusing about her music, raising her voice rather than turn it down, an alarming sound rose above both from behind the more distant of the two doors.

"What was that?"

She turned it down. "Oh, that's my friend Mikey. He lives here too. Uncle John's really his uncle, but I call him Uncle John 'cause he said I can, like, 'cause he loves me like a daughter, he says; except one time he touched me like I don't reckon he should of. But he never done it again."

The noise was awful, like someone straining on the toilet: a nauseating combination of gastrointestinal and vocal sounds.

Linus was unsure what to say, but the words "Where does he sleep?" came to his lips, and in an instant had passed them. Fi-fi's initial answer required some clarification, but it emerged that Mikey was an ex-boyfriend with whom nonetheless she still shared this apartment, but nothing else that she would divulge. (So it was a two-bedroom flat? No, just the one . . .) Apparently Mikey was to be departing, moving out, going somewhere far away in the near future. Then Fi-fi would need someone else to share with. No, Mikey would be fine with her bringing home a male guest.

"Come and meet him, Gerry!" she said blithely, then adding in a pitying tone, her hand on the doorknob, "Mikey's always sick; he just gets worser and worser."

Oh, it stank in there as well—stank like a sewer. In the bed was an obviously bedridden creature that Linus could only with difficulty, and given the context provided, identify as male and human. The man, for want of a better word, was weirdly misshapen in the face and neck, the substance of which bulged out here and there in a freakishly asymmetrical way. The skin was very blotchy, suggesting either that the man had recently been beaten up, or that he suffered from extreme circulatory problems. Overlaid were several scabs on the right-hand side of Mikey's face, where the texture of the skin looked horribly dry and flaky. There were hairy moles of abnormal size as well, and a nose and ears deformed by cauliflower growths. It was impossible to read the expression in those bulbous eyes, the right red and slack-lidded, the left glaucous, and both oozing rheum like a sick child's nostrils oozing snot. Besides whatever else was ailing him, Linus guessed that Mikey was a stroke victim, what with his mouth hanging wide open, lips slack and glistening with saliva which dribbled out both corners, but especially from the slacker and flabbier of the two, on the left. In addition, Mikey possessed the most disgustingly rotten set of teeth Linus had ever seen outside of a horror movie. Under the blankets were further amorphous shapes whose properties he could extrapolate better than he cared to. One hand lay atop the blanket, hairy and spastic. The hair, both here, on his head, and elsewhere, was variegated, and grew in weird-looking tufts all over the place, as though an ape were to suffer from alopecia.

Quivering all over, the entity made a pitiful noise, part grunt, part moan, part rattle. "Mikey's hungry," Fi-fi said, smiling back at her guest. "But," she addressed the creature, "it's not dinner time yet, silly! Here, have some water." She took the glass off the nightstand and poured some into the slack mouth, which made a very imperfect receptacle. She stood a moment stroking the hair on her pet monster's head, a few strands of which fell to the blanket below. Then she stroked his cheeks, each in turn. Linus suddenly felt as though he was intruding. Mikey seemed to agree. He was becoming agitated, grunting and gesturing with misshapen hands and weeping eyes in Linus' direction.

"Maybe I should . . ." but he found it impossible to say "go." All this stinking foulness and horror were of no account next to Fi-fi's extraordinary beauty, Linus realised. Incredible as it might seem, his attraction to her was actually greater in extent than his repulsion from Mikey, and in that moment he even believed that her departure from the median of human attractiveness was greater in the upward direction than that unfortunate creature's in the downward. The ghetto colloquialism according to which a very attractive girl is referred to as a "freak" came to mind.

Linus drew closer to his beloved, and therefore to the monster's bedside. Her perfume was unconquered by the foul air.

"Oh, don't cry, Mikey! What's that? You got a hair in your eye? Oh, don't worry, I'll get it out for you."

It looked like Fi-fi was plucking a stray eyelash—except that was not quite right. No, it was plain enough: the hair was actually growing out of the creature's one functioning eyeball! It was a huge black thing, like a wire; even in the twilit room, Linus saw it now clearly against the pallor of the rear wall. Then she confirmed what he might otherwise have convinced himself was a mistake: "Mikey hates it when they come out his eyes!"

Linus thought that the worst fate any man could suffer must be to exist in such a state in the bed and under the care of a beautiful girl. Mikey grunted in what might have been relief, raising a four fingered, purplish hand to touch Fi-fi awkwardly on the elbow. Far from flinching, she bent down and kissed her hideous pet on the forehead.

Where did she sleep? Did the couch fold out, or . . . Surely not!

Then she took a framed photo from the bedside table and brought it to show Linus. "This is Mikey and me when I met him." The man in the photograph was fit, well-built. The woman was a little dumpy. Not bad looking, tending towards voluptuousness, but only a distant relative of the stunner in front of him. Yes, there was some family resemblance—maybe a statue latent in the flabby stone—but what a transformation! He would not have thought it possible. No, she was playing a joke on him.

"Mikey wasn't smart like you; him and me's both, like, about the same dumbness. He used to make the pizzas, and that when uncle John had a shop here, and he got me a waitress job when we started going out. She paused and came towards Linus, wiggling her hips in a near-parody of seductiveness. "But don't worry, Gerry. I like smart men too."

THE BIRTH OF VENUS

I.

The early spring grass was high and green in the park by the creek which, according to the rusted sign over the entrance, had at one time been maintained by the Rotarians. That must have been a while ago, since the equipment was similarly rusted, and it was said locally that fingers had been lost and tetanus contracted here by small children. As a result, today the two girls and Paul, the older brother of one, had the park to themselves.

Perhaps hide-and-seek was a little juvenile, but then the girls were only thirteen, and Kamala Williams, Paul's sister's friend, loved to play all kinds of childish games despite, or perhaps because of, her precocity in other ways. Any time Paul thought that he really could not, in all dignity, participate in some little game of hers, she would enlist him, pushing, pulling and teasing. And though Edwina was always there, always between them, it was Paul with whom Kamala had shared the blood from her pricked finger in that strangely earnest little ceremony that had taken place behind the shed at his home the previous week.

He was almost eighteen now and in his final year at school. Shy, awkward, and bookish, he evoked little actual hostility from his peers, and scarcely more interest. Only in his dreams had Paul ever had anything to do with girls, apart from Kamala, and even there everything was done under an innocent pretext.

Contrasting with Kamala's childlike enthusiasm for games was a physical maturity that grew more astounding almost by the day. From some angles it was hard to believe that she was still in school, let alone in Edwina's year. This initially had bothered Paul, who knew that he would still have been attracted to her even had he felt able to approach girls his own age. Yes, he would have fallen in love with her sultry playfulness, her bright eyes and exotic, Mediterranean complexion, her wild dark locks, regardless. But then it was obvious that she was no ordinary thirteen-year-old.

The playground was bordered on two sides by tall pines. Alongside one of these borders ran the road to Paul's and Edwina's home, to which the three of them would soon be returning as the overcast continued to darken. On the opposite side, behind the play equipment and rotunda, was a kind of overgrown path of native scrub with small trees that coalesced into a denser growth out of their smattering throughout the park. This terrain lay to the far side of a small creek with high banks that flowed out of a culvert beneath the road with the entrance sign, and away into the more rural side of the hilly district where sheep paddocks were broken up by stands of eucalyptus. It was a free ranging game that the three of them played, finding their hiding places around the perimeter of the park, crouched against the steep gradient of the flat-topped rise on which the rotunda stood, in the trees and creek bank, or (a higher risk strategy) in amongst the play equipment, and even behind the rotunda whose front steps were designated "home."

Something uncanny was going on between him and Kamala, Paul knew. He had only to close his eyes, and, without any prior notion of her location, he would infallibly sense it with an inner compass that was like a sixth sense. But after several rounds playing out like this, the final one went differently. Paul found his sister first and suggested they search for Kamala by splitting up to right and left, leaving his sister to check the creek margins while he searched among the trees on the road side. As before, he had a preternatural sense of her whereabouts: it was a feeling that rose up along his spine from the groin upwards to the chest, yet it had something of light and vision, if only by analogy, about it.

This was when he turned and saw the figure of death, standing looking up at his beloved, who was sitting on the top of the Rotunda steps. As the two of them conversed, her skirt opened up like a corolla to give death a clear glimpse of polka dot-clad receptacle. The hooded figure was one of the local youths, some of whom Paul knew, slightly or by reputation, from before they had dropped out of school. They would hang around in the rotunda after dark, always several to a group, leaving bottles, cigarette butts, and sometimes condoms behind. Their presence was usually announced by an aggressive blare of ghetto beats from a car stereo or boom box. Yet it was silent at the moment, and the youth seemed to be on his own, nor could Paul identify him individually.

Paul stood still for some time, apparently unseen, though completely exposed. Then he found himself walking away whence he had just come, back towards the trees to pretend to look for Kamala. It was ridiculous; he knew they had seen him and that the laughter he now overheard was at his expense. His eyes rolled back in his head. If only he could shut off his other senses the same way, so as not hear the reproaches of the wind and of the twigs under his feet, or taste the rotten flavour of cowardice in the back of his throat.

Another moment, though, and his eyes, refocused on the external world, seemed bizarrely enough to meet Kamala's behind him. They opened, Paul breathed in the humus and pine scent, pivoted, and reversed his steps.

The two at the rotunda were apparently engrossed in conversation. She was laughing—nervously, was it?—at something the hood had said, with an accompanying gesture that suggested a recount of some violent episode in which he had prevailed over a presumptuous adversary. Paul heard the tail end of some utterance: someone was "gonna get fucked up," in whatever sense was intended. The hood pivoted slightly to face Paul at about 45 degrees, thrust out his chin, and said nothing before turning back to Kamala.

"Who's this?"

"He's just my friend's brother," she explained in her big-girl voice.

"Not your boyfriend, then?"

She laughed, raising her eyebrows and making a face. "He's my brother too now; I've adopted him. We were playing."

"Playin', huh?" The hood made an obscene gesture.

She laughed. "Hide and seek, you naughty boy! Want to play too?"

"Hide my dick," the hood chuckled, shooting Paul another unbelievably truculent look. Here for the first time during the exchange Kamala looked directly at Paul. She wanted, whether for amusement or edification, to see what he would do. The hood turned lazily, almost facing him now. Paul, not knowing what else to say or do, uttered some standard remonstrations about his indisposition towards any kind of trouble; the hood replied in turn by spitting, very close to Paul's toes.

Paul heard a strange little squeak from the vicinity of the creek. Was it Edwina, or a bird cry?

"Fuck off, poofter" sneered the hood decisively; then, turning back to Kamala, "Give us your phone number."

A phenomenon Paul had seen before in other boys and which inspired him with terror as if they were skin changers, was a certain skill, or instinct, which he lacked: the ability, predicated on the willingness to use violence, to turn absolutely mean at a moment's notice. In other words, Paul was a coward, and he knew it. He opened his mouth to speak again, but Kamala spoke first. "Look, Pauly, Eddie looks kind of freaked out about something over there. You should go . . . look after her." No, the irony was not lost on the tittering little demoness above him.

And there she was indeed, running toward them with, he now could see, an expression of panic on her face. He hesitated but did as he was told, not missing the mixed laughter behind him; "I'll count to ten—nah, make it three," he heard the hood say.

Edwina's distress, it turned out, was due to some kind of animal she had seen, or more strictly, deduced, or imagined, to be present on the far side of the creek behind a bush. All her experience amounted to, it seemed, was a rustling of foliage. Typical hysteria from the sister he at that moment resented, irrationally, more than her friend. Like plenty of other stupid girls, Edwina had a juvenile crush on one of those creeps, he recalled.

When next he turned around, the hood was gone; whether having achieved more than a rival's humiliation Paul was loath to contemplate. On the way home he ruminated on what had happened. Kamala had been far from taking his side; had she done so he might have managed a more robust intervention. But things had just happened so quickly, and he was only just now thinking clearly enough over a rapid, almost deafening heartbeat, to realise the probably undying significance of the event.

Meanwhile, behind him Edwina was raving on about her imaginary experience by the creek. Now, apparently, there had been a spot of intense blackness amidst the rustling foliage. Then it had blinked. "So basically you saw a one-eyed monster," Kamala summarised, and laughed and teased, explaining the joke, until she carried Edwina along in her gaiety.

About half a kilometre away by the gravel road that led from the park gate to Paul's and Edwina's parents' house, a car was parked outside. It was a grimy old white Toyota Corona adorned with several bumper stickers whose general purport was that its owner lived in an enchanted world of untold possibilities and wonder. The other noticeable thing about the vehicle was the amount of rubbish inside: parking tickets, take-away wrapping, and sundry items of women's clothing.

". . . You know how the Eskimos have a hundred words for snow? Well, these people, they've got a thousand words for what they can do to you, the kinds of pain they can inflict. There's a different vocabulary for boys and for girls, and different ones again for women, and men. Like dialects. I used to know the one for little girls pretty well, when I was little, but they must've wiped my brain at some point, because when they were all standing around in a circle outside the house that night, just before we ran away, singing or chanting like they do, I couldn't make out what they were saying they were going to do with her . . . Poor Kamala!"

Here, and not for the first time that afternoon, her mother Faye Williams, started crying. Paul and Edwina's mother, Carinne Hardy, spoke what comforting words she could, which were not many, given the extreme remove of the situation described from anything in her own experience.

"Even now, since the memories started getting stronger, since I realised who—who Kamala's father is, I know I'm remembering maybe only a thousandth fraction of what actually happened, what it felt like when I was little. I think he's their leader now, like Dad used to be. They didn't want to use me when I was older; when I grew past Kamala's age they only wanted me to watch . . . So why would they want her?" Faye was strongly opposed to uttering her ex-husband's name under any circumstances.

Besides the sexual abuse, she also told of a number of other perverse rituals to which she had been subjected as a child. These included being forced into coffin along with a large spider, being made to sleep outside while tied up like a dog, having darts thrown at her naked body, and far more than Carinne had the stomach to hear of. There were animal and yes, occasionally human infant sacrifices as well. There was no overt or clichéd satanic imagery involved, but at the same time, there certainly was the suggestion of a supernatural dimension to it all. For example, the spider in the coffin with her might not have been merely an earthly creature; it was actually "something like a spider but so, so much worse." Also, among the more readily comprehensible tortures Faye described was this one: "They'd paint my face in these . . . colours and shapes, I guess they were, or lines, and then they'd make me stand in front of a mirror, and it was just . . . horrible! I can't even tell you!" From the way she told of it this seemed to have been the most traumatic experience of all—which of course made no rational sense, and tended to strengthen Carinne's partial incredulity even while it contributed to her perturbation.

This was the first time her frequent guest had fully opened up about her past like this, which was surprising to Carinne, since the last descriptor she would have applied to this woman, of whom she had seen a lot in recent weeks since their daughters became friends at school, was "reserved." She and Kamala had appeared suddenly in their lives after moving to town and starting school mid-year.

As the story went on, Carinne more than once had the urge to spring up and leave immediately to find their children in the car. But no, she told herself, she must not over-react (also, she must stop thinking of Paul as a child *per se*). How much of all this narrative was strictly, factually true she did not know, and it was hard to credence the fantastic details of her friend's story. Kamala was more often a guest here than Edwina at her house, but had Carinne previously known as much as was now being divulged to her, she would not have allowed it.

"I thought I was escaping, going off with Kamala's father. He was so tall, dark, and handsome, and nice to me at first! But, of course, they never would have let me get away like that. Back then I'd already started to forget, whether it was me doing it or some mind-control spell, I don't know, but I sure knew I wanted to get away from home. Out of the frying pan and into the fire!"

This reminded Carinne that dinner was in the oven. She got up and checked the roast chicken, finding that it was a little over-done, and that the potatoes were in worse condition. She felt momentarily annoyed, and inwardly censured herself.

On the ex-husband's recent reappearance, which Carinne had already known was the trigger for the move that brought mother and daughter to town, Faye had attempted to take out a restraining order, but that was impossible since the name he had been using during their entire relationship turned out to be an assumed one. He had been involved in illegal activities of various kinds back in the day, and certainly had known people who could organise fake ID, so that was not too hard to believe. Nor could she give his address or employer.

Back when she was pregnant with Kamala, Faye said, she had run away suddenly when he had taken her to a party where she recognised faces of people who had been involved in her parents' cult. Memories had flooded back, and in moments she had grown convinced that the assembled revellers were about to seize and cut her open, and sacrifice her and her baby, right then and there. Surrounded, she began to panic; but then an extraordinary stroke of fortune occurred. The police arrived to raid the party, finding sufficient quantities of drugs to take everyone into custody, and in the process separating Faye from her husband. She took advantage of the situation to divulge the abuse she was currently suffering, which was of a more mundane type than that she remembered from her childhood. She was referred to a social worker, who assisted in her flight.

Seeing her husband at that party surrounded by her parents' horribly familiar-looking accomplices, all of whom treated him with great respect, she had suddenly realised that this was not the first time Faye had seen him so surrounded. He had been there years before, had solemnly received the infected, serrated knife from her father's hand. And furthermore, was it possible that her husband was in fact, her own brother: the one she had been told about but had no recollection of ever having met? There was no resemblance she could see, but certain half-remembered utterances might be interpreted as pointing towards her mother having been inseminated by a third, possibly non-human party.

The other thing that had precipitated Faye's sudden recollection during the party was the sight of some very young kittens in a basket with no mother to be seen. Once when she was a child she had had to watch as a very brutal and no doubt medically unnecessary caesarean was performed on a mother cat. It had been her own job afterwards to bottle-feed them something rather less wholesome than milk until, at length, they died.

There had been no overt pursuit, but occasionally Faye would see or hear things that suggested that she and her daughter were under surveillance: familiar faces watching her in the street, overheard snatches of conversation in mysterious languages, but otherwise the next decade or so had yielded them a normal life. Faye had had a couple of boyfriends, but no one special, and now she considered herself done with all that.

The first sign of a return of trouble was something Kamala had said upon coming home much later than expected one night during her penultimate year of primary school. Faye was a permissive parent, less in spite than because of her experiences as a child (why fear strangers when worse dangers had existed for her at home?); even so, when her daughter was not home for dinner, fear rapidly became terror. When she did show up, Kamala appeared shaken: her eyes were huge and red, her complexion relatively pale. She said that she had gone with a man who picked her up outside the school gates, and that he had taken her to a house and shown her things that were hard to describe in words. No, not male genitalia, or not only that. Insofar as she could describe them, her words tallied with certain painful memories of Faye's own. There had been a book in which the writing was like horrible pictures of nothing she recognised exactly: the more she looked at it the less abstract (to paraphrase) the script had appeared, until there was not a straight line or simple curve to be seen. The letters now possessed intricate volume, shade, and colour, as if they were photographs of organic, irregular, and highly unpleasant three-dimensional objects, but without losing their identity as letters in some vast, intricate alphabet or system of hieroglyphics. Just what they had meant, the girl was unable or unwilling to say.

Kamala had got her first period in the middle of that night, and the bleeding was so severe that she had to be taken to hospital to receive a transfusion.

It was in the uneasy year following this event that Kamala came prematurely into bloom. It was not only the looks her daughter was starting to receive from grown men; it was moreover a horrible sense Faye had that her daughter was in some sense, as she put it, "being fattened for slaughter." Had not something similar, though less remarkable in extent, occurred to Faye at the same age, right after her father had taken her on his knee and read to her from a strange book in some respects like a diagnostic manual, and not for the squeamish, in which pictures and text bled together into something resembling a mess of carrion, their disorder and decomposition so far advanced that they seemed to come full circle back to order?

"You know, before we came here I sent her to stay with a couple of old friends out at Woodgrange; they've got no kids of their own . . . She was probably safer with them, way out in the country! God, I should just let her live with them permanently and stop being so bloody selfish . . ." Faye paused, assessing her own proposition. "Except, to be honest, Carrie, I feel deep down that whatever's going to happen is destined to be. When the time's right he'll come and take my baby and do what he wants with her, and just kill me. I just hope it'll be quick. Some hope."

Not for the first time, Carinne did not know what to say as her friend lapsed into weeping. She took her hand across the table.

After a minute or so she continued. "When he showed up again, at first I didn't want to let Kamala out of my sight, even to go to school, but after a while I started feeling differently; more afraid, less able to do anything about it. I see signs of him everywhere, you know . . ." She said these words impassively, trailing off this time not into tears but into a resignation her hostess found much more difficult to bear, before resuming some of her former pathos: "If it doesn't stop we'll have no choice but to move again. And I know I'll never see you again if it comes to that! You're such a beautiful friend to me, Carinne, and your beautiful children . . . Kamala and I, we love them both!"

She burst once more into tears, while Carinne, who comforted her this time a little perfunctorily, experienced more than one negative emotion as she contemplated again the possible danger in which her own children might have been placed as a result of Faye's fatalism, weighing this up against the likelihood that there was some amount of paranoid fabrication in her story. In any case, she wished that her own husband was not away for the night.

It was just then that the front door opened and they heard the sound of giggling girls.

Paul went straight to his own room, got into bed, and lay on his back to gaze at the ceiling in the dismal twilight. He thought of the strange connection he felt with Kamala, how at any time, on closing his eyes, he would feel her presence like a compass needle pricking at his consciousness. It had been like this since last week's finger-pricking ceremony. It was probably just his imagination, and yet there seemed more to it than that. Now wherever she might be, near or far, he found that his consciousness could progress through the darkness behind his eyes just as if his skull housed the real world in its entirety; then, as he approached his goal, something analogous to daylight would give him a sense of being physically in a definite place: a place filled with the glamour of her presence.

Currently Paul could hear Kamala's laughter through the thin wall between his and Edwina's bedrooms. Given the short distance it took only a split second, and he was there with them, seeing and hearing her as she talked about her encounter with the hood: "Yeah I gave him my number. I don't know if he's my type though. One way to find out!" Shrieking laughter.

Paul's consciousness recoiled from the shock and returned to himself. Looking inwards, he became aware of selves within selves; of a bodily self that cared nothing about honour or dignity, only what pleasures it could steal, up to and including the almost unimaginable ones that pertained to Kamala's person. Then his awareness shifted to an over-self that was engaged in bellowing recriminations at the preceding one in a language it was constitutionally incapable of understanding. Above these he found a third, looking down on the other two with sublime detachment, and seeing only something like a frustrated trainer abusing a dog. Then yet another self appeared and began critiquing that lofty attitude, asking rhetorically what such an view of things ever achieved in the struggle for life. Finally another, the primal, subterranean self, infinitely more powerful but slower to rouse than the others, began to stir, heaving up all the warring strata of Paul's personality and sending them sprawling. The feeling was more profound than any he remembered having experienced before, excepting only his passionate love for Kamala.

He, Paul Hardy, would this moment go and take a revenge so immediate and decisive that it would be as though he had gone back in time and chastised that delinquent hood in the park at the very moment offense had been given! He lay there for some minutes longer, checking his resolve and appreciating its unaccustomed firmness.

He stood up deliberately, walked out of his room, and, camouflaging his purposeful rage with a greeting for the two women in the kitchen, went out through the back door. Dinner would be served in a minute. The ute was absent from the big garage-cum-tool shed tonight (as a fencing contractor, Paul's father's work often took him far away, and tonight he would be staying in a motel somewhere near a cattle station some three-hundred kilometres from home). Paul looked over at the cluttered shelves and the garden implements leaning against the walls. No, he would not take some preposterous murder weapon: no hammer, axe, or hatchet. The spare hatchet handle leaning against the wall in the corner would do nicely, though. Hefting it, he felt that it was something he would be willing to bring down across any part of an opponent's body without the slightest qualm. Paul went through the side gate holding his weapon in full view before realising his mistake; then he went back in through the front door and marched directly to his room, where would put on a large jacket in order to conceal the weapon up his sleeve. He might even be back in time for dinner.

"Close the door, sweetheart, it's getting chilly," called his mother.

Paul threw open his cupboard and paused a moment, suddenly hearing an engine outside that sounded like it must be passing at a highly inconsiderate speed. Instead, it came to a screeching stop. He heard the slamming of a door and a harsh voice (or was it voices?) like the cawing of a crow. The words he could not make out. His first thought was that either Kamala had given the hood his address, or he had followed them home. And just as if there were indeed a carload of teenagers loitering out the front, Paul could make out a drumbeat underneath the noise of an engine that now ceased while the dull, ominous rhythm continued.

The voices, which seemed to be speaking, threatening, quarrelling, he now realised, were indeed crows, or anyway birds of some kind, having been startled by the car.

But there was no mistake about the unapologetic footfall that was crunching its way up the driveway. At the same time there were excited voices in the kitchen. Paul went to the window of his room. There was a cotoneaster bush partly blocking his view, which revealed nothing, and the only car he could make out on the street was Faye's. The ineluctable knock on the door followed the resounding thud of heavy feet on the wooden veranda. Paul fancied he could feel the floorboards shake under him.

"I can feel it, it's him!" Faye whispered histrionically just as Paul peeked in the doorway to the kitchen, on his way to the door. "We can't let him in! You remember what I said: anywhere he goes he leaves a trace! It's like he never leaves! You don't want him in your house, Carinne! Don't let him in—please, pleeease!"

Her tone was exceedingly pathetic and alarming. Paul, who was on a first name basis with the familiar Mrs Williams, knew that she was eccentric, but had never seen her act this flaky before, not even when she had speculated—flirtatiously, Paul had felt—about his past lives and the uncommon age and wisdom of his soul.

"It's okay, Faye. We won't let anything happen to you. If it's him we'll call the police, and you'll be able to get your restraining order," said Carinne, trying not to sound nervous. Then another knock came. Paul stood poised, watching his mother stroking the other woman's hand which she held in hers.

"Paul, will you come and sit with Faye, please, while I get that?"

"Nooo! Pleeease!" the queer woman whined, regressing so abjectly that it was disturbing for Paul to listen to her nasal, high-pitched voice, and at the same time to see her tugging at his mother's sleeve like a distraught child.

There came another knock, louder this time and more sustained. Paul continued to the front door without a word.

The door consisted of a moulded wooden frame containing a large, arch-shaped pane of reinforced glass. The house's westward orientation resulted in a vivid yet obscure play of lights and shadows through the rippled surface patterning of this glass pane. A dark, man-sized shape was occluding the light of the orange sunset behind it that passed through the trellis which trailed hardenbergia around two sides of the veranda, leaves and flowers agitated in play. Another ripple occurred as the figure raised its hand to knock again. It appeared taller than the nuggety physique Paul was half expecting to re-encounter.

Nonetheless, he let the hatchet handle drop from his sleeve into his right hand, opening the door with his left, afraid but not frightened, ready.

What he saw was a dark, hooded figure, and literally nothing else. It seemed to Paul as if the figure in the doorway occupied the whole of the outside space, like a giant in a fairy tale. And yet, somehow, it was growing! Soon it was not even a figure, but an awesome presence that occupied his whole consciousness, so that he suddenly was no longer even aware of the house behind him, the piece of wood in his hand, the purpose in his heart . . . In a moment it had lifted him up out of his familiar world into a place of total darkness whose atmosphere was as unbreathable as the void of outer space.

Then it spoke, and its utterance was like the cawing of crows and the singing of crickets, and further removed than either from any language produced by human vocal chords. A million miles away, Paul felt the weapon drop from his hand.

On waking, he had only the vaguest recollection of the long, long night of terrors that had passed while that strange choir sang in the solid darkness that had pinned his limbs in place and piled its crushing weight on him. Kamala and the light of her presence were nowhere to be felt. His senses, apart from his sensitivity to every kind of pain, had been completely stifled throughout the interminable ordeal, which now he struggled to remember in any detail. Perhaps it had been some kind of interrogation involving torture, an operation without anaesthetic, or both. The location had been somewhere extremely hot, so that he felt soft, as if semi-dissolved. Hours seemed to have stretched out into years until finally, at long last, he awoke, gasping.

The return to this world was gradual; just opening his eyes was like trying to lift up the rear wheels of a car in a superhuman feat made possible only by dire extremity. Then Paul felt a prickling sensation on his cheek, which turned out to be caused by ordinary green grass. Somehow, after an unsuccessful attempt or two, he stood up and looked around. He was in the park near his home, the one he used to play in as a child, the one he had played in more recently with . . . someone, a beautiful girl, the love of his life—but that was probably just a half-forgotten episode of the dream, a pleasant interlude in the nightmare.

To his right was the old, flaking rotunda, and the rusted play equipment lay to his left. Paul experienced a sense of displacement in his perceptions: it was as if the familiar surroundings were looking at him, as much as vice-versa, and not liking what they saw. What was he doing here? Had he got drunk and passed out? He had done that once at his aunty Sandy's wedding back in May, but could not recall having drunk a drop since. Yes, he was coming back to himself. He was Paul Hardy of 11 . . . he had to think about it—11 Mistletoe Place. Of course he knew how to get there.

Crickets were chirping as he made his way home in a twilight that could equally have been morning or evening. When he reached home his mother's car was in the driveway, a small, reassuring sign of normalcy; behind it, in the garage, his father's station wagon. The front door was locked, and Paul was carrying no key, so he went around the back and let himself in the seldom locked rear entrance, not wishing to disturb his family or have to explain himself. He doubted that he would be able to form the words, if he had had anything to say. The recent past was a blank; memories of school, of family meals, of having to sit through his sister's primary school theatre performance . . . these were the nearest he could come up with, and they felt as though they must be years old.

He went straight to bed, where a long, dreamless sleep awaited him.

II.

His infirmity became suddenly apparent some weeks later. His mother found him lying in bed one morning when he had not roused himself by the usual time for school. He was on his back, staring at the ceiling, pale and unresponsive. Even Carinne's scream was not enough to rouse him.

By the time the family assembled, Paul started coming around. He was grunting in some distress, like a sleepwalker trying to talk. He was repeating some disjointed syllables that meant nothing to anyone in the family. After several minutes, having recovered to an extent, he began to blink and swallow; soon he was able to sit up in bed and to respond, albeit vaguely, to his family's pleas for reassurance.

A visit to the doctor ensued right away, and the basic examination revealed nothing obviously wrong.

Subsequently, his blood test showed a depressed leukocyte count. This was of some concern, but nothing more. Since the initial episode Paul had remained in a somewhat altered state, vague and staring much of the time, unable to complete any but the simplest of tasks. He stayed home from school at his mother's insistence, his father agreeing with her after the second fainting fit. He was referred to a haematologist, as well as to a neurologist, but before he had seen either, the results of the MRI came back.

Paul sat between his mother and father in their family GP's office, the adults deriving a desperate, subliminal reassurance from the familiar surroundings. A copy of the scan had been sent to the Hardys' doctor *pro forma*, but the next appointment was supposed to have been with the specialist. When they were summoned to the surgery no details were given over the phone, despite Carinne's almost hysterical pleading with the receptionist.

Then Dr Mulqueen, who had been the family doctor as long ago as Carinne's first pregnancy, with Paul, explained to them with the help of the images on the film, that throughout Paul's brain an incredible infestation of tumours had been discovered. They were linked together by tendrils branching out in all directions in a structure similar to that of a rhizome. How his condition might be treated, or what the prognosis might be, Dr Mulqueen was not qualified to say, but he had shared the images with a neuro-oncologist and it was evident that they were dealing with an aggressive form of brain cancer. Full diagnosis and prognosis were deferred until a trip to the hospital the following day.

Things progressed quickly over the following weeks and months. The rate of growth was indeed amazing, and what was now believed to be a single tumour was extending down his spinal cord. No one was prepared to hold out even the faintest hope on Paul's behalf, other than to affirm that as his case was in many ways unique, a clear prognosis was more than usually difficult. Surgery was out of the question, so chemotherapy was promptly tried. The only evident results were that Paul's hair fell out, and less typically, that his scalp broke out in a very nasty scabrous rash and an odd swelling at the top of his head.

Meanwhile, another abnormality was manifesting which under different circumstances might have attracted more attention. As it was, Paul's parents pointed it out to doctors who did little but raise an eyebrow and rule out in principle any connection between it and the tumours. This was a mutation in his standing posture that went well beyond any common teenage slouch, even taking into account the misery for which Paul, as well as both his parents, had been prescribed anti-depressants. The patient seemed to have lost his lumbar lordosis, which development bestowed an increasingly C-shaped spinal alignment and a resultant simian posture.

Paul spent much of his time curled up in bed, in foetal position. He was now largely bedridden, the bouts of fainting paralysis lasting longer and longer, now interspersed with violent seizures. These symptoms would likely continue to worsen until one day soon Paul would simply stop breathing. His doctor was willing to help this eventuality along by providing powerful sedatives to help with the growing intracranial pressure. The dosage had to be continually increased.

His autonomous reflexes soon began to suffer even between bouts of paralysis and seizures, Paul's movements alternating between a sluggishness that was understandable given the severity of medication, and abrupt loss of motor control which, after one shocking near-miss that almost blinded him in one eye, precluded Paul from using a knife and fork.

It had been the beginning of spring when the whole tragedy began to unfold; by summer he was bedridden. Strangely, as Paul lay in bed his long, thin and never especially powerful frame seemed actually to put on muscle weight at a time when by rights his muscles should have been atrophying. Given his family's stupefied mental condition on the one hand, and the highly specialised nature of the contemporary medical profession on the other, it was perhaps not overly surprising that this development failed to attract much attention.

After a period of total mutism lasting about a fortnight, Paul now began to make inarticulate noises that apparently signified his physical needs. His facial expression at such times was fearsome indeed, his voice inhuman, like the squawking of some dreadful bird, and no one liked to be on nursing duty or failed to wake as from a nightmare on hearing those noises, especially at night.

A short while later, there was much consternation when Paul began to be found in different positions to those in which he had ostensibly been left.

"Edwina, you didn't change him during the night, did you?"

"No!" his sister exclaimed, unable to disguise her repugnance. It was a task she refused ever to help with.

"It must have been your father, then. I must have slept through it."

For there lay Paul, diaperless and clean on his bed.

Then one morning Carinne found Paul lying more or less as she had left him in his bed. Having slept relatively well that night she felt the strength within her to savour, or try to savour, a moment of her dying son's company: perhaps he might even look at her with some recognition, even one last time. She had never ceased to love her son and to mourn the horror of what had befallen him, but had come increasingly to regard him, despite herself, as already dead.

Now, as she stroked the back of his limp hand with her thumb, Paul took hold of his mother's hand in turn, and squeezed—squeezed so hard that she cried out and tried to yank it away. He responded by pulling against her, using her countervailing force to pull himself up into a seated position. This was new. She looked him in the face. His expression was absolutely ghastly and manic.

Then his head fell forward as if he had suddenly lost consciousness, except that his grip remained tight. She stared at the horrible scabby eruption at the top of his head, and saw the angry node of flesh twitch, just as if it were connected to his somatic nervous system. Then it opened from the bottom up, slowly, to reveal a glistening black pupil.

Carinne screamed and struggled until the creature in the bed let her go, still grinning as she backed out of the room, wishing that the door could be locked from the outside. That was the only time she saw the pupil, the eye in the dead centre of her son's bald, scabrous scalp. She came to believe that she had imagined it under the influence of drugs and sleep deprivation, and told no one of it. Certainly she was not about to go and prise open the wrinkled mound and check!

The incident changed nothing, fundamentally; it only confirmed what she already knew; Piers, her husband, did not gainsay her, either, when she brought up how he had grabbed her.

No, she was not a bad mother, nor (unless she was mad and hallucinating) was this some self-justifying delusion: if the creature in his bed had been still her son, Carinne would have ministered to it until doomsday, but it was a changeling. It was more than just the terrifying facial expression she had just seen, the animal groans and weird squawking, barking noises, the physical fear he made her feel: it was what she somehow understood it all to mean, and that, paradoxically, was like a page of writing in an evil hieroglyphics she could not, and would not if she could, decipher. Her son was already dead, and the cancerous entity that had taken over his body was not dying at all.

In fact, though, Paul was still alive, and had never felt more so. The suffering of past months was over and meant nothing now. It had been so long since he was at liberty, yet he felt strong despite a numbness in the extremities. His heart was full of an obscure passion, his body its obedient tool. Where he was going and why he had no idea, despite a sense of a purpose so transcendent that he took little notice of his surroundings. His mind was not even a tool of the power that moved him, but rather an inexplicable gratuity, a free ticket to the show. The roadside continued to provide a little cover for a while, with its trees and sheltered walkways winding through the hilly terrain, although the warm night was not particularly dark, the moon just about full. But then the land flattened out into paddocks, leaving him relatively exposed.

What would anyone who saw him like this think? This was really no worry, more an idle speculation. Perhaps the answer would be amusing, as had been the case with his family towards the end of his gestation. He knew that even his mother had wanted to be rid of him, and that was okay; it mattered not at all, now that a new and better world had opened up. He had wondered if he was going to hurt his family, but the light in his head had told him that it was better to leave quietly, as there was something more important to do, far away. Going on all-fours came naturally now, nor was Paul bothered by the cuts and bruises that soon appeared on his hands: indurations would form in time, he supposed, and anyway flesh was for laceration, contusion, immolation: that was its purpose.

There was something like a lodestar before his new cyclopean eye that assured him of this, and in an obscure way the light it emitted was clearer than the moon and stars. No longer did he survey the world from the space just behind his eyes; now his consciousness opened up lotus-like, higher up, to provide a throne for some unfathomably exotic and barely anthropomorphic deity that showed him the hidden colours of the world as it really was.

Soon he heard a noise (or rather, since he felt a vibration, followed by his body's response to it). The car pulled over up ahead to one side of the strip of bitumen, and backed up. Then somebody got out and came towards him. He could not make out what the person was saying over the drumbeat in his ears, but it mattered not at all; he would know what to do—or what he had just done, in a moment. He remained on all fours and hung his head so that he must have looked like someone being sick. Everything was suspended within him while he waited for the animating impulse. The man approached him, knelt down and said something, taking one hand off his own knee and placing it on Paul's shoulder.

One advantage, Paul now discovered, of his servile condition, was that social anguish was precluded in much the same way as physical pain. Remorse, too, he found in a moment, was similarly left behind: after all, the physical strength he somehow enjoyed, along with the motivation to use it, were so unwonted that, even were he still minded in the moralistic human way, he would have found little difficulty in dissociating his conscience from their effects. He was no more troubled by the stranger's shouting or struggling than distressed at the look on his face, so full of uncomprehending revulsion.

Driving was a new sensation as well. His old self had never taken any steps to learn, despite his father's assays. The only thing that troubled Paul now, and that more with a sense of excitement than of anxiety, was the question of where he was going, eyes closed, guided by a light that was something other than light. It toyed with him and enraged him, zipping up and down his spinal cord, then going out suddenly and leaving him in the dark; then his eyes would start open on the moonlit road ahead, and in panic he would close them again to find that the light had moved to a different zone of that other world it inhabited, and into which it was drawing him: above, below, he had no notion. His hearing had been the first sense to experience muffling; now his mundane vision began to dull as his communion with the light grew stronger. It was no cause for alarm.

Crops and animals alternated across the surface of the rolling earth as Paul continued along one country road after another, the last of which was a dirt track full of potholes going slowly uphill through the long, dead grass. An old wooden gate stood half-open ahead, between posts topped with cow skulls. He drove through, knocking it off its hinges. Now the car was jolting over a driveway that seemed to go on winding past paddocks empty of all but trees, both living and dead, for ages.

At last he came to a stop in front of a farmhouse whose dark bulk he had seen far off on the horizon. Paul turned off the engine and leapt out of the car onto all fours. As his hands touched the ground the beacon in his head throbbed, wanting to spill out and illuminate the world.

A dog began to bark. Paul felt the muscles in his own throat contract in a strange fashion, and his mouth open to omit a semi-articulate, half-bestial sound that he could hardly hear, but which might very approximately have resembled the cawing of a crow. What he could hear, above the beating of his heart, was a noise like the shrieking of crickets; though he did not know if this was inside his head or out. No light was on in the house, or under the soft floorboards of the veranda on which Paul crouched, having mounted three decrepit wooden steps. He was no longer made for human posture, and instead of standing up to announce his presence by knocking or ringing, he simply waited, confident of having been heard. There followed a sound of footsteps.

Paul could hardly make out what the person before him was saying over the noise of the crickets, but this did not prevent him from answering. He spoke in a strange language that, as before, moved his organs of speech in a highly unusual way, while his ears failed to pick up much of the short conversation. And yet, with an awareness that was perhaps the auditory analogue of the lotus-light in his head whose roots extended down throughout his body, Paul understood (albeit with an instinctive humility that told him such was only the most exoteric translation) that what he said was, "You are not worthy that I should come under this roof!"

The person (hard to tell whether male or female) hung his head in submission, stepped aside, and showed the honoured guest in.

The moon was close to full, and a window in the front wall was not merely open but smashed, so that artificial lighting would have been unnecessary even if Paul had required it. He was in a large room that was in a state not so much of disarray as of decomposition, with assorted rubbish and filth so worked in everywhere that the place seemed more a lair than a human dwelling. The walls were smeared with some kind of writing or glyphs that simultaneously constituted a gruesome mural, painted in organic matter derived, at a guess, from the sheep that lay in the middle of the carpet. It had been eviscerated, butchered, and cooked in the most incomplete and piecemeal manner, so that with the remains of his olfactory sense Paul could the smell roast lamb mingled with other less wholesome odours. As he approached, the animal twitched feebly and tried to raise its head.

The expression shared across the two simpering human faces was loathsomely eager (though it was not Paul's place to feel any loathing). The one further back—call her female—ran forward and threw herself at Paul's feet, grovelling among the sheep's entrails. He snarled, and she withdrew. The one who had opened the door now led the way through the room and up a flight of stairs that commenced in the passageway to the rear. They stepped over the continuous piles of rubbish and filth that included large quantities of decomposing animal matter along with a variegated litter of commercial packaging, till the figure ahead of him stopped at a door that was bolted on the outside, unlocked it, and disappeared on command.

With only his human eyes for guidance, Paul would have found the room quite dark. There was a surge of both the cranial illumination and the cricket music in his ears. Inside the void behind that door Paul now lost all sense of his location in space; it must have been for some time, also, that he remained still, listening in wonder. His peripheral nerves had all but ceased to provide any data, and when finally he did move, he was just barely aware of his own bodily movements by the usual efferent pathways. The crickets were, he understood, actually stringed instruments playing terribly complex melodies and harmonies that created an impression of extra-dimensional space.

Yes and no; in fact, the strings were literally voices, a superhuman choir singing in a language so detailed in its reference to manifold existents and subsistents that, to the human mind, what they were saying could only be represented as a terrifying chaos.

Images came before his mind that were like mandalas composed of gore in infinite but clearly defined shades of decomposition. What he saw opened up, yielding its secrets at last like one of those "magic eye" pictures that had transfixed him as a child, but the secrets kept pouring endlessly forth. The pressure in his head intensified as if his frontal and parietal bones were being forced apart, and he felt a further veil of corporeal limitation fall away. His one eye facing toward the one goal, it was time, apparently, for the remaining scales to fall.

Inching forward, still he crouched on the floor, wonderstruck at the ineffable depth and breadth of the vision before his true eye that was opening more and more. At the centre of the field lay what he understood to be an almost life-sized doll lying stiffly—more so than any furniture in the room—on a raised platform, seething like everything else, which Paul supposed was a bed.

The eyes were lidless (he imagined that, were he to tilt the head backwards, they would close mechanically, like the eyes of those old-fashioned baby dolls his grandmother collected). The mouth was slightly open. Against the music a recitative dialogue in the awesome language he had already spoken and seen written on the walls was being sung between two entities that drew echoes and sympathetic motions from all lesser things around, including him and the doll. These immanent presences resided within the morass of forms that filled the darkness around the objects that filled the tiny room. Paul understood intuitively what they were saying.

A girl had been waiting here for her father, who had arrived at last bearing gifts. She was ecstatically pleased with the doll—actually it was more a kind of puppet—and with the pet that was something like a dog and also itself a kind of puppet, operated by her father; and although the four of them were there already, in the room together (indeed, in an unfathomable way the father and daughter were in a sense a single being), the dog-puppet now had a special role to play in ceremonially presenting the doll-puppet to the girl so that she could take possession if it—she who had waited so long without a body, without sensation, present only in a subtle way in the spaces between things. She wanted badly to play with the doll; her uncountable arms were reaching out for it from everywhere.

Paul advanced on all fours, covering the short distance between himself and the wide-eyed doll that was his mistress' gift. As he reached out it moved suddenly, flinching and writhing against its restraints, and his deaf eardrums rattled with its scream.

Eternal Sleep

He could hardly imagine how the statue had come to be here in this rustic little house consisting of two bedrooms, a kitchen-and-living area, and a lean-to that formed another pair of rooms out the back containing in turn a toilet, a claw-foot bath tub, and an old washing machine that leaked and had no spin cycle. It was of no consequence, about the washing facilities: clothes dried easily out in what might have been the post-apocalyptic sunshine, though unfortunately the plastic pegs he had been provided did not last, crumbling to pieces after the first few days of this interminable summer. The only other regular outside chore was taking the rubbish out and leaving the bags beside the already-full bin. Did the rubbish truck never come? The diurnal cycle seemed hopelessly confused, and days on end would pass (as measured by the highly imperfect rhythm of his sleeping and waking) before he was able to catch a dawn, or a sunset.

The heat was so intense that the only thing to do was to take refuge in the steady exhalation of the air-conditioners, curtains, and blinds that were drawn to create a cool, twilit haven. It was a heatwave beyond any he had ever experienced.

Thank God, his medication was there in plenty, in the fridge, where the heat would not denature it. Besides that, as far as he could remember, the fridge had been empty on his arrival here except for a carton of off milk and a few disgusting, unidentifiable items wrapped in plastic film. Also in the kitchen was a large cupboard filled with canned goods. He found that his caloric needs were less than usual, which was probably an effect of the heat. Actually, he felt as though he might be eating at all out of nothing more than habit, or boredom.

There was not much in the way of entertainment, only a small bookcase in the living room (or rather, a set of four breeze blocks supporting a pair of two-by-four planks) against the wall, which was papered in a very old-fashioned Rococo style with bountiful arabesques and cabbage roses. The contents of the bookcase were eclectic, consisting of a few best-sellers with embossed lettering on the covers, the authors' names bigger than the titles, some literary classics and obscure books with literary pretentions, and some old and slightly mouldy cloth-bound histories, one of which by chance provided the first and only clue as to the provenance of the statue with which he shared this accommodation.

The statue was easily the least comfortable fact about the situation in which he found himself; it made him feel as though he were under its hostile surveillance at all times—which made little sense, unless its pupil-less eyes could see through walls.

But there was nothing to be done. There was no working phone, no computer, and the prospect of an exploratory expedition was out of the question in this heat. For one thing, his shoes were missing, and the ground was covered in three-cornered jacks; for another there was nowhere that he could remember for him to go. He had spent a part of his childhood in a place like this, so that the arid landscape of unworked fields and sparse, ruined buildings was semi-familiar. Then, too, there had been nowhere to go, and nothing to do during the numbing summers when temperatures consistently reached above forty Celsius and difficulty sleeping melded the days together into a sluggish nightmare.

The only clue he had about the statue was found in one of the books of the small library. It was a history of the French Revolution in which, the first time he opened it, his eye alighted on the following passage concerning the de-Christianisation of France under The Convention:

> Burials were to be conducted without any religious ceremony, in fields planted with trees, "beneath the shadow of which shall be erected a statue representing Sleep. All other emblems shall be destroyed," and "The gates to this field, consecrated with religious respect to the shades of the dead, shall bear this inscription: 'Death is eternal sleep'."

After reading this he felt impelled to go and unfasten the heavy bolt on the outside of the door to the statue's room. Lacking a window, it was empty except for a bare, steel-framed single bed, and a pair of heavy red curtains that might by themselves have blocked out every last chink of light, although there was an external blind as well, which he had noted on one of his brief forays into the scorched back yard. Then, of course, there was the statue itself.

On the couple of occasions he had entered the room previously, he had not been game to approach its informal niche in the corner of the room by the far side of the bed. But now that curiosity demanded satisfaction, it was time to take another look. As he approached, the life-sized figure seemed to grow taller, until his impression was that it stood a head above him. He practically tip-toed around the room, eyes seeking the statue's (as if the empty sockets might be following him) until he stood directly before it, afraid to break the virtual eye-contact that he felt was somehow preventing the thing of greyish yellow material from springing on him.

When he had rounded to face it, astonishingly and despite his having failed to notice it previously, he found that the thing in fact stood on a low plinth engraved with the inscription "LE SOMMEIL."

The sculpted figure wore some kind of drapery suggesting a toga, in fact, though its posture was other than might have been guessed, a slouching mope with the shoulders lifted high, chin jutting out a little and lips parted. That expression seemed vaguely appropriate, or appropriately vague, except that the forehead was creased in an oddly conspicuous way. It was not a classical figure at all, more like the impressionistic sculptures of Rodin, or even of Rosso. But it was hard to describe further, since concertedly looking at the statue afforded a similar sensation of repulsion as looking directly at the Sun.

The crease in the forehead above the gouged eyes seemed a significant detail. Was Sleep having a bad dream? Was it angry—with him? He left the room quickly, running once his back was turned on the morbid figure, shut the door, and re-locked it with the heavy deadbolt that, suggestively enough, was on the exterior of the door.

What kind of joke had it been to bring that thing here? His working hypothesis was that this place in which he found himself was a halfway house of some kind, through which many others before him had passed in succession. And was the statue really an eighteenth-century French public sculpture? How so valuable and rare an historical artefact had found its way to wherever he was, out here in the middle of nowhere, was a first-rate mystery. Perhaps there was a graveyard nearby in which some eccentric local *philosophe* was buried, and for obscure reasons his ostentatious grave marker had been licitly or illicitly removed and stowed away here?

He might go back and ask the statue itself; he almost suspected that it would answer him in terms not soon to be forgotten.

Another troubling consideration was that each time he had viewed the statue, it seemed to occupy a slightly different posture; perhaps his memory was at fault, but the previous time its mouth had been closed, surely. And it had stood further back in its corner.

So the statue was alive. And what if those hands with their avid fingers were slowly, inexorably seeking his, the interloper's, throat? How had it advanced, though? Had the thing picked up its plinth and carried it a couple of steps? Or had the plinth sunk down and risen up out of the floor to meet it? The latter image was so ridiculous that he began laughing to himself for the first time since his amnesia. The laughter would not stop for some time.

He laughed until he slept, exhausted. On waking, as usual he had no very clear idea of the time of day or night, but understood that he would probably have continued sleeping if it were not time for another dose of medication. Resistance was increasing apace with dependence, he knew, having been through the process before with other prescriptions. But tonight he was mysteriously able to resist the urge to top up, enjoying in a strange way the heightened sensitivity to sensation thus afforded, while knowing that his supplies were within reach should that sensitivity spill over into actual pain. So instead he got up and went into the living room, where he wandered over to the window that overlooked the front yard of the house. He craved at least the image of space and air, and something told him that it might just now be evening for a change.

The noises inside his head could be disturbing, and they were growing in intensity. There was a creaking that made him think of bones shifting in their joints under a thin tent of dry flesh. That seemed to come from without him as well as within. As often before, he listened for any noise from the statue's side of the dividing wall, but as ever was unable to make out anything unambiguous. There was also a blustering, as though the window in the room looking out on the otherwise empty, rust coloured yard, towards the tree near the fence that was the only thing faintly living besides a few weeds, had been opened on a storm. The creaks and cracks were deep, low, and prolonged. All of this was strange since another atmospheric peculiarity of the location was the absence of wind.

Outside the desolate view was lit by a full moon and a fantastic cascade of stars, brilliant against the sky's blue-black. And then there was also what might have been the wind, if there had ever been any, blowing sustainedly through a crack somewhere, howling and moaning by turns, long and low, like someone with infinite lung capacity playing musical notes by blowing into the neck of a jug. He felt as if he were witnessing the end of the universe itself from somewhere outside it. There were no streetlights out here, and the moon was not in sight, yet things were visible. He then focused on the lonely tree against the fence that came before the dirt road down which no traffic ever came. There was nothing else to see, no houses or signs of recent human habitation or cultivation of the probably saline expanse that filled his field of vision. It was swaying slowly, rhythmically. He watched for a long time as its movements increased steadily, gradually. He imagined that the cool breeze from the air conditioner was really the same as that felt by the tree. Now, astonishingly, it was dancing like a bacchante, twisting and swirling its foliage and even its branches in a way that, although it must have been due to the wind, seemed possible only for a being endowed with volition.

Yes, it was dancing—even while no dust stirred and the salt bushes disdained to waver. He focused his eyes on the fence behind it, which was a makeshift thing of slack wire supported by irregular pieces scrap wood that had the appearance of alternately charred and whitened bones sticking up out of the earth. It was matched by some similar structure on the far side of the apparently disused road, on which flat, vacant land covered in low scrub stretched out indefinitely. He had no neighbours. Why did the wind, which must have been very high, not disturb the dust in the front yard?

Then there came another low creaking sound, this time definitely not in his head, but from the vicinity of the enshadowed doorway behind him. Unable to turn, his mind lengthened out the moment of fear, the reflection of the room behind him resolving in the window pane. He saw one of those grasping, straining hands of whatever strange, shifting substance it was, gleaming.

When he did turn around, of course, there was nothing there.

The blessed trance was permanently broken by that momentary shock, however; and, coincidentally, the wind had died down at the same time. When he went back to bed, fearful of shadows, he found it advisable to break a couple of blisters in the pack beside his bed, and swallow their contents.

As he sat in a depressed armchair, eating his breakfast of tinned corn, he contemplated the growing certainty that it was the medication that prevented him from understanding what the statue was, and what it meant. His brain would cloud over as soon as he tried to think about it, just as it did when he tried to think about how he had ended up here in this country retreat. Surrounded by mysteries, he realised what he had previously suspected, that he would have to stop taking the pills if he were ever to make sense of the situation or move on out of it. The question was whether he would have the willpower to do so on his own terms, or if he would have to wait for the pills to run out, as assuredly they were doing.

Food was likewise becoming an issue. Perhaps there would be some unforeseen incursion before things became dire; but no, that now seemed impossible. He knew why he was here.

The withdrawal pains, he was accustomed to, except that they now got worse and worse. His skeleton felt as though it wanted out from under his flesh, and he suffered from alternate bouts of hot and cold sweating all day and night. His head ached and throbbed, along with all the muscles in his body. His appetite waned, and he slept when he could, the rest of the time just lying there, staring at the walls and ceiling of his room. He could hear his close companion now, unmistakably, the creaking of the floorboards and a knocking against the wall like the branch of a tree in a storm, as well as low, unintelligible vocal noises that were like the rushing of wind through those branches. Sometimes he thought it might, at last, be raining outside, but when he staggered to the window to look, he was always mistaken.

In a paralysis of dread and resignation, he listened for these noises that were sometimes clear and sometimes indistinguishable over the severe tinnitus he had developed and the humming of the air conditioning, which he was now forever turning off and on again, struggling to cope with hot and cold spells in addition to the external temperature. What he felt sure would be the final, unavoidable confrontation could not be put off much longer, but the time was not yet quite ripe. Let him first sweat out the last traces of the drug that still clouded his mind.

He had a dream while in this state. In fact, there must have been many, but one alone carried over into his waking memory. There was the merciless heat of the day again. He had gone to the window in a moment of semi-respite from torment, and was drinking a glass of water held in a trembling hand. It was a physical shock when the brightness attacked his eyes. But there was a substantial hole in the centre of that brightness, within which blazed smaller but no less bright suns in the form of fenders, exhaust stack, side mirror, and grille. It was omitting a sound, too, which he had thought to be in his head, a roaring sound such as the truck would have made moving. And yet it was quite still.

Or was it? It seemed to be rolling slowly forward, as though the brakes were off. Presumably it would be hurtling under its own weight, if the ground were not so level. It was the first time he had seen any sign of human presence out there, and his heart thrilled with vague, unaccustomed hope. It was hard to make out the driver from this distance, though. He ran to the front door and out into the baking heat and mordant light. Straight away he had difficulty breathing and it was as though a stop watch had begun timing his last moments on Earth (if that was still where he was).

Nevertheless, he ran to the end of the driveway, which was like running across a stove-top. The heat made him cry out in pain and leap onto the bare, dry dirt of the front yard in preference, attempting to avoid the prolific three-cornered-jacks whose points were like mature rose thorns. He stepped on one and cried out again, reaching down to pull it out before mastering the pain. The moment demanded it.

He could not quite discern the figure of the driver, but saw that the shadowy head was turned in his direction, as one would expect in an otherwise featureless landscape. The driver neither waved back, looked away, nor otherwise moved a muscle that could be seen. No, as the monstrous machine crept forward like a huge, lethargic grub, the driver only continued staring out the open window with, as best could be made out, a face that might have been the statue's.

Terror sent him running back into the house, where he stayed, gasping, hands over ears to block out the noise of the engine that seemed to continue for hours.

It was lucky that his appetite had all but died, as he was down to the last few cans of food and would soon need to set out and face the rigors of the hostile landscape. That this would mean death seemed more likely the more he thought about it. To die without confronting the riddle of the statue now seemed far more horrible than death itself. It was a marginal and dreamlike impulse towards heroism that, he knew, was at a single remove from one towards martyrdom.

And so, one morning, trembling from fear and nausea, he decided that it truly was time. Although his head was by now relatively clear, there was a sensation as of a dripping tap at the back of his brain. As had been increasingly the case for some time, around him everything seemed to lack colour and, even in regard to household objects, some quality of vivacity. There were cracks in the walls that seemed to ramify more and more. There was also a musty smell about the place, similar to that which old, carpeted houses develop when unoccupied for some time.

He slid the bolt, and opened the door to his non-human housemate's chamber slowly and with his heart ringing the bells in his ears at high pitch, expecting at any moment a greyish, inhumanly powerful hand to wrap its fingers around the edge of the door and force it fully open.

But nothing stood where he had last seen the statue extend its avid hands towards him. There was a different, more intense smell in here which, also, he had not previously noticed. It was like the lair of an animal, and, something told him, a sick one. As well, there were now several dark, filthy looking stains and blotches on the threadbare carpet. The colours in the room, formerly a frigidly bluish scheme that set off the deep red of the curtains, seemed inexplicably to have faded to a vague and somehow terrible greyness, like the rest of the house, only more pronounced.

More surprisingly, where the rich-hued curtains had been, there was now a window that had been most emphatically boarded up.

He stood still in the threshold and looked around, fear rising more slowly than he might have expected, had he expected anything like the sight before him. His slow brain tried to make sense of the room's emptiness and sudden change. He had not taken down the curtains or boarded up the window, unless he had done so in his sleep. How long had he slept? And above all, where was the statue? A rattling noise like an unhealthily snoring beast was coming from the space beside the bed where it had first stood. It had escaped his attention at first, what with the assorted noises in his head. He moved slowly around the room. When his foot struck a groaning floorboard, something shifted in the same quarter, down there beside the bed, just below his line of sight. There was an intake of breath as the snoring stopped. Somehow, his resolve to face the truth did not weaken.

A moment later when he stood to the right of the foot of the bed, there it was in the nook beside the bed, lying on its belly now: an emaciated figure of a grey-haired man, or possibly a woman, dressed in rags and covered in bruises and filth, staring at him with an expression of terror, arms extended in pathetic supplication.

About the Author

J. A. Nicholl is an Australian writer of weird fiction. *Venus & Her Thugs* is his first book.

www.ingramcontent.com/pod-product-compliance
Lightning Source LLC
Chambersburg PA
CBHW030342131224
18858CB00004B/132

9 781940 933832